The One Who Sees Me

JOAN EMBOLA

THE ONE WHO SEES ME

SOVEREIGN LOVE. BOOK THREE

JOAN EMBOLA

Manuscript edited by Michaela Bush

Blurb edited by Abigayle Claire

Cover designed and illustrated by Elle Maxwell

For more information, contact;

www.joanembola.co.uk

ALSO BY JOAN EMBOLA

Fiction

The One Who Knows Me: Sovereign Love Book 1

The One Who Loves Me: Sovereign Love Book 2

The One Who Holds Me: Sovereign Love Book 4

Devotionals

Outpourings Of A Beloved Heart: A 30 Day Poetry Devotional About God's Love

The God Who Holds Me: A Companion Devotional & Journal

Also check out the merch store for cute faith-based merchandise such as t-shirts, stickers, mugs, notebooks and so much more.

Trigger Warning: This story involves sensitive topics such as parent abandonment, references to domestic abuse, the death of a loved one, substance misuse and human trafficking. I have done my best to treat these issues with the care they deserve. However, if these topics are triggers for you, I suggest you please pray before going any further, knowing that my intentions for choosing to address these topics are not to plunge readers into darkness, but to point them to the light and hope we have in our Lord and Saviour—Jesus Christ.

To my Heavenly Father, the One who sees me

For by grace you have been saved through faith. And this is not your own doing; it is the gift of God, not a result of works, so that no one may boast.

— EPHESIANS 2:8-9

NAME PRONUNCIATION GUIDE

Chijioke (Chi-ji-oke)- An Igbo name for boys which means God gives gifts/ God is my guide/ God is the custodian for all talents or gifts

Madu (Mma-du)- An Igbo name which means beauty/good exists

Olanna (O-la-nna)- An Igbo name for girls which means 'her father's jewel'

Akachukwu (A-ka-chu-ku) - An Igbo name which means 'the hand of God'

Amarachi (A-ma-ra-chi)- An Igbo name for girls which means 'God's grace'

Nwaeze (Nw-e-ze)- An Igbo name which means 'the king's child'

Adebisi (A-day-bi-si)- A Yoruba name which means 'added to the crown'

1

HEATHER

Would it be so bad if I slap a rude customer? Well, I'm about to do that in the next ten seconds if God doesn't help me. My thoughts run wild as I clench my fists and jaw at the rambling brunette standing across the counter from me. I've been listening to her endless complaints for the last ten minutes and I don't know if it's her squeaky voice or her barking dog that's making my head throb with pain.

Ten. Practice relaxation techniques.

"I already told you I can't drink this." The blue-eyed brunette pushes the cup of tea toward me and almost spills it on the counter—the same tea that took me ten minutes to make and the same tea she has now left to go cold.

"I'm lactose intolerant," she continues. "Are you trying to make me sick?" She holds her white Chihuahua close to her chest as the animal growls at me. I bet only the dog can see the steam coming out of my ears right now.

Nine. Think before you speak.

I open my mouth to say something, but bite down the curse words and sarcastic comments threatening to fly out. Instead, I force a smile and, with the last bit of strength in me, I speak.

"Ma'am, you asked for a honey chamomile tea latte with hazelnuts and that is exactly what I gave you. It comes *with* milk."

"Yeah, but I said *non-dairy* milk," she interjects, her high-pitched voice turning the heads of the dozen seated customers toward us. Even the music playing from the overhead speakers isn't loud enough to disguise the scene this woman is trying to create.

I let out a heavy sigh, my frustration at its peak now. "Ma'am, I don't remember you mentioning non-dairy milk when I took your order." I raise my notepad to show her where I scribbled her order fifteen minutes ago.

At this, the woman scoffs and takes a step back. "Are you calling me a liar?" She shakes her head and then paces the length of the counter. "I want to speak to your manager."

Seriously? There are five people behind her waiting to be served, and she holds the line like this? Heat flashes through my body as I gather my thoughts, but I can barely hear myself think over her barking dog.

"Heather, do you want me to get Eddie?" Abdul, my co-worker, whispers next to me.

"No, I can handle this. Please, keep serving the others." I point to the couple waiting directly behind my unsatisfied customer. It's not fair that the pressure is now on Abdul to serve the others while I deal with this issue, but I have no choice. I'll be disappointed if I don't sort this out quick enough and we lose our customers.

Eight. Identify potential solutions.

After exhaling a sharp breath, I turn to the woman again. "Ma'am, I'm happy to make you another cup of tea with non-dairy milk." I grab the warm cup of tea from the counter, but before I can turn around, the woman holds her hand up.

"No, you've already done enough damage. I'm done talking

to you. Get me your manager," she says as her dog's barks intensify.

In situations like this, I always hope that people would be more appreciative of my efforts to rectify the situation. But I've learnt that some people feel entitled, and this makes them come across as insensitive.

You can't choose how people act, but you can choose how you react to their actions. Meredith, my therapist, would say if she was standing next to me right now. But these things are always easier said than done–even Meredith knows that.

My gaze sweeps through the small coffee shop as a dozen pairs of eyes stare at me. Some customers look away while others keep staring as they sip on their hot drinks and bite into their pastries, watching the scene play out as if it's a movie.

A tingle creeps up the back of my neck and across my face as embarrassment takes over my anger. I should be able to handle this like others would, but I've tried my best and sometimes, you just have to give up.

Seven. Take time out.

"Okay. Suit yourself." I throw the cup of tea in the trash can behind me before heading out back toward the staff office. It's my last day on this job and I don't have to stand here and take any more insults.

"Heather, is everything okay out front?" Eddie's heavy steps rumble across the corridor as he walks out of his office. Like me, he's also wearing a burgundy t-shirt with the Café Express logo printed on the front pocket, except his t-shirt also has the word 'manager' printed across the back.

Apart from Eddie's tall, broad frame, which gives him a commanding presence, he has a frown which can put anyone in their place and also a friendly personality which always pacifies volatile situations. After one year of working here, I thought I would know how to deal with difficult situations too, but it always ends up the same way–Eddie coming to my rescue.

Six. Know when to seek help.

I shake my head at Eddie's question, giving myself some time to find the right words. "It's the same woman from the other day. She's back and..." My throat closes up and I bite my bottom lip to fight back the tears.

"Say no more." Eddie raises his hand. "Take a quick break. I'll sort this out."

"Are you sure?" I ask, as if I have a better solution.

"I'm serious. Go on now. I'll come and get you when she's gone."

"Thanks, Eddie," I respond as the middle-aged man walks past me and heads out front. Without waiting to hear how their conversation goes, I take off my apron, grab my coat, and take a left down the hallway to get away from the noise.

When I push open the double doors leading to the backyard, a black stray cat scurries away from the pile of trash bags in the corner before leaping over the wooden fence and disappearing from my sight. It reminds me of Phoebe, my dad's cat who would do the same thing whenever she's caught in the middle of her shenanigans. But no matter how mischievous Phoebe gets, she would never make a mess outside. I've taught her better than that.

It's Stacy's turn to put away the trash bags today, but she had a family emergency and left early. That's why Eddie asked me to come in this morning to fill in for her. If I had known my day would turn out like this, I would have declined and stayed at home.

The cold Brooklyn air envelopes me as I tie the trash bags and place them in the garbage can. That will stop the cats from scavenging in it for food. When I straighten my back, my eyes catch a glimpse of a used cigarette in the corner with a steady stream of smoke floating away from it. It's the source of the pungent smell in the backyard—the smell that refuses to go away, and the smell that used to be home for me.

Eddie is the only smoker here, so it must belong to him. This is where he spends all his smoke breaks and that's why I never come out here. *Flee away from temptation* is what the Bible says and for four years, I've done exactly that. It's a lot easier to run than to stare at your demons face to face, like I'm doing right now.

I have so many reasons to walk across the yard, light that cigarette and have a quick smoke. It won't take long before it finds its home again between my fingers. It'll help take the stress away and it'll help calm me down. No one will ever know and it'll be a secret I'll carry with me to my grave. *But at what cost?*

I've been at this junction too many times, and I know how it ends. It only takes one moment of weakness before I start waking up at five a.m, roaming the streets of Brooklyn, trying to find a lighter and a cigarette because the cravings are so strong I can't sleep. It only takes one moment of weakness before I can brand myself a failure.

Five. Get some exercise.

I let out another heavy sigh and peel my gaze away from the cigarette before shaking my hands and legs to distract myself. Since no one is out here with me, I can focus on the sirens going off in the distance and the gray clouds hovering above my head.

It's the second week of March and with spring being only a week away, I hope the chances of rain are low because the thought of sunshine and flowers is already slowing down my heart rate, relaxing my jaw muscles and taking away the tight-ness in my chest.

Four. Once you're calm, express your anger.

One bitter truth I've learnt over the past year is that the world—not just New York City— will still go on without me no matter what challenge I'm facing. When I started my social media marketing business a year ago, I never imagined I'd end up here.

Things weren't supposed to turn out like this. I only meant for this job to help me out temporarily, so I could pay my bills until I had enough clients to become fully self-employed. I never expected my life to turn into this big mess.

"Heather?" Eddie's voice shakes me out of my thoughts, and I turn around to find him at the door. *How long has he been standing there?* "You can come back inside. She's gone now." He rubs his palms together and blows into them before taking a few steps toward me.

Three. Stick with 'I' statements.

"Eddie, I'm so sorry about that. I could have handled the situation better and I..."

"Nah, don't worry about it, kiddo." He waves his hand dismissively. "That's what we get for choosing to work with people." His hearty laugh brings a smile out of me. I don't know how I would have survived this last year if I didn't have a manager as understanding as him.

Two. Use humor to release tension.

"You're right. I'm sure these customers will be relieved to know that this green-eyed, red-haired trouble maker will no longer be working here." I chuckle, but Eddie doesn't laugh with me. Instead, the expression on his face turns serious.

"Don't be hard on yourself, Heather. You know we've all loved having you here." He turns around. "Come on, I need to show you something."

I follow him inside as he leads me to the staff office, where Abdul is waiting. The seventeen-year-old boy runs his fingers through his silky dark hair before handing me a white sealed envelope and Eddie ushers me to sit down.

I stare at the envelope in my hands and I don't have to look twice to recognize Stacey's cursive writing spelling out my name across the back. Stacey has always been the innovative one who remembers birthdays and organizes staff social events. I know this was her idea, too.

"Go on. Open it," Eddie says, and Abdul nods before flashing me a bright smile.

"Okay." I tear open the envelope to reveal a beautiful card with the words "We will miss you" at the front. When I open the card, the stack of cash is the first thing that catches my attention before the hand-drawn social media logos at the center and the kind messages from my colleagues written all across the card.

"Please accept this little token of our appreciation," Eddie says as a tear slides down my cheek. "I'm sorry not everyone could be here today, but as you can see from the messages, we're sad you're leaving us."

"Yeah," Abdul chips in, and I turn to look at him. "I've only worked with you for three months, but I've learnt a lot from you. Please don't forget about us when you become a six-figure business owner."

We all laugh as I swipe my tears away. "This is so sweet, guys. Thank you so much." I stand up and hug Eddie and then Abdul. "Don't forget to thank your mom for sharing her Gulab Jamun recipe with me. It's quickly becoming one of my favorite desserts."

"I sure will, and she'll be happy to hear that," Abdul says before leaving the room.

"Thanks for your help today. I think Abdul and I can take it from here," Eddie says.

"Are you sure?"

"Absolutely. Jane will start her shift in half an hour. We can hold the fort until she gets here. Please go home and get some rest. I'm sure you have a lot of packing to do." He smiles before walking out of the office.

I spend five minutes reading all the messages on the card and counting all the cash before placing it safely inside the envelope. Now I can finally buy those vacuum storage bags I need to pack my clothes. After grabbing my backpack from my locker and returning the key to the staff office, I pop my head into the shop to wave Eddie and Abdul goodbye.

"Don't forget to call me if you need any help moving your stuff," Eddie says and I nod at him before taking one last glance at the small coffee shop. After one year of calling this place my second home, I'll definitely miss its brown walls, the sound of crockery, fingers tapping on laptop keys, and all the interesting conversations I've eavesdropped on from the counter. As sad and scary as it feels to leave this all behind, Eddie is right. It's time to go.

Stepping out through the back door and taking the path around to the front of the building, I turn around to look at the bold Café Express sign shining in white lights above the front door. Abdul waves at me from inside, and I wave back before walking to the parking lot.

One. Don't hold a grudge.

This has always been easier said than done and this is the reason for all my problems. If I can go away from this scene, forget about the rambling brunette and her barking dog and embrace the winds of change taking over my life, then maybe I'll feel better about this whole situation.

But as soon as I shut my car door and turn on the ignition, a surge of despair washes over me and I burst into tears, my head falling into my palms. Sometimes I wonder whether things will ever change because every time I try to fight, I always end up back here—feeling sorry for myself and remembering how much of a failure I am.

2

HEATHER

I t's after seven p.m. when I park my car in front of my apartment building. After stopping at the grocery store, it took me two hours to get home, not because there was traffic or because I lost my way, but because I kept driving around the block until I felt I could form a sentence without crying.

There's a high chance that someone will talk to me when I get into my building and the last thing I want to do is cry in front of my neighbors. I've felt sorry for myself enough for one day and it's time to move on from this stage. I knew it was going to be hard, but nothing prepared me for these tears.

I used to be the girl who would rather lash out at others, curse, or throw sarcastic comments than shed a tear. But Jesus and therapy have taught me that anger isn't always the answer. So my alternative for dealing with pent-up frustration is to cry or cook. I've done enough crying for today, so it's time to cook something.

"Hi, Heather." An African-American man smiles at me as he descends the stairs carrying two empty boxes of pizza.

I stand at the bottom of the stairs to give way for him. "Hi,

Mr. Jackson." I smile at him and then tilt my head. "You didn't finish two boxes of pizza on your own, did you?"

The elderly man laughs and his gray mustache spreads out across his face. "I wish I had that much of an appetite, dear. I had some friends over from the community center where I volunteer. It was the only thing I could provide for them without breaking my back. Things haven't been the same since my wife died. We used to work so well together and these days I haven't had the motivation to cook."

"Aww, I'm sorry to hear that." If I didn't have the motivation to cook, I don't know what I'd do with myself. "Listen, I'm about to make some lasagna. Do you think you'll have an appetite for that?" I lift the plastic bags I'm holding to show him the groceries I bought.

His eyes light up. "I haven't had a home-cooked meal in a long time. You know I always love your food. I can't say no to that."

"I didn't think you would. I'll bring it to you when I'm done."

"Thank you, dear," he says as he heads toward the garbage room.

When I get to the top of the stairs, I turn right and walk down the hallway to my apartment. After placing the grocery bags on the floor, I rummage through my backpack to find my keys, but before I can open my door, the adjacent door opens up and Mrs. Andrei pokes her head through. "I thought it must be you, Heather."

"Hi, Mrs. Andrei. How are you?" I smile at the middle-aged blonde woman. She, her husband, and her children have all been so kind to me since I moved into this apartment a year ago. They helped me settle in and showed me all the best places to eat, buy food and groceries.

"I'm good," she responds as she ties her hair up into a messy bun. "Have you bought those vacuum storage bags yet?"

I groan and lean my head back before covering my eyes with my palm. "*Ugh*, I knew I had forgotten to buy something."

Mrs. Andrei smiles. "Okay, wait a minute." She disappears into her house and then reappears five minutes later, holding a cardboard box. "I saw these storage bags at the supermarket the other day and I thought of you."

"Aww, that's so sweet of you. Thank you so much." I take the package from her. "These will help me save a lot of space in my car."

"They sure will. Now you get some rest and let me know if you need any help packing, okay?"

"Of course I will." I nod and then enter my studio apartment. After locking the door behind me, I hang my coat up before leaning the cardboard box against the wall. Then I walk a short distance to my kitchen area and place the bags of groceries on the counter.

Turning around, my gaze sweeps through the apartment I've called home for the past year. I put so much love into decorating it and making it my own. Everything from the gray couch to the round coffee table, the small flat-screen TV and the cupboard with all my favorite souvenirs from New York City, was intentionally picked out, so I could make this small space feel like home.

I was so excited to get an affordable studio apartment in Brooklyn because I thought it would help me stay afloat until my business set off. I can't believe that next week, I'll be leaving all this behind and moving back to Jersey City to live with my dad.

Since graduating from college almost two years ago, I poured out my heart into my social media marketing business and took a giant step toward my dream of becoming a full time entrepreneur. But unfortunately, all I'm doing now is taking ten steps backward and I don't know how long it'll take me to get to this stage again.

My vision blurs and another tear threatens to fall, so I shake my head and turn around to focus on the cooking, which always makes me feel better. Starting with the side salad, I cut up some red onions, crisp lettuce, and some crunchy sliced radishes into a bowl. Then I mix everything up and place the bowl in the fridge to cool.

After frying some onions, carrots, garlic and chopped up mushrooms in a pan, I add in the minced meat and let it brown for a few minutes. My mom taught me how to make lasagna when I turned eight and she loved adding brown sugar to the salt and pepper mix. I've made lasagna at least a thousand times since she left and each time, I choose to use her recipe. I've always wondered why I hold on to little parts of her when I'm still so angry at her.

I stir the mix in the pan and add tomatoes, oregano, thyme, crumbled stock cubes, and Worcestershire sauce. After assembling the lasagna layer after layer in my rectangular enamel roaster, I sprinkle some cheese at the top and place it in the preheated oven, together with some buttery garlic bread.

My phone rings in my bag as I shut the oven door and when I take it out, a photo of Dad's smiling face is staring at me. He has the same auburn hair as me, but he doesn't look as pale. *How fortunate for him.* "Hey, Dad." I bring the phone up to my ear and hold it in place with my shoulder as I try to wash the dishes in the sink.

"Hey, honey. How was your last day at the coffee shop?"

I shrug. "It was okay, I guess. Just the usual."

Dad pauses. "You sound a bit deflated. Are you sure you're okay?" His worried voice comes through the phone. He's so good at picking up stuff like this and he never minces words, always very direct and straight to the point—just like me.

"Yes, Dad. I promise I'm fine." There's no way I'll add to his worries by telling him I cried for two hours straight.

"Okay, how's the packing going?"

Seriously, can everyone just let me go through today without asking about packing? "It's going," I say. "But I've made little progress." I place the washed dishes on my plate rack and turn around to look at my room, which is still well-put together and doesn't at all look like I'm moving next week.

"You're sure you don't want me to come and help you?" he asks. "We could drive back in two cars, so it'll be easier to carry all your stuff."

"No, Dad, I'll be fine." I walk toward my round table and pick up the bunch of letters I've been avoiding for the past week. "I'm only bringing my clothes and shoes. You don't have to worry about that because I'm selling all my furniture this week."

"You'll let me know if you need anything, right?"

"Of course I will. Now let me continue packing, and I'll speak to you later."

"Okay, then. Have a good night. I can't wait to see you."

I end the call and tear open the envelope from the New York Department of State, which contains a letter confirming the dissolution of my limited liability company—HO Marketing. Even though the words bore a hole in my heart and shred it into a thousand pieces, I choose to believe that this won't be the end.

I'm moving back to Jersey City because I'm starting a six-month paid internship. When it's all over, I'll have enough experience to apply for a marketing job and after a few years, I would have gained enough experience to set up my business again.

My dad has been kind enough to let me live with him rent-free, which will help me save money for a new apartment and a new car. So yes, things haven't gone according to my plan, but I won't stop fighting.

3

EMMANUEL

Once a family, always a family, and you never let family down; that's my dad's favorite quote. The old man has lived and moved that quote every day of his life (or so he says). In fact, he has lived out that quote so perfectly that sometimes I wonder if I'm really his son. Everyone says I look and act like him, but I can't disagree more.

No true son of Chijioke Madu, the chief executive officer of Madu Health, wouldn't want to take over the family business and carry on the legacy. I haven't told Dad yet that my dream is to use my skills in the charity sector, but Mom knew, and she would have understood my reasons. Her death was an excuse for me to take time off to grieve, but it's been two years and I'm sure Dad is sensing my hesitation.

He has said nothing to my face (not yet at least), but every time we have the conversation about starting the transfer arrangements and I say 'not yet,' the stress lines deepen on his forehead and the muscles twitch in his jaw. No true son of Chijioke Madu wouldn't want to help his family.

"Emmanuel?" Dad's voice transports me out of my thoughts and back into the conference room, where the rest of the team all have their eyes on me. "We're ready for your presentation." He smiles before smoothing his two piece white kaftan and adjusting his black hat.

To everyone else in the room, they see Dad's smile as that of a loving father who is encouraging his son, and they are right. But what they're not seeing is a son who is practically crumbling under the immense pressure to fill his father's shoes. This is our biggest client and there's no way I'm going to mess this up and disappoint Dad.

After pulling on my suit jacket, I adjust my tie and walk to the front of the room where my laptop is. I bring up my presentation and when the PowerPoint comes up on the projector screen, I pick up the pointer and turn around to face my audience, trying my best to avoid eye contact with Dad.

"Good morning, ladies and gentlemen. My name is Emmanuel Madu and I'm the managing director here at Madu Health. Please join me in welcoming Mr. Brown and Mr. Chen, the representatives of Long Term Health—our potential client." I gesture at the black-suited gentlemen sitting on my right and everyone in the room gives a round of applause while the men smile and nod at us.

Turning around, I press a button on my laptop to change to the next slide of my presentation. "As some of you know, Long Term Health is a medical device company that has been in the business for over twenty years and they specialize in long-term conditions such as diabetes, asthma, and osteoarthritis, to name a few. They will use their newest product in the surgical treatment of severe osteoarthritis, which will hopefully provide a better prognosis for patients and improve their quality of life."

I pause before continuing. "Here at Madu Health, we focus on healthcare marketing, advertisement and communications, but just like you," I point to our clients, "the wellbeing of patients is our main priority, so I'm here to tell you why you should choose us to help you market and launch your newest product."

After a few minutes of talking, my mind stops worrying about the intensity of Dad's gaze on me as well as everyone else who is furiously making notes on their tablets and notebooks. Over the years of delivering presentations, I've learnt how to block out the facial expressions and focus on the heart behind my words because if I don't believe what I'm saying, then my words do not matter.

"To conclude." I click to the last slide before facing our clients again. "Madu Health understands that though each medical device is unique, the key to selling to target customers is making sure we make a compelling case for the product's potential. We have an excellent team here who will use various tools and skills to show your customers how your product can solve their problems, what the specific benefits are, and why they should buy from you and no one else. Thank you." I nod and close my presentation as everyone breaks into another round of applause.

"Thank you very much, Emmanuel, for that wonderful presentation," Dad says as I walk back to my seat. "As you can see, Mr. Chen and Mr. Brown, our team is prepared to take on this task, so we would love to know whether you're ready to get on board with us."

The two men whisper among themselves for a few minutes, and my heart thumps as we all wait. I grab my glass of water and gulp half of its content to get rid of the dryness in my mouth. This is always the hardest part for me—waiting to see if the client will choose us after pouring out my heart to them.

If they decide not to go with us, it wouldn't be the first time a potential client has turned us down. But I know how much having them on board will help our company and how much Dad was relying on me to bring this deal home.

At the end of their conversation, Mr. Chen turns to us and says, "We have decided to go with your company. Emmanuel, your presentation was excellent and we believe that Madu Health understands our vision, so we're excited to work with you on this project *and* future projects."

Thank You, Jesus.

Everyone stands and claps before going around the room to shake hands with our new clients. "We will be in touch with you soon to complete the contract and the details," Mr. Brown says to Dad and I.

"Take as much time as you need," Dad responds. "We're ready when you give us the signal and my son will handle everything." Dad pats my back and gives his nod of approval.

"You're an expert in the business, Mr Madu," Mr. Brown says. "We're glad that we finally get to work with you. I'm sure your protégé here is going to deliver excellent service."

Here we go again with the comparison. Even after working here for four years, most people still only see me as Chijioke Madu's son. Once it starts, it doesn't stop.

Dad turns to one of the team members standing behind him. "Mr. Garcia, please, could you give these gentlemen a tour of the facility? When you're done, please bring them back to the communal area so we can have some refreshments."

The two men follow Mr. Garcia out of the room, leaving me alone with Dad. I loosen my tie and let out a deep sigh before relaxing in my seat and finishing my glass of water.

Dad sits down again before speaking. "*Nwa nwoke*, you know I'm proud of you, right?" The older man trains his dark gaze on me.

"Yes, I know that," I say with a low voice, my heart already dreading the next part of this conversation.

"You have proven that I made the right decision by choosing

you to take over this company. My days in this business are numbered and soon, you will be the one in my place."

I shake my head and push my chair back. "Come on, Dad. I don't know what you're talking about. You still have a lot of time to be here. We need you, so you're not going anywhere."

Dad leans forward and places his hands on the table separating us. "Of course, I'll always be here for you. We're family and family always sticks together. But you need to work with me to learn all the managerial aspects of this company, so you'll be ready when I retire. We don't have time."

"Dad, there's no rush. The contract with Long Term Health is very important to us. I have an entire team to lead, so I'd like to spend the next six months giving it my best."

Dad pauses for a few seconds as he studies me. Then he speaks again. "So you promise that after the product launch in six months, we can finally kick-start the process of making you the C.E.O?"

Oh no, why didn't I think of this? Of course, he'll give me a deadline.

"Yes, Dad. I...I promise." My words falter as they come out of my mouth. I don't know what I've just gotten myself into, but I have six months to decide. I can either choose Dad's approval and stay with Madu Health, or disappoint him and go with the dream that has been tugging on my heart since I was eighteen years old.

"That's perfect." Dad rises to his feet. "Oh, that reminds me. I knew you were going to get this deal with Long Term Health and I knew you would need extra help with it, so I took it upon myself to get an intern for you. She'll be starting in two weeks."

I frown and lean back, trying to remember if I ever told him I wanted an intern. "An intern? In two weeks? Dad, I don't need an intern."

"Well, you think you don't, but now is the best time to flex those managerial muscles."

"But Dad..."

"May I remind you that one of your duties as a managing director is to supervise the marketing team, and this includes hiring and training—"

"Dad, I know what my duties are," I interject. "But I already have a lot on my plate."

"Emmanuel, it's a temporary internship and she'll leave when the launch is over."

"But this is going to be too much for me."

Dad sighs and walks around the table to meet me. "Emmanuel, *ekwenyere m na gi*. I believe in you." He squeezes my shoulder and holds my gaze. "I know your mother would have been proud of you. She believed in you too, so please give yourself some credit."

He can't bring Mom into this. He doesn't understand.

"Dad, that's not the point." I sigh before lowering my gaze. "You should have talked to me first. We said we would hold back on hiring any interns this year, so this is taking me by surprise."

"Well." Dad straightens and walks toward the door. "You'll soon learn that sometimes things will take you by surprise, so you need to always be prepared." He pauses and then turns to face me again, his graying eyebrows drawn together into a frown. "I spoke to Olanna today. She said she has been trying to call you for the past week and you promised to return her call, but you haven't done so."

Ugh. I totally forgot. Again, this just goes to show how much I have on my plate.

"Isn't she visiting Aunty Agnes in Ohio for Spring break?"

"Yeah, she's there already, but that doesn't mean you should ignore her calls."

"Dad, I wasn't ignoring her calls. I was busy preparing for

this presentation. I'll call her when I get home tonight." *Hopefully, I remember.*

"You better call her. You know family is everything. Join us for refreshments when you're ready." He nods toward the door and then heads out, leaving me alone in the room.

I lean my head on my palms and rub my temples. This isn't working for me anymore. Time is running out and I need to make a decision. The thought of even approaching Dad to tell him I want to go a different path sickens me. I can already see the disappointment in his face and sometimes the pressure weighs so heavily on me, I want to walk away from everything.

But I'm a Madu, and Madus never let anything or anyone faze them. So I stand up and walk out the door with my back straight and my chin high, hoping that someday my strides will be as confident as Dad's.

4

HEATHER

P eople say you should forgive and forget, but I say whoever came up with that quote doesn't know what it means to be hurt, betrayed, and abandoned.

How can I forget when each day brings back the memories which pushed me down this destructive path? How can I forget when everything reminds me about what I've lost, the mistakes I've made, and the one person I hate? How can I forget when I've found myself back at the very place where all my pain started?

This was a terrible idea. I grip my steering wheel as my car squeaks to a stop at the red traffic light. When I lift my head, my gaze settles on a woman who is walking across the street, holding her daughter's hand. I cock my head to one side as memories fill my mind, transporting me back to those monthly Saturday trips I used to take with Mom to the salon, where she allowed me to sit next to her as she had her haircut.

It always starts with the happy memories of Mom, Dad, and I cooking together, or them reading my favorite Bible stories to me before bed. But it always ends with the painful memories of them arguing, shouting, calling each other names and then Dad telling me Mom had left us.

My eyes prickle with tears as I shake my head and dab on the moisture on my cheek with the sleeve of my t-shirt. She doesn't deserve my tears. She left Dad, and she left me. I refuse to shed any tears because of her.

A string of curse words and the sound of a car horn fly into my ears from the car behind me, jolting me out of my daydream. I face the front again to find that the traffic light has now turned green, so I take my foot off the brake pedal and step on the gas. I glance in my rearview mirror before rolling my eyes at the driver behind me. *Someone's a little grumpy today.*

Signaling left, I turn into the road leading to my childhood home, the familiar landmarks of my childhood passing by on my left and my right. There's the hair salon, the pizza place, the coffee shop and then the transition into the apartment buildings. Here in Jersey City, I once held on to hope, but life shattered my hope into pieces before my eyes. Jersey City used to be home for me until it quickly became the place I was glad to leave and vowed never to come back to.

As my car slows to a stop in the driveway, I say a quick prayer, thanking God for helping my car make it this far. I need to take it to the garage when I get paid from the internship before I can drive on the road again.

Turning off the engine, I stare at the front door, its familiarity stirring up mixed feelings inside me. I haven't lived with Dad for longer than a month since I left for college six years ago and our relationship was very rocky back then.

If not for my college roommate, Teeyana, who encouraged me to reconcile with Dad, things wouldn't be going this well between us. I'm excited to live with him again, but I'm also nervous about living in this house, which still reminds me of Mom.

Last year, I suggested Dad find a new place so he can get a fresh start, but he insisted on staying here for reasons best known to him. This might be a terrible idea, but it's too late now. I can't go back to Brooklyn. There's nothing waiting for me there. Not now anyway. Every good thing takes time, they say, so I need to be patient and wait for the right time to try again.

"Heather?" The white door swings open, hitting the wall with a gentle tap–the same way it has always done for the past fifteen years. Dad's red head pops out, a massive grin on his face and his arms spread out wide as if I'm a prodigal daughter returning home. Actually, maybe I am. When I left for college, I was the rebellious teenager who couldn't do without drugs, alcohol, and boys. But that girl is long gone and God knows how much I'm fighting for her not to come back.

"Dad." I force a smile as I step out of the car. But before I can close the door, Dad's strong arms wrap me up in a hug, almost lifting me from the ground. His familiar smell of spices wafts into my nostrils, announcing the fact that I'll be getting a good meal tonight.

For a moment, I stand there, stiff as a rock, not knowing what to do with my arms. But as the seconds pass, Dad's emotions seep through to me and I wrap my arms around him, too. *I've missed him.*

"I'm so glad you're finally home." He breaks the hug and when his soft brown gaze meets mine, there are tears lining his eyes. "Thank God for bringing you back safely to me."

I smile at him again, a genuine one this time, because as much as I have my reservations about this next stage of my life, God made this moment possible and I still have my dad in my life. That's enough reason for me to be grateful. "It's good to be back home."

Dad swipes a tear under his eye and then pats my arm gently before shutting the car door for me. "Come on, let's get all your bags inside. I'm sure you're very hungry."

"You got that right." I chuckle as he helps me take my bags

out of the trunk. After making two trips, we carry my two large and three medium-sized suitcases into the house. I didn't realize I had so many clothes and shoes until I was fighting to zip up the suitcases and carrying them to my car.

After stacking the last of my suitcases downstairs, something catches my attention in the corner of my eye and I turn to find our ginger cat Phoebe strutting toward me in her glorious white and orange fur. I gasp and sit on the floor as she makes her way into my arms, purring and rubbing her whiskers on my arm. "Hey there, little girl. Did you miss me?" She meows in response. "I missed you too. Yes, I did. Ooh, I got something for you."

I take out a treat from my pocket to see if she remembers all the tricks I taught her years ago. When I hold the treat between my right thumb and index finger, I form a full circle in the air and, to my surprise, she follows the treat and does a full spin before meowing. "Oh, well done. You're so smart." I give her the treat as a reward and then rub her ears before standing again.

Dad and I make our way to the kitchen, which is the source of the spicy aroma that's making my mouth water. "I couldn't decide which of your favorites to make for dinner, so I went for double bean and roasted pepper chili." Dad turns to face me. "It's still one of your favorites, right?"

I nod and smile at him. "Of course it is." *He remembered.*

Dad picks up his apron and ties it around his waist and, as if he knows what I'm thinking, he brings out an extra apron from the drawer and passes it to me. "Would you like to join me?"

"It would be my pleasure." I take the apron from him and tie it around my waist before joining him at the counter. "What would you like me to do?" I ask, staring at the onions, celery, and red peppers on the chopping board. He knows I can never be too tired to cook, and he knows this is one thing I do to relieve stress.

"Well, it looks like you already have an answer." He nods at the vegetables in front of me before opening the cupboard and bringing out a saucepan.

"So, how are you feeling about this internship?" Dad asks as he pours some oil into the saucepan.

I shrug and pick up another pepper to chop. "I'm glad *something* is happening in my life, you know? The last few months have been hard because I felt stuck and helpless. I'm tired of feeling that way, so I'm excited about this next step."

Dad turns to face me while wiping his hands with a kitchen towel. "Honey, it's a significant step. You're so brave for doing this, and I want you to know that I'm proud of you. Please never forget that."

I stop chopping and lift my head to meet his gaze. Again, like he always has, his facial expression is serious and the care in his voice melts my heart. "I know, Dad."

We finish cooking our meal and after an hour, we're both sitting at the table, eating our chili served with sour cream while Phoebe plays with her rainbow ball on the floor.

Dad always makes fun of me for topping up my chili with Greek yogurt instead of sour cream, but he needs to try it first before passing judgment. "This is so good," I say after taking a spoonful and savoring the spice mixed with the creamy and tangy flavor from the yogurt.

"I know." Dad nods and dabs the corners of his mouth with a napkin. "It tastes just like your..." He pauses for a second before continuing. "Just like your mom's."

The food turns sour in my mouth, and I force myself to swallow it. I knew cooking with him would make him think about Mom. We used to cook together all the time before their relationship broke down, but things are different now. It's just me and him. If both of us can't accept that, then being back in this house is going to be very challenging.

Clearing my throat, I speak up to disperse the awkward silence. "Do you still think about her?"

He looks at me and nods. "I do. All the time," he says. "Do you?" he asks, a tinge of hope radiating in his voice.

My jaw muscles tighten and I frown. "No," I lie.

"I see," he says and returns to his food. The new tone of his voice carries disappointment—as if he wanted me to say I'm thinking about her too. If I tell him the truth, we'll go down the rabbit hole of reminiscing about the time she was here and I don't want that. It's not healthy for me and it sure isn't healthy for him. Mom leaving had a negative impact on both of us–one that took years to recover from. I'm not about to open those wounds up again.

"You never liked talking about her after she left," Dad adds. "I thought maybe that would have changed."

I shake my head and shove another spoon of chili in my mouth, trying not to roll my eyes or stand up and walk away. "That's because I don't like reminding myself about painful memories."

"That's fair," he says and another minute of silence passes between us. "Well, I'm glad you're here and I'm going to support you all the way." He changes the subject and a wave of relief washes over me.

"Thanks, Dad." I smile at him before we return to our food. Given how terrible the last week was for me, I don't know what I would have done if Dad wasn't as supportive as he is. I regret all those years where I treated him badly and blamed him for mom leaving. I should've been more grateful and stuck with him because he was hurting, too.

I still wonder to this day how he could forgive me so easily. God has given me a fresh start even after all the mistakes I made in the past, so I don't want to mess this up. "Dad?"

"Hmm?" He looks up at me, his forehead creasing as he raises his eyebrows.

"We're going to be okay, right?" I stretch my hand to him, my heart desperate for more reassurance.

He reaches out and squeezes my hand. "Of course we are," he says and holds my gaze without faltering for a second. "I trust God. Everything will be okay."

5

HEATHER

After dinner, Dad helps me carry my suitcases up to my room, then I spend half an hour packing my clothes into my drawers and wardrobe. I start my internship at Madu Health on Monday, and I want to make a good first impression.

It'll be amazing if they offer me a job after the internship, but even if they don't, I won't let that deter me. I'll keep fighting and I won't stop until HO Marketing is up and running again in a few years.

After packing away the clothes from the first suitcase, I open the bottom drawer of my dresser and a pack of cigarettes slides into my view, causing me to pause. *Oh, no.* I forgot I used to hide cigarettes around my room so Dad won't find them.

They used to be my comfort on those mornings when I woke up with a powerful urge to smoke. I thought they were my life-line then and that I couldn't do without them, but I was wrong.

Heather.

I shake away the still small voice as I stare at the pack of cigarettes. Not even Phoebe's continuous meowing outside the door stops me from reaching out to hold it. As the tips of my fingers brush against the pack, my breathing becomes shallower and faster, but then I stop.

Pulling back, I sit on the floor and lower my head–memories flooding in from all the weeks of rehab, all the years of therapy and all the progress I've made. It can't be all for nothing. *I refuse to go back there.* "Dad?" My voice comes out shaky, but I'm hoping he heard me and I'm hoping he'll come to my room quick enough before I change my mind.

"Honey, did you call me?" Dad pokes his head through the half-open door a minute later, his eyebrows furrowing.

"Please, can you take these away?" I point to the drawer and his gaze follows my finger.

"Of course." Dad walks in and grabs the pack of cigarettes, asking no questions. He understands, and he knows I've come too far to slip up.

"Wait." I hold out my hand when he turns around to leave. "I think there are more." I push myself up and uncover my hiding spots—behind my trash can, behind my flat screen TV and on the top shelf of my bathroom cabinet.

"Is that the last one?" Dad looks at me after stacking the packs in one hand.

I nod.

"Okay. I'll get rid of these for you."

"Thanks, Dad." I say, and he kisses my forehead before walking out of the room. I let out a sigh of relief as an invisible weight falls off my shoulders. *Thank You, Jesus.*

My phone vibrates in the back pocket of my jeans and when I take it out, I smile as Teeyana's name flashes on the screen. She couldn't be video calling at a better time. "Hello?"

"Hey, Heather. How are you? Are you in New Jersey already?"

"Yeah, I got here a few hours ago." I lean the phone against the dresser before going back to folding my clothes.

"Aww, I'm glad you arrived safely. How's your dad? I bet he's happy you're back."

"He really is and I have you to thank for helping us mend our relationship all those years ago. I'm seeing now how God planned everything. He knew I was going to leave my job, and He knew my business would fail, so He made sure I wouldn't end up homeless." I chuckle, even though the realization hits me deeply. "I can't thank you enough for talking to me that night. You changed my life, Teeyana."

"Hmm hmm," Teeyana interjects. "Correction. God changed your life. He only used me as a vessel and I wasn't even compliant initially. It took a lot of going against my will before I spoke to you that night. I would never have done it if it was up to me," Teeyana says and she couldn't be more right.

I still remember that night like it was yesterday. Freshman year was challenging for me and not only did I have to deal with family issues and my addictions, but experiencing a break up messed up my mind. I was so close to giving up, and I felt empty. But God used Teeyana to show me that there was so much more to life than drugs, alcohol, and boys.

"Thank you for listening to God and being obedient," I say to Teeyana as my gaze slides down to the tattoo on the inner part of my right wrist. It's the word "beloved" in cursive writing and a cross on the right-hand corner. "You know, every time I look at my tattoo now, I think of you, right?"

Teeyana chuckles. "Well, soon you won't have to just think of me because we would be talking in person. I haven't seen you since the wedding. We need to plan another meet up."

"Of course," I say. Teeyana got married to her college sweetheart, Jayden, three months ago. They live in Boston and with the distance, it has been difficult to see each other regularly. "Me, you, and Amara should meet up at some point this year." Amara is Teeyana's best friend, and she lives in Atlanta.

"Oh gosh, Amara is knee deep in wedding planning right now," Teeyana says. "She's your typical Bridezilla. I'm surprised she hasn't pulled her hair out already and if she wasn't my best friend, I would have smacked some sense into her, so she can calm down." We both laugh.

"Aww, I can imagine. Planning my move back to New Jersey was stressful and for weeks, I felt numb and couldn't do anything. I can imagine why Amara would be stressed about planning the wedding."

"Yeah, and she has to plan three different ceremonies because of her Nigerian culture. She has the civil wedding, the traditional wedding, and then the church wedding."

My jaw drops open. "Three ceremonies? Why?" I can barely plan a birthday party—let alone three wedding ceremonies.

"The traditional wedding is very important in her culture, so they can't skip that. Her extended family in Nigeria is stressing her out with a lot of demands," Teeyana says.

"Wow." I didn't realize how heavily the family got involved in Nigerian weddings. "Well, God has brought her this far, so I'm sure He'll see her through it."

"Amen," Teeyana responds as a door opens behind her to reveal her husband Jayden poking his head through.

"Can I come in, babe?" he asks in a hushed tone.

Teeyana's face lights up as she responds. "Of course you can. Come say hi to Heather." She beckons him over.

"Hi, Jayden." I wave at the camera and he waves back. "How are you?"

"I'm doing great." He wraps his arms around Teeyana and crouches behind her so I can see his face. "Congratulations on your move and your new job."

"Aww, thank you. I can tell you've been looking after Teeyana really well. You should have seen the smile on her face when you walked into the room."

Jayden smiles and shrugs. "Well, she means the world to me, so I have to do my best." He turns to Teeyana and asks in a low voice. "Are you okay?"

She nods. "Yeah, I'm good. Thanks, my love."

"Okay, great." He kisses her cheek and stands up. "I'll leave you two alone, then. Take care, Heather." He waves at me and then exits the room.

Teeyana waits for him to leave and then she turns to me with another big smile on her face. "Okay, there's one last piece of news I have to share with you." She pauses. "I'm pregnant."

My eyes widen as I bring my hands up to cover my mouth. "No way!"

"Yes way!" Teeyana squeals.

"Congratulations. That's amazing."

"Thank you so much. Jayden and I have been holding on to the news for a few weeks now, so I'm glad we're finally telling close friends and family."

"Aww, now you're making me even more excited to see you. How far gone are you?"

"Only six weeks, so we have plenty of time to meet up before the baby arrives. I'll speak to Amara and we'll plan a video call soon, so we can catch up. How does that sound?"

"That'll be great. I can't wait."

"Okay, I'll let you go because I'm sure you're exhausted from your trip. If I don't speak to you before Monday, I hope your first day at your internship goes well. I'll be praying for you."

"Thank you so much, Teeyana. I'll speak to you soon." I end the call and drop the phone on my bed.

Sometimes people move on with their lives, seasons change and they make new friends, but Teeyana and Amara aren't friends I would ever want to leave behind. They've been there for me in ways I can never imagine and distance has only made my heart fonder of them.

I can't believe Teeyana is going to be a mom and Amara is going to be a wife soon. It was only yesterday when we started college as eighteen-year-olds who didn't know their left and right. But inspite of everything we've been through, God has smiled on us. It's such a blessing.

I place the last piece of clothing in my drawer and head to the bathroom to shower and brush my teeth. In half an hour, I'm lying in bed with my bedside lamp on and my Bible in my lap.

"Knock, knock."

"Come in. The door is open." I lift my head and smile at Dad as he peeks his head through. "Everything okay?"

I frown and tilt my head. "Dad, you know I'm twenty-four years old and I can say my own prayers and tuck myself in bed, right?"

He chuckles and leans against the door frame before putting his hands in his pocket. "Of course I do. I just wanted to make sure you're alright... and also to tell you before I forget that we'll be having a visitor on Monday. She'll be having dinner with us and... I'd love for you to join us when you come back from work."

My eyes widen as I stare at him in shock. "She? Dad, I didn't know you were dating again." I throw my covers off and shuffle toward the edge of my bed, unable to contain my excitement. "Who is she? How did you meet? Is she pretty? Does she have any kids of her own? What does she look like? Show me her photo."

"Okay, okay, calm down, honey." Dad raises a hand up. "When you meet her on Monday, I'm sure she'll be happy to answer all your questions."

"Come on, Dad." I stand eye to eye with him. "You have a photo of her on your phone somewhere. Okay, is she on social media? Just send me a link to her profile and I'll do a background check for myself."

Dad shakes his head. "I'm afraid she's not on social media."

"*Ugh.* Why do you have to be so old-fashioned?" I whine.

Ignoring my plea, Dad stands there and crosses his arms, his auburn hair glowing under the light. "You'll meet her next week," he repeats before a sly smile crosses his face.

I throw my head back and let out a dramatic groan. "Fine. Have it your way. But you better keep your phone with you every second because trust me, I'll be investigating." I squint at him before getting under my covers again.

"Goodnight, honey." Dad closes my door, plunging the room into partial darkness again. So much good news in one day. My heart is so full of joy. It's been sixteen years since Mom left and I think it's time Dad moves on. I can't wait to meet my potential step-mom.

6

EMMANUEL

Dread, dread and nothing but dread. That's the only thing that engrossed my entire being as I dragged myself out of bed this morning. I remember the season in my life when all I did was pray for God to get me to where I am today. Like any other son born to Nigerian parents in the US, a very important goal to me was (and still is) to make my parents proud—especially my dad. In my case, this meant eventually working with my dad and helping him run the family business.

The desire to make my parents proud was what got me through college during the hard days. Having Dad pat my back and say, *"Well done, Emmanuel,"* was what I strived for, and hearing Mom say, *"I'm so proud of you, Akachukwu,"* with the beautiful smile on her face, made the blood, sweat, and tears all worth it.

Mom preferred to call me by my middle name. It means "the hand of God" and she insisted on giving me that name when I was born because of how (in her own words) the hand of God miraculously saved both of us from dying. She had many pregnancy and delivery complications and when both of us survived, no one could convince her that God's hand wasn't in it.

So while growing up, every time I went to Mom with a problem neither of us could solve, she always said, *"Don't worry, Akachukwu. The hand of God is on you. He will help you find the solution."* Sometimes, I felt she was only saying those words because she was being a good mom. But I learned that she really believed those words and, like she said, God always helped me find the solution.

Everything made sense then. I had a happy family, and I knew what my specific purpose was (well, at least I thought I did). But Mom's unexpected death made me question my 'why' and for the past two years, all I've done is compromise, so I can please Dad.

I should have told him what I really wanted to do two years ago. It's my fault for letting it drag on this long and it's my fault for letting my fear of disappointing him keep me rooted to this spot. I thought it didn't matter, but my life is slowly turning into a nightmare I can't wake up from.

"Morning, boss." Yin's voice brings me out of my thoughts as I step out of the elevator. He is our digital marketing manager and the closest friend I've had since I started working here four years ago.

"Hey, man. How you doin'?" I walk to his workstation and pump his fist. "How was the praise conference on Saturday?"

"Dude." Yin drops the folder he is holding on the desk and pushes his glasses close to his face. "It was amazing. MercyMe was there, Casting Crowns, and even Maverick City Music. You would have loved it. I was hoping you would come, you know?"

"Sorry, man. Maybe next time." I wave my hand dismissively and force a smile as I ignore the guilt clawing at my insides. "At least it gave you more one-on-one time with Jess. The last thing you want is an annoying third-wheel coming between you and your fiancée." I lean against his desk.

Yin shakes his head. "Come on, man. You know we love hanging out with you. It's been a while. You need to make time."

He's right. I haven't been to church in the last year and I haven't felt motivated to attend any other special programs and events since Mom died. It started off with me choosing to work from home one Sunday instead of going to church, then the next Sunday and then the next. I thought it was part of my grieving process and I needed time alone, but I've become so comfortable not reading my Bible and praying that it's scary.

"I know, I know." I push myself away from the desk before placing a hand in my pocket. "Let's make this launch successful for Long Term Health and after that, I'll have time to get more involved."

Yin sighs and runs a hand through his silky dark hair. "You really think you'll have more time after this? What happens when you get the next project and then the next one and then the next?"

"Whoa, slow down there, man." I force a laugh to convince myself it's not that serious, even though I know he's right. "I'll make time. In fact, I'll clear out my Saturday evening plans so I can hang out with you and Jess."

"Okay, boss." Yin finally lets it go. "By the way, I heard a new intern is starting today. Did you know about her?"

Ugh. For a moment, I forgot about that. "Yeah." I sigh as my jaw and neck muscles tense up. "My dad mentioned her two weeks ago, and I'm not looking forward to it."

"Why not?" Yin crosses his arms against his chest. "Come on, it'll be fun to have another person on the team. The more the merrier, remember?"

"Yeah, like I don't already have enough of you to supervise and worry about." I roll my eyes.

"But boss, you know we never give you any trouble." Yin

smiles before turning to the woman sitting at the workstation next to him. "Melissa, do we ever give him trouble?"

The woman who works with the digital marketing team lifts her head and smirks at Yin. "Of course not," she says and they both burst into laughter.

"Alright, lady and gentleman, get back to work." I shake away the smile on my face before heading toward my office. "Yin, don't forget the report needs to be on my desk before lunch time, yes?"

"Yes, boss." He laughs behind me.

As I walk down the open-plan workspace, I smile at everyone who locks eyes with me and greet them good morning before entering my office. After placing my briefcase on the single sofa, I take off my jacket and hang it on the jacket hook.

A heavy sigh escapes my lips as I look around the office and admire the set up. This space used to hold a special place in my heart when I first moved in. I made so much effort to customize it to my taste as I thought it would be a reminder of everything I have achieved. But none of this matters to me anymore because this same space which used to motivate me now only stirs up feelings of confinement.

Apart from the perfect view of the Jersey City skyline and Hudson River outside my window, there's a well-organized bookshelf next to the window with all my folders and files. Sitting beautifully next to the shelf is the only other living thing in this office, my large Kentia palm plant. I've been wanting to give her a name for the past three months, but I can't decide.

The sun's rays are filtering through the window and shining on her dark green leaves, which look much healthier today as all the brown tips are gone. She's also almost at the height of the bookshelf now, which means I'm doing something right. Grabbing my spray bottle, I mist the top and underside of the leaves to boost humidity and when I'm satisfied with their dew-covered look, I place the bottle back on the shelf and walk over to my desk.

You need to make time. Yin's words float around in my mind as I lower myself on the chair. My gaze drops to the folder in front of me, which is labeled "Long Term Health" and then to my planner, which has my to-do list for today. If I can make time to take care of a plant in the middle of this madness, then surely I can make time to spend with God.

Speaking of time, I still haven't called Olanna after she reported me to Dad. The girl can push my buttons sometimes, but I still love her. "Hey, Siri," I call out to the virtual assistant on my phone. "Call *Little Sis*."

The phone lights up and then rings, but she doesn't pick up, so I ask Siri to call her again. This time, she picks up. "Hello?"

"Hey, Trouble." I open the folder in front of me and flip through the pages.

"Manny, I'm still sleeping," she says and a rustling sound follows.

"Well, since sending you text messages wasn't enough, and you had to run to Dad, now is the only time you can get a call back from me."

She chuckles. "Nice of you to *finally* call back. It's a bad time, though. I studied until two a.m., so I've not had any sleep."

"I'm sorry," I say, remembering my own struggles when I was in college. Olanna is in her junior year and she's studying marketing and business administration. "Are you okay, though? It seemed you wanted to talk to me about something when you called."

"Yeah, I needed help with my project and wanted to ask for your expert advice. You weren't picking up, so I panicked a little and called Dad. He told me you were fine, and he answered the question I had, so it's all good."

Oh, no. She needed my help, and I wasn't there for her. Great!

Not only am I a terrible son waiting to disappoint his dad, but I'm also a terrible brother. "Olanna, I'm so sorry. I should have picked up when you called me."

"It's okay, Manny. I know you're busy."

Finally, someone understands. "Okay, I'll let you rest now, but please let's catch up on Saturday, okay?" Olanna snorts. "That's if you'll remember."

"I'm setting a reminder on my phone right now as we speak."

"Okay, if you say so."

"Please look after yourself."

"You too, Manny. Don't work too hard and don't forget to drink water."

"Yes, *Mom*," I say and she giggles. The older she gets, the more she reminds me of Mom.

"Love you."

"Love you too, sis," I respond before ending the call.

Don't work too hard. I wish it was that easy. I sigh and turn on my computer, but as I type in my password, Dad's gray two-piece Kaftan catches my attention as I spot him through the glass wall. He is talking to Yin and there's a woman standing beside him with shoulder-length red hair and bangs. That must be the new intern. I can't believe this is really happening.

Frowning, I avert my gaze and get to work. Maybe if he sees how busy I am, he'll finally believe me when I say I don't have the time or the energy to supervise an intern. Five minutes later, Dad knocks on my door and walks in with the girl following closely behind him.

"Here's our last stop and where I'll be handing you over to the managing director." Dad holds open the door for the intern and she walks in with a big smile on her face. Her aura screams confidence and the ambitious look in her green eyes catches my attention. "This is Mr. Emmanuel Madu, my son, and the next

CEO of this company," Dad says as I stand up. "Son, meet Miss Heather Osborne, your new intern."

"Very nice to meet you, sir." She extends her hand, and I shake it briefly without responding.

"Well, Emmanuel. I'll be having meetings all day, so she's all yours." Dad nods at both of us before exiting the room.

"I'm so excited about working with you," Heather says, still smiling. "I've read a lot about your company and I admire how much growth you've achieved over the last few years."

Okay, so she's keen. That's good, but it doesn't change the fact that I'm swamped right now. I only agreed to do this because of Dad and now I wish I had just said no. "Listen, Heather." I tap a finger on my desk as I try to choose my words carefully. "I'm happy you're excited to work with us, but I'm afraid I can't squeeze you into my day."

"Oh." Her smile fades, and she straightens her back before tugging on her backpack strap. "But Mr. Madu said you were going to supervise me directly."

"Yeah, well, my father is not involved in the day-to-day operations of this company. I am," I snap at her before I can stop myself.

"I apologize, sir," she says, still maintaining eye contact with me. "I was just under the impression that—"

"Listen," I cut her short, the irritation obvious in my tone. "I believe I've already explained myself, so now that we're clear, please come with me." I walk past her, open the door, and lead her back to Yin's workstation, where we meet him talking with Melissa.

"Hey, boss. Are you ready for our meeting?" Yin asks before turning to Heather.

"No, let's push that forward an hour. Please, could you do me a huge favor and do an introductory session with Heather? Also, while you're at it, please give her a tour of the facility as well."

"Erm... okay, sure," Yin says before gesturing for Heather to sit in the empty chair behind him. "Is everything okay?"

"Yeah, everything is perfect. See you later, Heather." I send her a half-smile before turning around and walking back to my office. There was nothing perfect about that and I'm mentally kicking myself for being unnecessarily harsh, but at least this will give me time to clear out the tasks on my to-do list with no distractions.

7

HEATHER

What a jerk. The words pierce into my thoughts as I struggle to listen to Yin tell me more about Madu Health. It's a good thing I already know this information because my attention and gaze keep drifting toward Emmanuel's office.

He is back at his desk now, wearing glasses, which he didn't have on before, and he is typing away on his computer while simultaneously taking notes on the pad next to him. After every five minutes, he pauses and stretches his neck before continuing, and I can't help but notice how good he looks in his blue pin-striped suit. He looks very busy, but there was no reason for him to snap at me. *So much for trying to make a good first impression.*

Apart from Dad, I've not had many good experiences with men in the past. But that was only because I put myself in a vulnerable position, so my high school and college boyfriends could treat me like trash after they got what they wanted from me.

I'm not that girl anymore. I know better than to let what someone else thinks of me affect how I do my work. Today has not started the way I wanted, but this only means I need to prove that I have what it takes to be here. I'm ready for that challenge.

"Heather?" Yin's voice breaks into my thoughts and I peel my gaze away from Emmanuel. "Is everything okay?" Yin raises his eyebrows before checking out the subject of my attention. Turning back to me, he sighs. "Look, I don't know what he said or did in there, but Emmanuel is an amazing boss and friend."

Well, I'll believe it when I see it. The words creep to the tip of my tongue, but I purse my lips and take them captive.

"He has a lot going on with him right now and he is over-seeing the Long Term Health project, so he is trying to juggle it all like any human would."

He can juggle his problems alright, as long as he doesn't pour out his frustrations on me. "Thanks for caring enough to explain, Yin. I'm just here to learn, and I don't care who supervises me."

"That's the spirit." Yin says before turning to the brunette in the workstation next to him. "Melissa, she's a keeper," he says, and the woman, who seems to be in her early thirties, smiles at me.

"We're happy you've joined us, Heather," she adds before shaking my hand. "I'm Melissa and I'm part of the digital marketing team. We're not perfect, but we treat each other like family here. Just make sure you carry your weight and always ask for help. I'm sure you'll have no problem fitting right in."

"Yeah, that's right," Yin chimes in. "Also, if you sense someone is projecting negative vibes, stay away from them and if you feel it's affecting your work, let me or Emmanuel know immediately."

Melissa nods vigorously before responding. "Oh, and always keep your lunch on the bottom shelf of the fridge because lunch thieves are too lazy to search there. The best place to eat your lunch in the communal area on the first floor because it's quieter and has a good view of the city."

"Wow, thank you so much for the tips, guys." I smile at both of them.

"You're welcome. By the way," Melissa glances over her shoulder and pulls her chair closer before reducing her voice to a whisper. "I heard Emmanuel doesn't want to take over the company anymore."

My eyes widen and Yin frowns at Melissa. "Why would you say that?"

Melissa lowers her voice even more. "Well, Neil, who is our PR manager by the way." She says to me before turning back to Yin. "Neil said he heard Emmanuel and the Chief Executive talking in the conference room after the meeting with Long Term Health two weeks ago. Neil went to use the copier just outside the room and he overheard their conversation. He said Emmanuel seemed reluctant to accept his dad's offer to start making the transfer."

Hmm. The plot thickens.

Yin clears his throat before looking at me. "Well, I hope Neil knows that it's rude to eavesdrop on other people's conversations, let alone spread rumors with no evidence."

Melissa straightens her back. "Well, I hope it's just a rumor because if it is true, Mr. Madu will be very disappointed. The poor man has been telling everyone that Emmanuel will take over soon."

There's a brief silence before Yin speaks again. "We have a lot of work to do, Melissa. Can you please continue working on those LinkedIn campaigns?"

Melissa opens her mouth to say something, but closes it again. "Yes, boss," she says before wheeling herself back to her workstation.

"Sorry about that." Yin turns to me. "I just don't like gossip."

"Me neither." I smile, but all I keep thinking about is

whether there's some truth to this "rumor." *Is Emmanuel struggling so much that he is planning to quit?*

"Here's some information about our newest client, Long Term Health." Yin hands me a green folder. "You might work with us on some of their projects, so it'd be good to familiarize yourself with who they are, what they do, and what products they make."

"Of course."

"I have a meeting with Emmanuel in..." He glances quickly at his watch. "Forty-five minutes to give him a marketing update on our current clients. Then I'd like to finish my report for our other clients before lunchtime and return it to Emmanuel. If I find you a workstation, are you happy to spend some time doing some research and exploring our system?"

I nod. "Sounds good to me."

"Great. After lunch, I'll give you a tour of the office and introduce you to the rest of the team. You'll also need your own login details and a staff badge, so we'll sort that out before the end of the day."

Yin walks me further down the open-plan office and lets me settle into an empty workstation with a computer and also a laptop. He gives me a temporary login for the computer and once I'm settled in, he returns to his workstation.

My workstation is far away from Emmanuel's office and he is no longer in my field of view, which is great. I take a deep breath in and exhale slowly. I'm so proud of myself for not snapping back at him or ranting about it to Yin. Some battles are just not worth fighting. Meredith will be so proud of me when I tell her about this experience at my next therapy session.

I smile to myself and look out the glass windows at the skyline of Jersey City. The view of the sun's rays reflecting from the skyscrapers and the Hudson River is so calming and good for clearing my mind. The view also causes nostalgia to rise in my chest as memories of New York come to me. I'm so close, but still so far away.

This is my new life now and I'm choosing to embrace it. It won't be easy, but I'll keep fighting. My gaze sweeps around the entire office and as I observe everyone at their workstations typing, writing, and talking to each other, gratitude fills my heart. This place will be my home for the next six months and I'll make sure I make memories here.

After browsing through the Long Term Health website, ideas pop into my mind about slogans and campaigns we could use for social media marketing, so I bring out my notebook and start drawing out the designs. The excitement to do what I love again takes over and before long, time slips away from me.

8

EMMANUEL

"*Stop trying to be a jerk. It's not who you are,*" Mom would have said if she had seen how I treated Heather this morning. I told myself the same thing when I got back to my office, but if I hadn't handed Heather over to Yin, I wouldn't have done as much work as I did. Sometimes one just has to do what needs to be done.

"Emmanuel," Yin calls out to me from a table in the communal area. He texted me half an hour ago and told me he was getting lunch. I promised I'd join him in ten minutes, but I had to finish looking over the marketing budget plan for Long Term Health campaigns, so I can present it at our meeting this afternoon.

"Sorry, I'm late." I sit in the white chair across the table from him before placing my lunch on the table.

"All good," Yin says as he bites into a carrot. "You just missed Heather, though."

I snap my head up to look at Yin. "Heather? You were having lunch with her?" I ask before my gaze drops to the chair next to Yin. There's a black backpack on it. "Is she coming back?"

Yin shrugs. "She went to take a phone call from her dad five minutes ago, so I'm sure she'll be back soon."

I fidget with my Ziploc bag before finally taking out my sandwich. When I lift my head, Yin is staring at me with his head tilted. "What?" I frown as I try to swallow the dry chicken sandwich I made in a rush this morning. I didn't have the time to add sauce like I usually do, but at least I made the chicken flavorful.

"You're hoping she doesn't come back, aren't you?" Yin asks, chuckling. "So, you're not happy with your dad for springing an intern on you, but please don't turn on the poor girl who is just here to learn."

"I'm not..." I straighten my back and force myself to swallow the pieces of bread in my mouth. "I don't know what she told you, but all I asked her to do was come to you just for today because I was busy. I'm her boss and if she doesn't like the way I manage this company, then she can walk out."

Yin lets out a sigh and leans back before closing his lunch box. "All I'm saying is that whatever you're doing, make sure you're doing it for the right reasons." He stands and pats my shoulder. "I'll see you inside."

"Wait..." My gaze darts from Yin to Heather's bag on the chair. "Aren't you going to take her bag?"

Yin scoffs. "No, she's coming back. You can watch it until she comes, boss." He smirks before walking back into the office.

Why does Yin always have to be right? How many reprimands can I get in one day? I drink half of the water in my bottle and clear my throat. *I really need to cook proper meals again because this sandwich business is not working.*

I glance at my watch to check the time before looking over my shoulder for the red, flowy curls or the piercing green eyes, but there's nothing. I stare at her bag, tapping my fingers on the table as I wait. Five minutes pass, and then ten and fifteen and still no sign of Heather.

A pang of guilt rises in my chest as I stare at her bag, and soon the object becomes a source of torture for me. She did nothing wrong, and I could have relayed my instructions without snapping at her. I exhale deeply and pick up the bag before heading back inside. Halfway to the door, I stop in my tracks, realizing that Yin never mentioned where she went.

I walk back down the corridor toward the open-plan office to give the bag to Yin, so he can give it to Heather when he sees her. But as I pass by one of the unused meeting rooms, a flash of red catches my eye and I stop.

There she is, standing in front of the window and looking out at the view of the city. She's still on the phone and the door is slightly ajar, so when I move closer, I can hear her hushed conversation.

"Thanks for praying with me, Dad," she says before exhaling.

Praying? She's a Christian? Cool.

"I've survived way worse situations in the past, so I have a thick skin. Rude bosses won't deter me."

Rude? I was not rude.

"I've come too far to let anything get under my skin, so I'll be fine."

Hmm. Tough and resilient. That's admirable.

"Okay, I gotta go now. I can't wait to have dinner with you and your special lady friend." She giggles. "I love you too. Bye." She ends the call, but instead of turning around to head back out, she stands there for a minute, staring out into the city. She looks so peaceful as the wind blows her hair.

As I watch her and the view, not thinking about work, or deadlines or numbers, I can imagine why she would want to stay here and not come back out. But I can't stay here forever, so I clear my throat and open the door wide before stepping in.

Heather turns to look at me and steps away from the window. "I'm sorry, sir. I was just—"

"Please... call me Emmanuel," I interject, trying to redeem myself and taking the first step to building the bridge I burned.

She nods and draws her eyebrows together. "Okay... Emmanuel. I'm sorry. I was just leaving." She walks toward me before her gaze drops to her bag in my hand and she frowns.

"Oh. Right." I raise the backpack. "I met Yin for lunch and he told me you were coming back, but when I didn't see you, I thought I'd come find you."

"Thank you, sir. I mean... Emmanuel," she says as she takes the backpack from me. "I better head back to Yin." She nods and heads for the door.

Come on, Emmanuel. Just apologize.

"Heather?" I spin around to face her and she turns. "About this morning, I just wanted to say I'm—"

"Please, you don't have to say anything," she cuts me short. "I'm just an intern. It's my first day and you're the boss, so I do as you say." She presses her lips together in a thin line. "It's all good," she says and before I can put in another word, she walks out of the room with her backpack slung over her shoulder.

Well, that was... easy. She seems to have forgiven and forgotten so soon. But she still thinks I'm a rude boss, which is not true, so I need to fix that. I walk back out to the main office, but when I get to Yin's workstation, he and Heather are walking toward the reception.

"Yin, wait up," I call out and they both turn to face me. I quicken my steps and when I get to them, I ask, "Are you taking Heather for her tour?"

"Yes, I was just about to—"

"Leave that to me, buddy. I'll take it from here."

Yin raises his eyebrows, and so does Heather. They both look at each other briefly before Yin turns to me. "Really?" he asks.

"What about our virtual meeting this afternoon with Long Term Health?"

I pull my shirt sleeve up to stare at my watch. "We have thirty minutes. I've been working here for four years, so I think I can manage a tour in less time. Is that okay with you, Heather?" I turn to her, hoping to see some appreciation for my efforts, but she responds with a blank stare.

She shrugs. "You're the boss," she says simply.

"Well, then. See you later." Yin gives me a thumbs up and whispers in my ear. "Please, don't be a jerk." He pats my back before walking away.

My dad always says that it's good to have friends who will have your back and cover your loopholes. Yin is that friend for me. Sometimes, you need someone else to make you see things from a different perspective.

"So," I begin as Heather and I continue walking to the reception. "What did you study at college?"

"Marketing and business management at St. John's University," she responds without looking at me. "I moved back from Brooklyn two weeks ago for this internship."

"Really? Well, nice to have you back here in Jersey City. I majored in public relations instead, but my little sister Olanna is in her junior year at NYU studying business management."

"That's cool." Heather lifts her head to look at me and her smile returns. "Is she going to work here when she graduates?"

"Yeah, that's the plan." I open the door for her, and she steps into the reception area. "But ultimately the decision will be hers to make."

"Of course." Heather stops at the reception desk and turns to face me. "It must be nice working with your family. I've always wished for something like that, but unfortunately I don't have any family members who are into marketing."

"Working with family has its ups and downs. The saying is

true that you have to be careful what you wish for." I hold her green gaze for a few seconds and a moment of silence passes between us before I speak again. "Well, let's begin." I avert my gaze and show her around the reception area and the waiting area before we make our way back to the office.

"This is where you'll be spending a lot of your time." My hand makes a sweeping motion over the open-plan office. "We have five departments out here, including digital marketing, content marketing, branding, public relations, and advertising." I point to each of the sections of the office before turning to her. "Any idea what area you are interested in?"

"Social media marketing will always have my heart," she says without hesitation, her mouth curving into another smile. "I ran my social media marketing business for a year, but unfortunately it didn't work out, so I had to close it down a few months ago."

"Wow, your own business? That's impressive. I'm sorry it didn't work out."

"It's okay." She shrugs. "It's all water under the bridge. I'm happy to be working here."

After making our way to the communal area, I show her all the meeting and conference rooms and we finally stop in front of my office, where Yin is already waiting for me. "Now that you've seen it all, I suggest you spend a day with each of the department managers this week, and then Yin and I will assign some projects to you next week."

"Really?" Her smile broadens. "That would be awesome. Thank you so much."

"You're welcome. Oh and I know you said your business didn't work out, but... I'd be interested in learning more about it someday... when we get the chance."

"No problem. Thank you again."

As she walks away, Yin squeezes my shoulder gently. "Glad to see you patched things up. Everyone likes a good boss." He winks at me, and I kiss my teeth as he laughs.

When I glance back at Heather again, she is talking and smiling with Kelsey from the branding department. There's something about her I find intriguing, but I can't figure it out. Whatever it is, I'm glad she's no longer having a bad day because of me.

9

HEATHER

Bars used to be my favorite place to unwind while I was in college. Even though I wasn't old enough to drink in my freshman year, my college boyfriend—Connor, who was in his junior year—always sneaked me in with a fake ID. My heavy make-up, piercings, and skimpy clothes made me look older than I was, so it was easier to blend in.

I used to crave everything about the interaction, from the clinking of the glasses, to the warm air radiating from the crowd of people, the laughing, the state of euphoria and the burning taste of the alcohol running down my tongue. Everything about that gave me false hope that my problems didn't exist.

But as soon as I was sober—as soon as I woke up on the other side, with the pounding headache, the muscle aches, and nausea—I realized one thing: my problems were still staring at me and my life had not changed.

For many years, I thought there was no other way to deal with the anger and hurt until that night when Teeyana reminded me about what I'd been running away from. I knew it was the only way, but I was too angry to believe, too angry to accept it and too angry to submit to a God who had let me miss out on the love of a mother.

It was a miracle that my heart changed after Teeyana spoke to me. She made me reconsider my stance and encouraged me to take one step toward the light. So here I am, casually walking past Ignacio's Bar without giving it a second glance. Okay, I have given it a second glance more than once today and the colorful lights at the entrance make me want to walk across the road and buy a drink, but I'm not going to. I know better.

I close my eyes briefly and exhale before continuing my walk down the road. My childhood neighborhood hasn't changed much. I still remember Dad and Mom driving me down these same roads to school and church every week. The streets are still the same, but I'm not the same. I left New Jersey a broken, hopeless girl, but today, I'm taking determined steps toward healing.

I know I'm healing because of how I handled the situation with Emmanuel today. After he apologized, I saw a different side to him. He is nothing like I thought he would be. Maybe I misjudged him, but I still need to put my guard up because I've only been working there for one day. I don't know him that well and he might be pretending.

Ranting to Dad for half an hour was very useful, but in the end, I couldn't bring myself to stay mad at Emmanuel—not after what Melissa said about him. It's none of my business and he was wrong for snapping at me, but if the rumor about him not wanting to take over the company is true, then he must be miserable. There's nothing worse than feeling like you're being forced to do something. Anyway, I'm happy my first day is over and I can't wait to meet Dad's special lady friend.

I breathe out a sigh of relief when I reach the house. Sending a quick glance to my car parked in the driveway, I climb up the stairs to the front door and scramble around in my bag for my keys. Taking the bus to work today wasn't bad, but I can't wait to fix my car so I can start driving around again.

When I push open the front door, the warmth of the house welcomes me and the sweet-smelling aroma makes my mouth water. "Dad?" I take off my jacket and hang it on the hook next to the door.

"Hey, honey." Dad walks out of the living room and stretches his arms out, inviting me in for a hug. "How was your first day?"

I take off both of my boots and place them next to Dad's pair of sneakers before wrapping him up in a hug. "Let's just say God came through for me. But I'll tell you all about it later. I just want to meet your special friend. Is she in the kitchen?" I wiggle my eyebrows before trying to walk past him, but he stops me.

"Heather, before you go in, I just wanted to tell you that—"

"Dad, it's okay." I cut him off, lowering my voice. "You don't have to explain anything to me. I know I never mentioned this before, but I want you to be happy and I want you to move on."

"Wait, but I just wanted to say..."

"No, Dad. Forget it. I'll just hear from the woman herself." I wink at him before heading for the kitchen, but when I get there, I freeze in my tracks as I stare at the green-eyed brunette woman sitting at the table.

I shake my head and blink multiple times, wondering whether my eyes are deceiving me and I just walked into a nightmare. But when Dad's footsteps get closer, I realize this is not a dream.

"Hi, honey," she says with a smile and in that moment, all the hope and joy I felt only seconds ago dissipates and anger replaces it rapidly, my chest bubbling and a lump building in my throat.

Words elude me, and I shake my head to steady my breathing. My jaw and fists clench and I turn around to face Dad. "Is...is this a joke?" I point a shaking finger at her.

Dad steps forward. "Heather…"

"Why is she here?" My voice breaks as my eyes well up with tears.

"Honey, please, I can explain."

"Explain what? That you tricked me? That you brought me back here to dump this on me?"

Mom stands up and inches closer, but I step away from her. "Honey, please." She stretches her arms out. "This was all my idea. Please give me a few minutes to explain."

"No…" I shake my head and lose the battle against my tears. They run down my cheeks freely as I struggle to let my words out. "You…" I say through gritted teeth. "You have no right to be here. You have no right calling me that and you certainly have no right asking anything of me, so get out."

Dad tries to hold my arm, but I jerk it away before brushing past him. "Dad, get her out of here right now, or I will." I say, before dragging myself up the stairs, my knees weak and my head light from all the emotions building inside of me.

When I get to my room, I slam the door shut, lock it, and pick up a pillow from my bed. I lean my back against the door and slide down to the floor. Then I bring my knees up to my chest and rest my shaking hands on the pillow. In between sobs, I scream into the pillow and pound on it many times, only lifting my head when I run out of air. The cycle continues until my energy is gone and my voice reduces to a whisper.

10

HEATHER

"Heather?" Meredith's voice jerks me out of my thoughts and I shift my gaze to focus on her face on my laptop screen. The middle-aged blonde woman leans forward and rests her chin in her hand. "Are you okay?" she asks. "You seem distracted today."

"I'm sorry. There's a lot on my mind." I rub my sore eyes, which have been staring at screens all day. The last thing I want to do now is be in front of a laptop but I don't have a choice.

Meredith has been my therapist since my first year of college. Dad's friend recommended her to us and she has been a pillar in my life these past four years. I always look forward to speaking to her because her caring attitude gives me a glimpse of what it could be like having a mom in my life.

We had to pause our weekly virtual sessions when I moved back to Jersey City because I needed time to settle into my new routine. I was excited to restart them, so I could tell Meredith about the little victories I've made at work.

But since Mom showed up, my thoughts have been all over the place. I can't think straight and I can't stop my heart from pounding every time her face pops into my mind. I should have postponed today's session. Meredith can see through me like an X-ray and I want her to know I'm making progress, not retreating. *Everything is messed up.*

"Would you like to share?" Meredith's voice pulls me out of my thoughts once again. "That's why we're here." She tilts her head and waits, staring at me as I stare back at her. She has never pushed me to talk, never pressured me to say or do something I've never wanted to do, but she has always been direct and honest with me.

I shake my head and cross my arms against my chest as Phoebe's head pops out from behind my laptop. The last time I saw her, she was rolling around on my bed and I didn't even notice when she climbed on the table. I can't resist her meowing and her round green eyes, which are letting me know she wants to cuddle.

As I extend my hand to her, she walks onto my lap and curls into a ball, my sweatpants providing warmth for her. "I think I'll stick with what we planned for today," I respond as I pet Phoebe, her soft fur sending tingles through my fingers, up my spine and slowing my heart rate down. "Sorry, what was the last question?"

Meredith places her pen behind her ear before asking again. "How did you feel after applying the anger management techniques when the dissatisfied customer at the coffee shop challenged you?"

Images from that encounter flash through my mind and I sniffle before wiping my runny nose with the sleeve of my sweatshirt. "I didn't count it as a victory."

Meredith frowns. "Why not?"

"Because... I still let the woman get to me. I applied all the techniques we talked about, but I still got angry."

"I beg to disagree, Heather. You were able to compose yourself, you stepped away when you needed to, and you let someone else take over so you could calm down. You controlled your emotions, which sounds like a win to me. Remember, the aim of this is not to stop you from getting angry. Anger is an emotion like love and sadness. The whole point is not to let the anger control you and lead you to sin."

Meredith is right and I want to focus on her words, but the more I try, the more I fail. I can't stop thinking about the audacity my mom had to show up after all she has done to me and Dad.

"Heather, listen. If you're not in the right mindset to talk today, then you know I'm more than happy to reschedule this—"

"My mom is back," I blurt out the words as my hands ball into fists and I lean my head back to fight the tears. I can't hold it in anymore. I can't talk to my dad because I'm mad at him and if I keep bottling up these emotions, I'll explode. I don't want that to happen. Not now. Not ever.

"She is?" Meredith straightens and takes her pen from behind her ear. Out of everyone in my life, Meredith is the only one who knows how I truly feel about my mom. Meredith knows how much I resent her and how much her leaving affected my life. "How long has she been back for?"

"I don't know. I came back from work three days ago and she was sitting in our kitchen, smiling at me and calling me 'honey' like she doesn't know what she has done." I grab some tissue paper and dab under my eyelids as my tears fall.

Meredith sighs softly and asks, "How do you feel right now?"

"Angry. Furious." I choose simple words to stop me from saying something I would regret. We agreed during our first session that I would never use curse words during our sessions and that has helped me apply that to my everyday life.

"Why?" Meredith asks and I lift my head to look at her. This would be a good time to throw in a sarcastic comment or scream and yell to tell her it's obvious why I'm angry, but that is why I'm in therapy—to learn how to talk through things.

"Because she ruined my life before, and I don't want her to ruin it again. She says she wants to explain. I don't need her explanation, and I want nothing to do with her."

Meredith sighs softly before giving me the look, which says she's about to say something I don't want to hear. "But Heather, she's your mother."

"No, she's not," I interject. "She stopped being my mother the day she walked out on me. A woman who abandons her eight-year-old daughter without batting an eyelid is not *worthy* of being called a mother."

Meredith pushes a few strands of her curly blonde hair behind her ear before leaning forward and looking me straight in the eyes. "Do you think there's a possibility you're angry because you never got closure? You mentioned that while she was away, you wanted to know why she left and you dealt with feelings of rejection by turning everything into anger. So, do you think now is a good time to address the source of the problem?"

"No, I don't." I swipe a tear rolling down my cheek and avert my gaze. Meredith is right, but I don't care. I will never speak to that woman again. "I don't need her. My career is on the right track. My dad loves me and would do anything for me. I have friends who care about me. I don't need some woman who doesn't know how I've survived for the past sixteen years. She can't just waltz in here and demand to speak to me. She has no right. I can't control my anger around her and all she'll do is bring out the worst in me. She'll cause me to sin."

"Hmm." Meredith pauses before she speaks again. "I see where you're coming from, but I have another question. What if God has brought your mom back into your life to make you confront your demons and to deal with the one thing that you've been avoiding for most of your life?"

"God would never do that. He would never put me in that situation."

"And how would you know? You're not God." Meredith's eyebrows furrow. "Heather, the things that scare you are things that will grow you. Could your mom coming back be the break-through you need in your healing journey?"

"No, I need to let sleeping dogs lie."

"Not when you let the memories of these sleeping dogs give you nightmares." Meredith holds my gaze and I open my mouth to speak, but the words elude me.

I know she's right, but I can't do this. I can't do what she's asking of me.

"Please, take the time you need. Think about it and most importantly, pray about it."

11

EMMANUEL

I tap my foot silently underneath the table as I watch Dad's facial expressions while he flips through the document in his hands. This document contains the official marketing plan for Long Term Health and every time I find myself in this situation (that is, waiting for his approval), I can never decipher what his facial expressions are saying.

Unlike me, who can't resist wearing my emotions on my face, Dad knows how to keep a neutral expression whether he is looking at my grades, or in this case, a marketing plan the team and I have worked on for the last week. It's always the same expressions from the furrowed eyebrows, followed by a nod, and then raising his eyebrows before pressing his lips into a thin line. Dad's facial expressions are the very definition of 'mixed signals.'

The worst mistake someone like me can make is to work under your dad when you know just how much his opinion can influence not just your working life, but your personal life, too.

The problem is, I feel like I don't have a choice, and with this new dark-clouded promise hanging over my head, if I don't come up with a plan soon, I'll be on the way to taking over this company in six months, which is *not* what I want. But does what I want really matter?

"Well done, son," Dad says before dropping the file on the table separating us. He leans forward and interlocks his fingers before looking me straight in the eye, his brown gaze penetrating my soul. "This looks great."

A soft sigh of relief escapes my lips, and I smile. "Thanks, Dad."

"You have my permission to implement these strategies and you can report back to me next week? Is that a plan?"

I nod. "Yes, sir," I respond as we both stand and walk out of the meeting room. Out in the office, Dad pats my back and heads for the exit while I walk back to my office. Heather's red hair catches my eye and for reasons not known to me, I pause in my tracks and start walking toward her workstation.

"Hey," I say when I get to her and she turns away from her computer to face me, her bangs almost covering her eyes and her hair tied up in a bun.

"Hey," She sweeps the bangs across her forehead, revealing her green gaze.

"How's it going?" I roll the marketing plan document in my hand and tap it lightly on her desk.

"Good," she responds before pressing her lips together. Something about her response is different today. What happened to the broad, enthusiastic smile she had at the start of the week? Even her eyes have lost some of the sparkle. *I wonder why.*

"What you working on today?" I look over her shoulder as she faces the computer again.

"Well, I'm working with Neil from PR today and he let me have a break to experiment on Canva, so I've been making some slogans and campaigns."

"Hmm." I inspect the work on her computer as she scrolls through. "Are these all for the Long Term Health project?"

"Yeah, but this is just a practice run for me."

"I see. Today is your last day shadowing, right?" I ask, and she nods. "You can start working with Yin and me next week and show these to him. They look good."

For the first time in five minutes, she cracks a weak smile. "Thank you, Emmanuel."

"You're welcome and I guess I'll... see you later." I nod and walk away toward Yin's station. As I approach him, he turns his chair around to face me.

"Hey, you okay, man?" Yin asks, and I sigh before trying to form the right question to ask.

"Yeah... erm, is Heather okay?"

Yin turns his head to look at her before facing me again. "I think so. Why do you ask?"

"I don't know." I shrug. "There's something about her demeanor today which seems off."

"But you just spoke to her, so why didn't you ask her?" Yin laughs and I use the rolled up document in my hand to smack his shoulder.

"*Ha ha ha*. Very funny!"

"No. I'm serious, though. She said nothing about not feeling well. The only thing she mentioned was that they changed her church Bible study from Wednesdays to Fridays, so she'd like to leave early on Fridays."

I raise my brows. "Wow, so I was right about her being a Christian."

"Yeah, we had a long conversation during lunch about the Bible and she is so cool. She's happy to come with us to the next conference we go to, and I know she and Jess will get along."

"I'm glad she's fitting in well into the team," I say before glancing at her. Her green gaze is now on her computer screen and even though there's determination written on her face, there's another expression I can see, but can't explain. Let's just say I'll never be good at reading facial expressions.

Before I can take my eyes off her, she lifts her head and locks eyes with me and instead of averting my gaze like any normal person would do, my body refuses to cooperate and I keep staring until she smiles. It's the same smile she gave me earlier— one that seems like a mask meant to make others believe she's okay. I smile back and send her a small wave before turning to face Yin as embarrassment twists my insides. *Oh, Lord, I hope she doesn't think I'm a creep.*

After work, I return to my apartment and fix a quick meal for myself after remembering I have some packets of noodles left in the cupboard. This, and fried rice, are my go-to meals after a long and tiring day at work.

In an ideal world, I would cook in bulk over the weekend so I don't have to worry during the week, but since I now spend my weekends checking and double checking all my tasks, I haven't incorporated that into my routine yet.

I eat dinner while watching yet another true crime documentary on Netflix and considering how many hours I spend watching these, I could become a detective. After an hour of TV time, I make my way to my plant babies in the guest room, which I have now turned into a plant sanctuary (as I like to call it). I bought a round wooden bookshelf and stacked all my eleven potted plants onto the four horizontal shelves instead of having them all scattered around my apartment.

I need to buy one more plant to make it up to the perfect number twelve, but I haven't decided what plant I want yet. Starting with Pepper, my peach Anthurium, I feel her soil for any dryness, but it's still moist, so I won't be watering her today. Carla, my Caladium plant, Anna, the Aglaonema pink Dalmatian, and Camilla, the Cereus cactus, all need watering today, so I use my mini watering can to moisturize the soil in their pots.

Some others like Othelia—my Opuntia cactus—only need to be watered every month, so they're good. After turning on the air purifier, I leave my plant sanctuary and make a cup of coffee before retreating to my bedroom.

I shouldn't be drinking coffee this late, but I need to stay awake to finish looking into Long Term Health's SEO optimization. Tomorrow, I'll focus on reviewing their conversion rates on their landing pages, so I can discuss optimization techniques with the team on Monday.

Settling behind my work desk, I open my laptop and place the cup of coffee next to me. But as I click on the folders, Yin's words pierce into my thoughts again. *You have to make time.*

I pause for a moment and after battling with myself for a few minutes, I give into the urge and close my laptop. Maybe I'll regret pushing my workload until later, but this is something I can't keep ignoring. I've spent the last two years admiring how intentional Yin and Jess are when it comes to their relationship with God. Now Heather has come in showing full confidence in her faith and it feels like someone is pouring hot coals on my head. I have to do something.

Opening my drawer, I take out my iPad and click open the YouVersion Bible app before searching up "How To Have A Closer Relationship With God." A list of plans come up on the screen and after scrolling through several of them, I pick the top one and start reading the devotional for the first day.

Half an hour later, after going back and forth between my Bible and the devotional, I read out the prayer points before continuing into my prayer session. "Lord, please help me. The pressure is too much. I don't know what to do. I don't want to make a mistake and walk away from everything I've ever known. Please help me make the right decision."

I stay there with my eyes closed as satisfaction and peace encapsulate my heart. I still don't have an answer, but the fact that I've prayed and handed it over to God makes the weight so much lighter. How could I have forgotten about how beautiful it feels to be held in the arms of God? How could I have let sadness and grief push me away from the only God who can help me work through it?

I open my eyes and my gaze lands on a family photo taken at my college graduation four years ago. I wore my best suit, which Dad bought for me, Olanna wore a peach-colored floral dress, while Mom and Dad wore a purple matching ankara outfit.

It seems like it only happened yesterday because I still remember the laughs, the smiles, the hugs we shared, and the tears of joy in Mom's eyes. She always told me it was one of the proudest moments of her life—watching her first child succeed at what he was good at. But was she right? Is this what I'm good at?

You don't need to ask what Dad is good at because business is what every bone of his body is made of. And for Mom? Her heart for helping people was what she was good at. Every year, she traveled back to Nigeria for the annual campaign of her charity, which is called A Widow's Comfort.

She set up that charity over twenty years ago before she moved to the US and married Dad. She has helped better the lives of many widows, single mothers, and their children. During the summer break before I started college, I wanted to do something different, so I offered to go with her to Nigeria. It only took that one visit for me to realize I wanted to work in the charity sector, too. When I told Mom about it, she only smiled and said, *"Akachukwu, if that is what God wants you to do, then so be it."*

Six years later, we got the news that Mom died in a car accident on her way to the same annual campaign event and everything stopped making sense. How am I supposed to find God in all that?

You will seek Me and you will find Me, when you seek Me with all your heart. The Bible verse from Jeremiah 29:13 drops into my mind and I look at my Bible again. They say all the answers I need are right here. I've been running away for too long. I have to seek so I can find.

My iPad vibrates, and a photo of Olanna's beautiful smile appears on my screen. In the photo, she's wearing the necklace I bought for her on her eighteenth birthday. She has worn it every day ever since.

"Hey, Trouble." I smile at her when her face pops up on my screen.

"Hey, Manny." She sits up and adjusts the satin bonnet on her head. "You call me *Trouble* again and I'll fly down there and whoop your butt," she says in the same tone Mom once used on us and we both laugh.

"Well, it's a good thing I'm the older one here because I'll *never* let that happen. Are you okay?" I ask, noticing her slouched posture.

She sighs. "Yeah, I guess. I can't believe spring break is over."

"Did you enjoy spending time with Aunty Agnes and her family?"

"Yeah, she and Uncle Gideon are so nice. Michael and Faith are so grown now. Those twins kept me on my toes the whole week and I need time to get my energy back." She laughs. "I can't believe they are already eight years old. Time flies so fast."

"It does indeed. You only have three months left and you can enjoy your summer vacation."

She groans and lets her head collapse in her hands. "I just want to be done with college, you know? Start working with you and Dad?"

"Well." I pause before clearing my throat. "All I can say is, enjoy the free time you have now. Trust me, this is as good as it gets." I smirk at her and she clicks her tongue at me.

"Just because you're so busy and can't find time for anything or anyone doesn't mean I'll be like you. Dad always has time for me because we're family."

"*Aye*, spoken like the true daughter of Mr. Chijioke Madu."

Olanna laughs before changing the subject. "Have you eaten?" she asks with the same care in her voice Mom had. Olanna is becoming more and more like Mom as she grows older, and that makes my grieving heart feel so much better as I know Mom left a part of her behind.

"Yeah, I made some *Indomie*." I smirk and Olanna rolls her eyes.

"It's noodles," she says, emphasizing on the word 'noodles.' "I don't know why Mom insisted on calling it *Indomie*." She shakes her head and there's a shared silence between us—a silence we both understand and know.

"You miss her a lot, don't you?" I ask, and she nods. "She'll be so proud of the woman you've become, you know that, right?"

"Yeah, Dad always says the same thing. She'll also be proud of how much of a wonderful cook I am. I tried her *egusi* soup recipe the other day, and it was delicious."

I raise my eyebrows. "Wow, look at you go. You need to share that recipe with me, or better still, show me how to cook it."

"Nuh-uh. You can use YouTube and Google and find your own recipe." She waves her finger in front of her face.

"Oh, come on, you know it won't taste as good without your womanly touch."

She rolls her eyes again, and I laugh. "Fine. We'll cook together when I come home for summer vacation."

"Who's the best yet the most annoying little sister in the world?" I lean back in my seat and smile.

"Take out the annoying part, and that would be me." She grins and makes a peace sign with her fingers.

"Oh, by the way," I shuffle back in my chair. "Are you busy Friday or Saturday evenings?"

She scrunches her brows. "No, I'm free unless I have to meet up with a friend to study."

"Okay, that's great, coz I was thinking, maybe we could meet up once a week like this to catch up and also to do some Bible study together?"

"Bible study?" Her eyes widen. "You serious? Manny, you haven't been to church in ten years."

"Correction," I raise my hand. "I haven't been to church in a year and that was wrong of me. I'm glad you didn't follow that example and stop going to church, too. There's a lot going on in our lives and we need to make sure we're seeking direction from God."

She remains silent for a few seconds and then speaks. "Yeah, you're right. I'm happy to do Bible study with you. Just know you're going to lead all the sessions because you're the older one."

"That's fine with me. I like the challenge."

"Okay, we can start next week because I have to... meet with a friend tomorrow evening." She looks away and picks up a bottle of water before sipping on it.

"Huh." I tilt my head as I study her body language. "So, what's the name of your boyfriend?"

Olanna chokes on her water and starts coughing. A minute later, after clearing her airway, she stares at me with wide eyes. "What boyfriend?"

"The one you're going on a date with tomorrow evening."

"What? A date? *Pfft*... I don't... I..."

"Olanna Gloria Madu, I wasn't born yesterday. What's his name?"

"Okay, fine." She places the bottle on the table and fiddles with her fingers. "His name is Alex Obeng."

I frown, trying to remember whether she's mentioned him before. "Wait a minute. Is this the same Alex you've been friends with since freshman year? The Ghanaian guy?"

"Yes, the one I met in church. Apparently, he's liked me since freshman year, but he only found the courage to tell me two months ago."

"Do you like him? Does he treat you well?"

"Yes, I like him a lot and yes, he treats me like a princess."

"A princess is not enough. He better treat you like a queen because if he breaks your heart, I'll break his face."

Olanna bursts out laughing. "Okay, *Dad*. I'll make sure I tell him that."

12

HEATHER

No one should blame me for using Bible study as an excuse for escaping Mom tonight. It was always my intention to attend Bible studies when I moved back to Jersey City, so there's no way I'll be missing that *just* to speak to a woman who doesn't care about me. But what good is it coming to Bible study if I'm going to spend the entire hour and a half thinking about her?

"We have a few minutes to spare, so if anyone has any questions about our study today, please ask." Samuel, the middle-aged pastor, says his last words as he closes his Bible. There are approximately twenty people here who look to be in their twenties and thirties. I don't know anyone, but I chose this Bible study group because I assumed I would relate with them a lot more, given that we're all around the same age.

Could your mom coming back be the breakthrough you need in your healing journey? I fidget in my back row seat as a weight of mixed emotions shifts around in my chest. Meredith's words fly around in my head, but each time, my own thoughts trump them with my justifiable reasons, if I do say so myself. I don't need this stress right now. All I want to do is forget my past hurts and live a Christian life without struggling so much. Is that too much to ask?

"I have a question." A girl in the front row with long black braided hair and glasses raises her hand. My phone vibrates again and I ignore it, knowing fully well who is calling me. Dad knows better than to expect me to give in—especially so soon. I just hope she's gone by the time I get home.

"Yes, Vanessa," Samuel says, and the girl asks her question.

"Is it possible to stop sinning completely?" Vanessa asks, plunging the room into complete silence. "I surrendered my life to Jesus over a year ago, but I'm still struggling with the same urges I had before. I always thought that knowing Jesus will completely crush all those urges, so I don't have temptation. Does that make me a bad Christian?"

Wow. This girl looked into my heart and asked a question I would have had if I had been listening to the Bible study. How does she know what I ask myself every day?

"That's an excellent question, and I'm so glad you asked it," the pastor responds. "It's important to understand that no human is above temptation. The devil tempted even our Lord Jesus three times when he was in the desert. Being tempted doesn't mean you're sinning, but giving in to that temptation and acting on it is what counts as sin." He turns to look in my direction.

"Unfortunately, as long as we're on this side of eternity, there'll always be the temptation to sin. That temptation is from the devil and not from God, but that's why Jesus died for us. He is the only one who walked this earth without sinning and by conquering death, He showed us a way of escape. Sometimes we may give in to sin knowingly or unknowingly. But the good news is that even when we sin, God is faithful and just to forgive us again and again and forever again as long as we acknowledge our sins and confess them with our hearts.

"Psalm 103 verse fourteen says that God knows how weak we are on our own. He knows we are only dust because He formed us. That's why, when temptation comes, He will empower us to overcome. He will have compassion on us and help us. So instead of putting a heavy emphasis on sin itself, keep your eyes on God. He has given us freedom from sin and freedom to live a righteous life."

Hearing this reminder fills my heart with relief, knowing that I'm not the only one struggling with my old habits. It also fills my heart with hope that God has promised to give me victory. Hopefully, someday, this journey won't feel like I'm fighting my demons all by myself.

On my way home, I walk past Ignacio's Bar again, only looking at it for a few seconds before continuing on my journey. After today's Bible study, I'm even more determined not to give in to my cravings. I've made so many mistakes in the past and now is the time to correct them as much as possible. I won't let my mom come in and ruin this for me.

"Heather." Dad extends his arms when I walk into the house. He gives me a warm hug and rests his head on mine. The thrum of his heartbeat saturates my ears as I lay my head on his chest.

"Dad, I'm sorry I missed your calls. I was at Bible study. They moved it from Wednesday to Friday."

"It's okay, honey. I'm glad you're home," he says and releases me before staring into my eyes. "Your mom left thirty minutes ago."

"Okay." I sigh and walk past him to the kitchen, hoping he wouldn't bring her up again. Dad enters the kitchen as I grab a glass from the cupboard.

"She really wanted to speak to you," he says as I turn on the faucet and fill the glass with water.

I turn around and meet his gaze before gulping down the water. "Why is she really back?" I ask, trying to keep calm.

"She wants to fix things. All she's asking for is that you let her explain."

I scoff and turn around again, rinsing the glass and placing it on the kitchen counter. I cross both my arms and stare out the kitchen window, refusing to look at him. "The damage she did when she left can't be fixed."

"Honey, please don't say that."

"Dad, whose side are you on?" I snap and turn my head to face him. "Why are you acting as if I was the only one she hurt? Have you forgotten what she did to you? She cheated on you, desecrated your marital bed, abandoned you with an eight-year-old daughter and ran off to China to live with another man for sixteen years." A lump rises in my throat as my voice cracks. "Sixteen years, Dad. You expect me to forget about that and accept her like nothing ever happened?"

"No." Dad shakes his head and inches toward me. "That's not what I'm asking you to do, honey. That would be very insensitive of me."

"Then what are you asking me to do? What do you want from me?"

"Just to have lunch with her." He holds my hands. "You don't have to say anything. Please, let her explain. That's all I'm asking."

I shake my head as I look at him, tears blurring my vision. I can't believe he has taken her side. We were supposed to be in this together. All these years, when she abandoned us, we survived without her. Yes, I know I abandoned him too at some point, but God helped me realize my mistake and I came back. Now she turns up, and he's already running back into her arms?

"Dad, you don't need her. You have me and we can do this together. You've been doing just fine for the past sixteen years and—"

"Heather, this isn't about me and her. This is about you and her. I'm sorry I didn't tell you she was coming, and I'm sorry for springing the news on you like that. Please give her a chance. That's all I'm asking." His eyes moisten as his gaze stays on me. I would never have imagined him asking this of me.

It won't be easy, but if this is what God wants me to do in order to face my fears head on, then I'll try. "I'll think about it. I need time to mentally prepare myself." *Or time to change my mind.* I push myself away from the counter and walk past Dad. "I'm not making any promises. I just said I'll think about it."

13

EMMANUEL

A soft knock on my door jolts me awake and I shake my head to orientate myself. Staying awake until the early hours of this morning to finish work was not a good idea. I knew I would regret it with the back-to-back meetings I have scheduled for today, but I did it anyway. I guess I only have myself to blame for me struggling to keep my eyes open.

"Yes, come in." I clear my throat before taking a sip from the stained cup of coffee next to me. *Yuck, it's cold. How long have I been dozing for?*

"You wanted to see me?" Heather pokes her head in and a sudden urge to make my desk look tidier overwhelms me. I knew about my meeting with Heather. That's why I opened the windows to let cool air in. Obviously, that wasn't enough to stop me from dozing off.

"Please take a seat." I point to the chair across the desk as Heather closes the door behind her. Adjusting in my seat, I arrange the stack of papers on my desk and push away the cold coffee mug, which has the words *"world's best boss"* written across it.

"Am I in trouble?" Heather sits down and fixes her ponytail.

"Huh? Oh no, no." I shake my head. "This is your one week review meeting. I do this with every new employee."

"Okay, good." She exhales sharply. "When Yin told me you wanted to see me, it felt like all those high school days when the principal summoned me to his office. Trust me, those meetings always ended up with me getting detention." A slight chuckle escapes her lips and the sparkle in her eyes returns.

"Well, in this case, I bring good news. You're not in trouble and there'll be no detention for you." I smile back at her before continuing. "So, did you find shadowing the different managers last week useful?"

Heather nods. "Yes, it was good to put all the theoretical parts of my studies into practice."

"That's great to hear." I rest my elbows on the desk. "I'm guessing you haven't changed your mind about staying in digital marketing?"

She nods. "Yes, it's the area I've always been passionate about."

I knew she'd say that. It's inspiring that she knows what she wants and still sticks to it no matter what else I offer. "Very well then. Today, you can work with Yin on some of the Long Term Health projects. He'll explain to you what you're going to do."

"Really?" The corners of her eyes crease up as a wide smile spreads across her face. "Thank you so much."

"Wait..." I place a hand up, stopping her from exploding with joy. "Before you thank me, I'd like you to understand that this is a lot of responsibility. Long Term Health is our biggest client and there's a lot of pressure on us to make their launch a success. You can choose to scale back and work on the other smaller projects we have going on..."

She shakes her head and cuts me off. "I understand how

important this is for the company. You won't regret letting me work with you, I promise."

"Okay, then. Yin and I will supervise you. If you need any help, let us know. Do you understand?"

"Yes, sir. I mean Emmanuel." She nods vigorously, and I chuckle.

For a few seconds, I just stare at her, in awe of her enthusiasm, confidence, and determination.

"Is there anything else you wanted to tell me?" Her voice pulls me out of my daydream.

"Oh... erm..." I pick up my pen and start tapping it on the table, an internal war going on within myself about whether I should tell her all I want to say. "No, that's all for now."

She smiles and then stands up, but when she gets to the door, my mouth betrays me and speaks again. "Heather?"

"Yes?" She turns around and brushes her bangs away from her eyes.

Don't say it. Don't say it. Don't say it. "Please don't take this the wrong way as it's none of my business, but... I noticed you didn't look happy on Friday and it seemed like there was something bothering you. I hope that whatever it was, you've been able to solve it or at least talk it through with someone. I'm sorry if this is overstepping boundaries."

Heather's gaze softens, and she lowers her head. "No, you're right. There was something on my mind on Friday." She pauses. "I have to make an important family decision and... it's kinda stressing me out."

Wow. So I was right. Maybe I know how to read facial expressions after all. "You won't believe this, but I'm in the same position as you. It's always one thing after the other with family, isn't it?" I laugh and she joins me.

"We have counseling services for all employees if you need

them," I say. "We're a family at Madu Health and we always make sure our employees feel well supported. Please ask for help if you need it. I pray God gives you the wisdom to make the right decision."

Her green gaze moistens, and she exhales softly. "I really appreciate that, Emmanuel. Thank you so much," she says and then heads out the door. I watch her through the glass wall as she walks to her desk and just before she disappears from my view, she takes out a tissue from her pocket and dabs the corners of her eyes.

It must be something really important if me bringing it up has made her emotional. I'd have to remember not to bring it up again now that I know how much it affects her. *God, please help both of us get through our family issues. Amen.*

"I can't believe the world's best boss *actually* made time out to have dinner with us today. We are not worthy." Yin laughs before shaking my hand and hugging me.

"Look at this guy. You're not serious." I smack his head with a throw pillow.

"Welcome, Emmanuel." Jess, Yin's fiancée, gives me a side hug before sitting next to Yin on the sofa.

I take a seat opposite them, leaning back and spreading one arm across the back of the sofa. "Jess, you have a beautiful apartment," My gaze wanders around her living room, admiring her turquoise and white Chinese-inspired decor. I love how the curtains match the throw pillows and how the soft feel of the rug is doing wonders to my feet.

"Thank you," she says and holds Yin's hand. "Yin helped me pick out most of the furniture—especially that one." She points at the turquoise oriental cupboard. "It's my most precious purchase because it looks just like the one my grandma has in China."

"That's amazing," I say as I stare at the chandelier. "Yin, maybe you should take some lessons from Jess so you can revive your apartment."

It's Yin's turn to launch a throw-pillow at me and we all laugh.

"Okay, boys, please be respectful of the furniture while I go check on dinner." Jess sends a stern warning to Yin before walking to the kitchen.

"Seriously though, I'm glad you could spend time with us today," Yin says as I pick up the throw pillow he sent my way.

"Yeah, I did a lot of thinking after what you told me, and I realized you were right. It's true that I'm busy, but so are you, so is Jess and so is Heather. You all still find time to go to church, study your Bibles, and pray together. When Jesus comes back, being busy wouldn't be a valid excuse when I give an account of how I've lived my life."

"Preach." Yin clicks his fingers. "That's what I've been trying to tell you for the last year. Man, I'm so happy God made you realize it yourself. And the fact that He used Heather to show you that? Wow."

"Hey." I grab the throw pillow and launch it at Yin, but he dodges this time.

"What? I'm just saying you went from not liking her to noticing when she's feeling sad. That went from 0 to 100 very quickly." Yin laughs and I roll my eyes at him.

"In my defense, I was right. I asked her about it and she told me there was something bothering her that day."

"Really?"

"Yeah, she's dealing with some family drama." Who would have thought we would have something in common, huh?

"Wow. She must have a good way of hiding it, because I

didn't notice," Yin says before leaning forward and lowering his voice. "Speaking of family drama." He looks over his shoulder and continues. "There's a rumor going around the office about you not wanting to take over the company. Is this true?"

My heart drops to the floor as my eyes widen. All this time, these thoughts have been living in my head, but I'm sure I never spoke them out loud. "Who told you that?"

Yin shrugs. "Like I said, it's a rumor."

"Yeah, but who did you hear the rumor from?"

"Does it matter?" Yin straightens before looking me straight in the eye. "Is it true?"

No, is what I want to say, but my mouth betrays me yet again. I let my head fall into my hands and sigh. "I don't know what I want." It's easier to lie than to say I can't do what I want because I made a promise to my dad and I don't want to disappoint him. That sounds... weak, and yet, I can't bring myself to just tell Dad the truth.

"Madu Health is all I've ever known and I love working there." I lift my head to look at Yin. "But the prospect of taking over the company paralyzes me with so much fear."

"Fear is not of God, Emmanuel," Yin responds. "Are you sure this isn't the devil trying to discourage you?"

I shrug. "It's possible, but for years now I've had this tugging in my heart to do something else. Time is running out and when this launch with Long Term Health is over, my dad will kickstart the handover process. What should I do?"

"Pray," Yin responds. "Pray and keep praying until God shows you what you need to do. I'll be praying with you, too."

"Thanks, man. Please, can you keep this between us?" I say as Jess walks back in.

"Of course. You know I've got your back."

"I appreciate it."

"Are we ready for dinner?" Jess says as Yin and I spring to our feet.

"It's chicken chow mein to the rescue." Yin walks over to Jess and kisses her cheek before we all head to the dining table.

14

HEATHER

L ast night, I caught myself googling *"how to look busy at work"* and that was how I knew I had let the pressure get to me. I knew it would be hard work when I accepted the responsibility of working on the Long Term Health projects, but I have to prove to them—especially Emmanuel, since he didn't want me here initially—that I have what it takes to be on their team as a permanent staff member and not just an intern.

Yes, Emmanuel apologized, and he has been nice to me since then, but I can't take any chances. I won't let him sneak up on me and find me slacking. He's still my boss and I won't give him any reason to question my credibility. The quality of the work I produce has to speak for itself and that's why I need to work extra hard now.

"You good?" Yin asks as he walks past me.

"Yeah, I'm okay, thanks," I respond, and he heads back to his workstation, which is straight ahead. He loved my sketches of the slogans I did before, so my first assignment is to bring those to life and show him by the end of the day.

Since I already completed the details over the weekend, I've spent my entire morning observing everyone and pretending to look busy. It took me a while to get used to the open-plan office layout as it is significantly different to the workspaces I've had before.

Running my business from my studio apartment in Brooklyn had a cozy feel, and it comprised of virtual meetings, phone calls, and lots of screen time with soft worship music playing in the background.

The aesthetic at Café Express was the complete opposite with loud music, voices talking over each other, standing for long hours and ending most days with a headache and lower back pain.

Madu Health is the best of both worlds and its neutral tones and utilitarian furniture give the office space an industrial look. The good thing is we are not cooped up in cubicles and everyone has an assigned workstation. The workstations are far enough apart to not invade anyone's privacy but also close enough to build relationships.

The new sounds I've had to get used to over the last three weeks are ringing phones, tapping keys, and the never-ending grinding of the paper shredder. I'm pretty sure I still hear that annoying sound in my sleep some nights.

"Heather, are you busy?" Melissa's high-pitched voice pulls me out of my thoughts as she power walks toward me. If I didn't know any better, I would assume I'm in trouble judging from the urgency in her footsteps. But I've spent enough time with her to say she either wants to tell me something she heard or she wants to have food.

"Kinda. Everything alright?" I crane my neck to get a full view of her over my computer.

"Yeah." She stops in front of my desk before blowing out a breath. "Neil, Yin, and I are going to check out the new café across the street. Their menu looks great. Wanna come?"

If someone can give me a penny every time I predict what Melissa would do, I'd be earning six figures in no time.

"Erm... I don't know," I respond before looking over Melissa's shoulder into Emmanuel's office. I'm not sure what he would think about the new intern walking off with the experienced employees during working hours. If anything backfires, my neck will be on the line. "I think I'm okay. I'll just hang back here for a while."

Melissa raises her eyebrows. "Are you sure? It's not just coffee. They have panini, omelets, iced tea, shortbread, and even sandwiches." She leans against my desk. "Come on. You need a break."

"The woman is right, Heather." Neil appears from behind Melissa and smiles at me before brushing his curly hair away from his face. "Working hard is overrated. Working smart is the new thing and we all know that taking breaks is a smart idea. Come on."

"Erm..." I lean back in my chair as my gaze wanders to Emmanuel's office again. This time, Yin is also in there talking to him. Neil and Melissa both follow my gaze and when Yin finishes speaking to Emmanuel, he walks out to meet us.

"Are you guys ready to check out this new place?" Yin asks when he gets to my desk.

"You're going too?" My gaze darts between them.

"Of course. It's their opening day and the first fifty customers get fifty percent off. Emmanuel just reminded me to bring you along."

"He did?" My eyebrows pull together in a frown. "Is he going to join us?"

"Yeah, when he is done with his meeting. Let's join the line before it gets too long. We can hold a space for Emmanuel." Yin leads the way, followed by Neil and then Melissa, who lags.

As we head out the door, Melissa pulls me close and whispers. "I can't believe all I had to say to get you flying out of your seat was that Emmanuel had approved." She giggles and I smack her arm.

"Go away." I roll my eyes and suppress a smile. "I don't know what you're talking about."

Seems like Melissa might also be good at reading me, but I'm keeping my lips sealed.

Walking across the street, we join the line in front of Rosa's Café just before a large group of men, women, and children file in behind us. When it finally opens, it only takes a ten-minute wait before we are inside.

The first thing that hits me is the sweet savory smell that envelopes us as we walk in, and the saxophone music playing from the overhead speakers reminds me of my days working at Café Express in Brooklyn. It feels great to be on this side again, where I'm doing what I love and rediscovering my passion for social media marketing. A moment like this is God's way of reminding me that I made the right decision to leave Brooklyn.

The cozy aesthetic at Rosa's Café is right up my street, and I can't stop staring at the beautiful floral oil paintings on the green walls and the LED fairy lights hanging from the ceiling. Each wall also has a shelf with vines, whose stems and leaves hang downward, providing a beautiful wall decor. Bob was against the idea of putting up paintings on the walls at Café Express, so I wonder what he would think of this.

I take out my phone and record a short video of the café decor before sending it to Bob. I also send Abdul some photos of the Gulab Jamun dessert I made last weekend using his mom's recipe.

"Heather, what would you like?" Melissa's voice brings my attention back as I didn't even realize it was our turn to order. Yin and Neil have already placed their orders and are now walking toward an empty table.

"Erm…" I scan through the menu on the board. "I'm not too hungry, so I'll go for a caramel macchiato and some shortbread." I reach into my pocket to grab my phone, but Melissa stops me.

"Don't worry. I'll pay for this," she says.

"Aww, thank you. That's so kind."

We walk over to meet Neil and Yin at a round wooden table, surrounded by very comfy turquoise velvet tub chairs. Ten minutes later, a server brings our orders and we immediately dig in.

"This place is so cozy," I glance around the café again.

"Yeah, and their food is delicious," Yin adds as he bites into his panini.

"I bet you're glad you came here now, aren't you, Heather?" Melissa says before placing a forkful of scrambled eggs into her mouth.

"Yes, you were right. The shortbread is amazing. I think I'm going to buy shortbread here from now on."

"That's great," Neil sips on his lemonade. "How are you finding Madu Health so far, Heather?"

"Everyone is nice, supportive, and looks out for me. Exhibit A." I make a sweeping motion around the table and they all smile. "Thank you all so much."

"You're welcome," Melissa answers for the group. "Has anyone stolen your lunch?" She asks, and I chuckle. *Of course she had to ask that.*

"No, I took your advice and I've been keeping it on the bottom shelf in the fridge, so it's been safe so far." I sip on my macchiato and continue. "I think Emmanuel would love this place, too. Look at all these plants." I blurt out my thoughts as I try to steer the conversation away from me.

"You can say that again," Yin responds. "I hope he'll be able to get some time away to join us."

"Speaking of the boss," Neil turns to Yin. "Has he said anything to you about what I heard in the conference room a few weeks ago? Is he really not planning to take over Madu Health?"

Yin lets out an exaggerated sigh. "Neil, I don't think it's any of our business what Emmanuel does with his life. Let's give it a rest, please."

"Hmm, you didn't deny it, so it must be true," Neil smirks.

Melissa places her fork down and leans close to Yin. "Is it really true? Did he say why? What does he want to do instead? Who will take over the company now?" Her questions fly out of her mouth without giving her a chance to take breaths in between.

To be honest, I would like to know all the answers to Melissa's questions, too.

"Melissa, I can't comment on that. If you really want answers, you can ask the boss himself," Yin says as we all laugh. "Please, don't go around spreading any rumors if there has been no confirmation from Emmanuel. Okay?" He says while looking straight at Melissa.

"Of course." She pretends to zip her mouth and throws away an imaginary key over her shoulder as we return to our meal. I can only speak for myself, but I think after this, we might all be secretly hoping Emmanuel shows up, so the topic can come up again.

But unfortunately, our break time runs out and Emmanuel doesn't show up, so we all head back to the office. As we step out of the elevator, Emmanuel emerges from the corner and walks up to us.

"Aww, no. Did I miss the break?" He rubs his forehead before placing both hands on his hips.

"Yeah, but there's no line and you can still get something to eat." Yin points toward the elevator.

"Sorry, guys. My meeting with LTH overran. Heather, did you like the place?"

A warm sensation travels across my cheeks and up my neck as I look for the right words. "Yeah, the food was great and I think you'll love the aesthetic."

"Oh yeah? Awesome. I'll take your word for it. I think alone time would do me some good anyway. See you all soon." He nods at us, but his gaze lingers on me for a few seconds before he heads toward the elevator.

At this point, the warm sensation is now taking over my belly, my underarms and... *boy, is it hot in here?*

Melissa wastes no time in rushing to my side and whispering. "I don't see the boss asking me about how I found Rosa's Café and taking my word for it. Seems like someone is getting on his good side." She wiggles her eyebrows at me and, for the second time today, I smack her arm.

"Melissa, go away." I shoo her away and return to my workstation, but when I'm sitting down, I chuckle at how ridiculous I might have looked in front of him with my flushed cheeks.

There are so many questions I would like to ask him, too. Why did he look so tired? Is he working through the night? Is he eating enough? Are the LTH clients stressing him out? Is he worried the launch won't go well? *Snap out of it, Heather. It's none of your business and you're not Melissa.* I turn on my computer and pray I can focus on my work without thinking about Emmanuel Madu.

15

HEATHER

I lift my head and glance at Emmanuel for the umpteenth time this morning. Although I wouldn't trade my view of the Hudson River for anything, the downside of the location of my workstation is that it is directly facing Emmanuel's office, so watching him do his work has become my new hobby.

I'm sure I've been staring too much because I now know he stretches his neck every half hour and that he finishes at least two cups of coffee by the end of the morning. I also know that he likes walking the length of his office when he is on the phone and sometimes he stands at his window staring at the skyline and the Hudson River. One of these days, he's going to catch me staring and I won't know what to do with myself.

Well, maybe it won't be too bad if he catches me staring because he was also staring at me a few weeks ago. Maybe that was how he noticed how low I was feeling. That day, Dad called to check up on me during lunch, but he ruined the sweet bonding moment we were having by telling me Mom would drop by the house for dinner. We got into an argument and I had to cut our conversation short because I refuse to let Mom ruin my relationship with Dad.

When I got back to the office after lunch, I tried all the techniques in the books to help me calm down, but then Emmanuel showed up and started asking me questions. I wasn't in the mood to smile, so I gave him vague answers. I'm surprised that after all my efforts to hide my feelings, he still noticed that something was wrong.

The sound of a ringing phone interrupts my thoughts and I peel my gaze away from Emmanuel as Melissa picks up the phone. But when I turn my head to look at Emmanuel again, he is staring straight at me.

Look away. Look away. Look away. My brain screams at me, but my head doesn't move. So I keep staring until a small smile tugs on the corner of his mouth and he waves at me. I wave back and flash him a sheepish smile before turning to my computer and wishing the ground would open up and swallow me.

Without letting my gaze wander to Emmanuel again, I finish working on my e-newsletters, so I can show Yin later. After saving my work, I lean sideways to reach my bag on the side of my desk and, after rummaging through it, I take out my phone to check my messages. When I come back up again, I flinch as I meet a smiling Emmanuel standing in front of me.

"I'm sorry. Did I scare you?" He cracks a smile and all I can think of is how good he looks in his black turtleneck sweater and nude trousers. Give the man any outfit and he just *owns* it.

"No, I just didn't hear you coming." I try to stay calm and forget about the fact that he caught me staring at him earlier.

"It's lunchtime," Emmanuel says before looking over his shoulder and calling out to Yin, who responds and says he will join us when he finishes sending an email. Turning back to me, Emmanuel nods toward the door. "Are you coming?"

Oh my goodness. He wants to have lunch with me? "Yes, boss." I nod and grab my bag before following him out of the office, ignoring all the eyes boring holes into my back.

In the communal area, I take a seat across from him and bring out my lemon chicken wrap as I check out the food in his lunch box. "That smells delicious. Did you make it?" The spicy aroma of his chicken chow mein teases my nostrils.

Emmanuel snorts. "No, I'm not that talented. Jess, Yin's fiancée, made it. I had dinner with them a few weeks ago and the food was so good she promised to make some more for me, so here we go."

"Aww, that's so nice of her. Yin always talks about her and I can't wait to meet her soon." I bite into my sandwich and sip on my bottle of water.

"Yeah, she's cool. You guys will make good friends." He nods before putting a forkful of noodles in his mouth. "So, you owe me some information."

My eyes widen as I try to swallow the bread in my mouth. "Oh?" *Is he going to ask me why I was staring at him? Oh, no. I should have known this was a trap.*

"Yeah, you promised you were going to tell me more about your social media marketing business."

"Oh... right." *Phew.* "Yeah, about that..." I shrug as I try to find the right words. "I've always wanted to have my own business, so after college, I got my studio apartment in Brooklyn and set up my LLC. It was called HO marketing."

"What does the HO stand for?" Emmanuel asks.

"My initials. Heather Osborne."

"I see." He dabs the corners of his mouth with tissue paper. "So what happened?"

"Well, I secured a few clients, but the money I was getting wasn't enough to live on, so I had to get a job at a coffee shop. After a year of running the business, I realized things weren't as easy as I thought they would be."

"What didn't you find easy?"

I place my sandwich on the table before looking him in the

eye. "I hadn't mastered the art of knowing where to find my ideal clients. Most of the people I reached out to were on social media and they weren't interested in my services. After a year of struggling, I started to hate my job at the coffee shop and I couldn't keep up with paying my rent, so I closed down the business and moved back home to live with my dad."

"So, getting a corporate job is a temporary solution for you?"

I nod. "The plan is to relaunch my business someday. I still want to become a full-time entrepreneur, but for now, I'm going to learn from pros like you."

Emmanuel snorts and shakes his head.

"What? It's true. I admire your leadership skills. Everyone on the team loves you. You're the world's best boss, you know?"

A broad smile appears on his lips at my compliment. "For last year's Christmas Secret Santa, Yin got me a mug with those exact words written on it." We both chuckle before a moment of silence passes between us. "Heather, I have to say, I admire a lot of things about you, too."

My cheeks warm up as I try to stop myself from smiling too much. "Really? Like what?" I'd be interested to know what he finds admirable in this messed up life of mine.

"You are focused, determined and you know what you want. You're not afraid to take risks and even when life knocks you down, you get back up again."

Well, he's darn right about that, I think to myself before picking up my sandwich again. "My dad once told me that a bird will never learn how to fly if it keeps walking on the ground."

"Your dad is a wise man."

"He is indeed, and he's so supportive as well. He refused to let me call myself a failure even when I couldn't keep myself going."

"I'm on his side." Emmanuel leans forward and places his elbow on the table. "Trying and failing is so much better than not trying at all. Your determination shows slackers like myself that I need to wake up."

It's my turn to snort. "Slacker? Emmanuel, you're not a slacker. Look at you—the future CEO of this wonderful company. That's not slacking to me."

Emmanuel shakes his head as his smile fades. *Maybe Melissa was right about the rumor.* "Heather, there's always more to certain situations than meets the eye, but I think that's a topic for another day." He says and there's silence for a few seconds before he speaks again. "What about your family decision? Have you decided on what you want to do?"

"Yeah, I think I know what I want to do." I've decided to go for lunch with Mom, so Dad can stop bugging me about it. "What about you? Have you made your decision?"

He shakes his head. "Still praying. Still waiting on God for answers."

"I'm sure He'll come through. He always does." The certainty in my voice brings out calmness in Emmanuel's features.

"Thanks, Heather."

Yin joins us at the table shortly after and when he commends me for my e-newsletters, Emmanuel announces that I'll be working with him on the next project and he'll be supervising me. The prospect of working in close proximity with Emmanuel both excites and frightens me. Of course I want to learn all I can from him because he's the boss, but his being nice to me is not helping.

The butterfly feeling in my belly is back and the last person I had butterfly feelings for was Connor. Connor and I used to... *no, no, no.* I shake my head to expel the thoughts and force myself to focus on the current conversation. I refuse to go back down that memory lane. I refuse to remember what I used to do with all the boys I let come close to me.

Take every thought captive, Heather. I exhale and force a smile, still listening to the boys talking. *Make it obedient to Christ. Not today, satan. You're not ruining this for me.*

16

HEATHER

Mom's green gaze pierces straight into mine as she sends me a small smile. The corner of her lips still curve upward the same way I remember it, but sixteen years have plagued her forehead with more wrinkles, her eyes with dark circles, and her cheeks with more freckles.

When I don't return her smile, she exhales and looks out the window at the passing cars. It's spring, so the temperatures are still moderately cold, but the anger in my chest makes me so hot I'm sweating.

Dad was so happy when I agreed to have lunch with Mom and seeing the joy in his eyes gave me a tinge of hope that everything would be better when I sat in front of her. But I was wrong. This was a terrible idea. Every gesture she makes sickens me. Her smile disgusts me, and the sad look on her face irritates me to the core.

She turns to me again and this time, she flips her brown shoulder-length hair to the side before fiddling with her fingers. I've always known her to have short hair, so seeing her with long hair makes her unrecognizable and maybe that's how it's supposed to be. The woman sitting in front of me is not my mom and she'll never be.

"How are you finding your new job?" she speaks after our awkward ten minute silence. "Your dad told me they're treating you well at Madu Health?"

Dad also told me all I have to do is listen, so that's the only thing I'm doing today. All she'll get from me is a blank stare and sealed lips. I want her to know how much I don't want to be here, how much I don't want to talk to her, and how much I loathe her for thinking she can right all her wrongs by buying me a sandwich.

"Here we go," the server arrives with a tray holding two sandwiches. "One buffalo chicken sub for you," he places a plate in front of me, "and one eggplant parm sub for you." He places the other plate in front of Mom. "Enjoy and let me know if you need anything else," he says and then walks away.

She made the choices of sandwiches because that was what I always ordered when we used to come to Sandy's sandwich shop when I was younger. I'm impressed that she didn't forget what I like, but she can't buy my forgiveness with a sandwich.

"I know you're angry with me, but, honey—"

"Don't call me that," I speak for the first time in twenty minutes. She always called me that and letting her call me that again means I'm letting her be my mom again. That's not the case.

"I'm sorry," she whispers. "Thank you for agreeing to see me. You have no idea what this means." She looks at me and her green eyes mist up.

Is she being serious? Why is she crying? If this is all she's going to do, then I better be on my way because I'm not here to feel pity for anyone.

Ten. Practice relaxation techniques.

How can I relax when there's an obvious trigger in front of me? *Lord, please help me.*

"The night I left," she starts and my heart rate quickens as I brace myself to hear her sorry excuse for destroying my life. "I had given up on my marriage with your dad. We disagreed on a lot of things and I started having doubts." Streaks of tears run down her cheeks as she continues. "Instead of taking his advice and going with him to marriage counseling, I vented to my colleague David. My company hired him from China on a temporary contract and he was so nice to me. I started confiding in him about how terrible things were between myself and your dad. That was the first mistake I made."

She lowers her head. "I liked the attention David gave me and the more I used him as a source of release, the more I started developing feelings for him. We started spending too much time together. One thing led to another, and I ended up being unfaithful. Everything happened so fast and I didn't mean to hurt anyone." The tears pour out of her eyes. "I was too ashamed to face your dad, so when David asked me to move back with him to China, I took a risk and followed him. I didn't think my marriage was ever going to recover from my cheating, so I counted my losses and left."

Nine. Think before you speak.

I bounce my leg under the table, waiting, begging for the anger in my chest to subside, but it doesn't.

"You're despicable," I say through gritted teeth as tears run down my face. "You're selfish and you're…"

"Yes, I was," Mom cuts in and leans forward. "I blame myself and I take full responsibility for everything. It was wrong of me to leave, and I'm sorry."

My chest heaves as I swallow the lump in my throat. "Why did you come back? Why are you here?"

She leans back and sniffles before continuing her pathetic

story. "Shortly after we arrived in Beijing, I filed for a divorce from your dad. David was divorced too and his children lived far away, so I had nothing to worry about. But after the first year, David's attitude toward me changed. He started keeping late nights, drinking and complaining about every single thing I did. I kept quiet because I didn't want him to throw me out. I had nowhere else to go and I couldn't come back here to face the shame and guilt.

"Five years into it, he hit me for the first time. He was drunk and promised he would kill me if I told anyone. I couldn't do anything about it. He stopped giving me money, so I started using up the money I saved and since I had no job, David dictated my life." Her shaky hands wipe the tears sliding down her cheeks. She holds her chest, closes her eyes, and exhales before continuing. "I was so afraid to report him because I feared he was going to kill me.

"I tried to run away so many times, but each time he found me and locked me up for days without food or water." She coughs and dabs the side of her cheeks. "Two years ago, I found a church on my way back from the market and I got the courage to speak to the pastor. I snuck out of the house to attend the meetings and when I knew I could trust them, I confided in them about my situation. I rededicated my life to Jesus and, having received the assurance that God had forgiven me, I fought hard to come back home. I made a vow to God that if I were to leave China alive, I would reconcile with my family.

"The pastor helped me report to the police, and they found me temporary accommodation. They helped me find a job, and I saved some money to buy a ticket back here." She looks me in the eye and I turn my face away. "All those days I was lying weak in the room David locked me in, I thought about you, Heather. I thought about your sweet smile, your warm hugs, and your feisty personality, which always took my breath away. I've made so many mistakes in my life, but the one I regret the most is leaving you here."

She pushes her sandwich to the side. "Heather, please, I want to make things right. I know it'll take a lot of work, but I'm ready to do anything you ask of me."

"I love your dad." She sniffles. "And I love you." She reaches for my hand across the table, but I jerk it away.

The anger I've been suppressing for the last thirty minutes flares inside my chest. "You know nothing about love. God gave you a chance to be my mom, and you threw it away without batting an eyelid. So you expect me to feel sorry for you? Run into your arms like nothing ever happened? Would you have remembered you had a daughter if your lover hadn't turned out to be a beast?"

Her hands cover her mouth as she tries to quiet her sobs. "Honey, I thought about you."

"Where did your thoughts get me, huh?" I interject. "You have no idea what I've been through because of you."

"I want healing for you and for me. That's why I'm here."

"I don't need you." I push my chair back, my voice rising. "Dad and I don't need you. We've been doing just fine. We will continue to survive without you. God has changed my life and I won't let you ruin it again. Your apology is sixteen years late and I want nothing to do with you." I push against the table to stand up, but she reaches for my hands and holds them.

"Heather, please, I'll do anything you ask. Anything, please."

I look straight into her watery green eyes and say the words I never believed I'd ever say. "I want you to stay out of my life... for good." With that, I pick up my backpack and walk away with nothing but her muffled sobs etched in my memory.

17

EMMANUEL

"Thank you for coming, everyone." Dad beckons to the group of employees walking in a single file into the communal area. When we're all settled inside, he clears his throat and continues. "I know this is impromptu, but I wanted to treat you all to lunch," he says before pointing to the corner of the room.

We all turn our heads to find displays of different foods spread out across a long table. There are sandwiches, wraps, meats, vegetables, fruits, and smoothies, and the delicious aroma makes my mouth water. Dad must be in a good mood today; I know this because he is wearing his favorite kaftan, the royal blue one Mom asked our family designer to make for him during one of her trips to Nigeria. It was her last birthday gift to him.

"I know I'm taking you away from work, but there's an old saying that *all work and no play makes Jack a dull boy,* so I wanted to thank you all for working hard over the last month. I'm so happy with the progress we've made on the Long Term Health project and I'm proud of you all."

"Whoop whoop!" Neil starts clapping and soon everyone

follows. When the room goes quiet again, Dad continues. "I especially want to thank my son, Emmanuel." Dad locks eyes with me and every head in the room turns to me. "He has been working tirelessly and led you all fiercely in pursuit of success with this project. He makes me proud to call myself a father, and I just wanted to let you know I appreciate you, son."

"Go, Emmanuel!" Yin yells from the opposite corner of the room as the applause returns like a surging wave. Dad gets a small smile from me to camouflage the guilt in my chest. I wonder if he'll still feel the same way if he finds out I'm planning to turn down his offer. I wonder if he'll still appreciate me the same way he does if I don't follow in his footsteps.

"Finally, I want to say a special thank you to the newest member of the team, Miss Heather Osborne." Dad points to the red-haired, green-eyed girl standing in the front row.

She's looking exceptionally beautiful today and I'm not sure if it's because she's wearing her hair down or if it's her red lipstick giving off girl boss vibes. Whatever it is—she's a sight for my sore eyes.

"She has only been with us for a month," Dad's speech cuts into my thoughts. "But I've already heard about her hard work and determination. Heather, we appreciate people like you on the team, so thank you for all the work you do."

"Go, Heather!" The words come out involuntarily from my mouth and I clap, surprising myself as the rest of the crowd joins in the applause. Heather turns her head in my direction and when her gaze finds mine, she smiles—a sight that brings joy to me for reasons I don't understand. I have no choice but to smile back.

"Now, let's eat and be merry," Dad says his last words, and the crowd disperses. Soft music plays from the speakers as everyone walks over to the table. Chatters and laughter fill the room as we talk about our success so far and how amazing it'll be when the LTH project is over.

I should be in the same mood as well–happy and excited about what the future holds for my father's company (and soon-to-be my company). It's not that I don't want to be happy, it's the fact that I feel like an ungrateful son who is just waiting to disappoint his father.

By the time I get to the food table, my appetite is gone and in its place is nausea, which is churning my insides and threatening to make me bring up the porridge I had for breakfast. I walk past all the food and grab a smoothie before heading toward the door.

"Emmanuel?" Dad's voice stops me in my tracks, and I exhale before turning to look at him. "I hope it's not the food making you look so pale. Are you okay?" Dad's graying eyebrows crease up as he places his hand on my shoulder.

I nod and smile. "Of course, Dad. I'm fine. I'm just going to get some fresh air."

Dad tilts his head and squints. "Are you sure?"

"Yeah. You worry too much. I'm fine." I squeeze his shoulder and start walking away, but he speaks again.

"You'll tell me if something is wrong, right?" The man's piercing gaze forces more guilt into my chest. "Your mom loved hiding things from me because she didn't want me to worry, but I've always prayed that you and Olanna don't take that same attitude because…"

"Dad, Dad…" I cut him short so he can stop prolonging my misery. "I promise I'm fine and if anything is wrong, I will tell you. Okay?"

He finally sighs and nods. "Okay, then. I'm going to get myself some more food. You should try the chicken when you come back. I told the caterers I won't hire them again if they didn't make it spicy enough." Dad laughs as he heads back to the table while I make my way out of the communal area and up the spiral stairs to the first floor.

Walking down the narrow corridor, I unlock the double doors and step onto the balcony. Unlike the other popular balconies in the office building, this one is less frequented (at least that's what I think), but it has the best view of the skyscrapers and the Hudson River. I call it my secret hiding place and since I accidentally discovered it a few weeks ago, I've been coming here every day to pray about my dilemma.

Exhaling, I walk up to the bar and lean against it before admiring the beauty of God's creation. The sun's rays reflecting off the ripples of the water and the blue skies displaying their beauty are enough to distract me for a few minutes. I lift my head to the sky and whisper the same words I've whispered every day. "Lord, please help me. Show me what to do. I'm very confused. Give me clarity, so I can do the right thing without hurting my family."

Just then, a squeaking noise forces me to turn my head toward the door, and Heather stops in her tracks when she sees me. "I'm sorry. I didn't think I would find anyone here."

"No, please, you can stay." I straighten my back and nod for her to come in.

She turns to look at me, her fingers already wrapped around the door handle. "Are you sure?"

"Of course I'm sure. It's a free country, isn't it?"

She cracks a small smile and again, joy fills my heart. I like that feeling. It's a feeling I wouldn't mind getting used to. What I don't understand is why making her smile brings me so much joy.

Heather tightens her jacket around her waist and leans against the balcony, mimicking my posture. We stare at the view for a few minutes before she breaks the silence. "I thought I was the only one who owned this secret hiding place." She grins.

"I thought the same. I've been coming up here every day for the last two weeks. How come I've never bumped into you?"

"That's because I only come up here after work, so I can have some alone time and say a quick prayer before going home. That way, I feel I'll be ready for whatever difficult conversation I have to have with my dad."

"You and your dad have a rocky relationship?" I ask, glad to know she is comfortable enough to open up to me.

"No, not my dad. It's my mom I don't get along with, but hey, that's not important right now. What are you doing up here, boss?" she changes the subject.

Her question catches me off-guard, and I take a few seconds to decide how much information is wise enough to share, given I've only known Heather for a month. "Interestingly, I've been coming up here to pray as well, you know, for that family issue I mentioned before."

"I see," she says. "Does it have anything to do with your..." Her words trail off as she clamps her mouth shut with her hand.

I frown and turn to look at her. "My what?"

She averts her gaze and brings down her hand. "Nothing, erm... forget I said anything. I'll just head back to the..."

"Heather, we're friends, right?" I ask, placing one hand in my pocket.

"Erm, yes. I'd like to think so."

"So if you're my friend, you'll tell me if you have any information that will help me, right?"

"Yeah, I would, but I'm not sure if this information will help."

"Well, if it's about me, then I'd like to know. Please."

After a bit of hesitation, she finally responds. "Okay, fine. But please promise me no one will get fired?"

"You have my word." I smile to ease the tension, and she relaxes.

"On my first day here, Melissa told Yin and I that Neil told her he overheard a conversation between you and your dad in the conference room. He said you sounded like you didn't want to take over the company."

"Wow, so Neil's the source of the rumor?" I shake my head and laugh. "I have to admit, he has a hidden talent for making good assumptions."

"So, it's true?"

I shrug. "Apparently so." I turn around and lean my back against the bar.

"May I ask why?" Heather leans her hip against the bar too, her eyes fixed on me. For some strange reason, even though this is very unlike me, I feel the need to confide in her.

Maybe it's the fact that we both have family dilemmas, or that I find it so easy to talk to her. Whatever it is, something about telling her feels right.

"My dad grew up in a large family and, being the oldest of seven children, he had to work hard to look after his younger siblings and to send them to school. When he migrated to the US, he made a promise that he would work hard to build a legacy for himself and his family. So after completing his education, he set up Madu Health and built it from the ground up. He took big risks, invested a lot of money and he ignored the naysayers until he succeeded. When he married my mom, she helped him build Madu Health to what it is today.

"My dad is a family man, and he believes in the importance of sticking together and conquering together. My little sister Olanna and I have always been told that Madu Health is our legacy, so my dad brought us up using the high achievement parenting style. Do you know very much about it?"

Heather shakes her head. "Not really, but the name says a lot."

"Yeah, I don't think my dad knew that was the parenting style he used on us, but I've done a lot of thinking over the years and it makes sense. Dad never allowed us to make mistakes, and failure wasn't an option. He taught us to always aim for excellence and if the results of our efforts weren't up to his standards, he scolded us for it. Whenever I told my dad I got ninety percent on an exam, he always asked what happened to the remaining ten percent before congratulating me. With him, we either go big or go home. We have to shoot for the moon because there's no option to land among the stars." I let out a brief chuckle, hoping it would hide the pain in my voice, but the sympathy in Heather's eyes tells me I'm not doing a great job.

"My mom was more gentle with Olanna and I so we always went to her whenever we fell short of my dad's expectations. Mom knew how to break the news of our failures to Dad and pacify his disappointment." I clear my throat to take away a lump that has wedged itself in there as memories of Mom flood my mind.

"Dad believes that pushing himself beyond his comfort zone was what made him succeed in this country, and I agree with him. I don't think I would have achieved half of what I did in my academics if he hadn't pushed me the way he did."

"But?" Heather asks in a soft voice. Her attention is still on me and something about the way she looks at me encourages me to keep talking.

"But..." I sigh before continuing. "The truth is that all these years of working hard to meet my dad's expectations have drained me. Everyone focuses on the results and the outcomes, but no one sees the crippling anxiety I have about whether my hard work will ever be good enough to lead Madu Health the same way Dad has done for the last thirty years. The worst part of it is that every day when I come to work, I get the overpowering feeling that this is not what God wants me to do."

Heather is silent for a few seconds as she crosses her arms

against her chest, her gaze still on me. "Do you know what God wants you to do?" she asks, and I shrug.

"I have an idea."

"Does your dad know how you feel?"

I turn my head away before shaking it. "I've never had the guts to tell him because I know he would be disappointed."

Heather sighs and we both stare at the water for a few minutes before she speaks again. "Your situation reminds me of a Bible passage I was reading last night. You know the one where Jesus was twelve years old, and he stayed behind in the temple to teach even though his parents had traveled without Him?"

I nod. "Yeah?"

"Jesus never cared about what His parents would think. He just knew he had a mission to accomplish, and He did it no matter what people said. So there's one question I always ask myself whenever I'm unhappy doing something. 'Am I doing this because I feel guilty or obligated or am I doing this because of my own values and convictions?' If the answer is the former, then something needs to change."

Wow, such wise words. "I never thought about it like that before." Mom would have definitely said something along those lines. "Thank you so much. I appreciate your words and sometimes I wish I were in your shoes, you know?"

"Mmm-hmm." She shakes her head before saying, "It's like you told me before—you have to be careful with what you wish for."

"Yeah, but I'm sure your family isn't as dramatic as mine," I say, hoping that she would open up a bit more about her family too, but she only smiles and gives me vague answers. The fact that she's being so guarded makes me more determined to find out more about her. Why does she need to pray before going home? Why doesn't she get along with her mom? Will she ever tell me what her dilemma is, so I can help her out the same way she has helped me with mine?

Getting to know her is like peeling an onion, with every layer revealing something more exciting. It's like putting together the pieces of a puzzle and I know the final picture will be beautiful —just like the woman standing in front of me right now.

"Can I ask you a question?" Heather's voice jostles me out of my thoughts.

"Yeah. Sure."

"Remember, you promised no one will get fired, right?"

I chuckle and rub my beard. "Why do I have a feeling you're going to use that against me every day?"

It's her turn to chuckle. "No, I'm just curious to know why you were so cold toward me the first time we met."

"Oh, no." I drop my head in my hands as embarrassment washes over me.

"Was I too chatty? Did I give you a bad vibe? Was it my shoes? My hair?"

"No, it was neither of those things." I lift my head to meet her gaze. "My first impression of you was a confident woman who knows what she wants."

"Really?" A small smile forms on her lips. "So what was it, then?"

"I guess you could say it was... a transfer of aggression. I was not happy that my dad didn't tell me before hiring an intern, so I chose to..."

"Be a jerk?" She crosses her arms and tilts her head, her green gaze boring into my soul.

I wasn't expecting her to be so direct and I want to defend myself, but we both know she's right. "Yes. Yes, exactly. I was a total jerk, and I knew my behavior was unnecessary, so I apologize because you didn't deserve that. I appreciate your hard work, and I've loved working with you over the last month."

Her smile is wider this time, her red cheeks showing she has accepted my apology (well, I hope so). "Thank you. You're forgiven and I've loved working with you, too."

"Great. I'm glad we've gotten that off our chests." I push myself away from the bar and nod toward the door. "We better head back before the chief executive starts looking for us. I promised him I'll try the chicken."

"Yes, you should *definitely* try it. It's finger-licking good." Heather smiles as I hold the door open for her.

"Cool. I can't wait." I return her smile before we walk down the stairs and out into the corridor leading back to the communal area. When we get to the door, I place my hand on Heather's elbow, gently slowing her down in her tracks. "Heather?"

She lifts her head and meets my gaze. "Yeah?"

"Listen... you're the first person I've ever told this much about my family, so I would appreciate it if you keep this between us. I don't want—"

"It's okay, boss." She cuts me off with a smile. "Your secret is safe with me." She pretends to zip her lips and throws away an imaginary key over her shoulder before we share a laugh and join the others in celebrating.

18

HEATHER

Sunday has always been my favorite day. It used to be because I could lie in and have a lazy day and forget about my problems for a little while. But now I love Sundays because I get to fellowship with other like-minded people at church who help me grow in my faith.

Six months after Teeyana spoke to me about Jesus, I walked into church for the first time in over two years. It's crazy to think about how much my anger tried to steal away from me. But now that I've returned, I'm not going back to where I came from. Everything I need is in the presence of God.

Including the grace to forgive.

Dad squeezes my hand, and I shake the voice away. When I lift my head to look at him, he pulls his brows together. "Are you okay?" He asks and I nod before turning back to focus on the pastor's sermon.

I never imagined I'd end up back here in my childhood church, sitting in these pews and listening to this same pastor preach. When I left home for college six years ago, it was my intention to never come back, but God has a way of reminding me He is still in control. Everything about being here feels right and no matter how hard it is to admit, I'm glad I came back to New Jersey.

I never realized how much I missed this place until I came back. The white walls and stained glass windows are still the same and they remind me about how I used to stare at the windows for several minutes, wondering why they were so colorful.

I've changed so much in the last six years, but everyone here, even though they've aged, seems to be the same way I remember them. The pastor's children, although all teens now, still sing in the choir and play the drums, guitar, and piano. The kids who used to be teens are now all in college or working, but are still involved in the youth ministry. These are all children I wanted to be like, but the key difference is they had both parents while growing up and I didn't.

Every good memory I made here always brings with it ten more memories of sadness and brokenness because of everything I've lost and all the mistakes I've made. A part of me longs for the life I had before Mom left, but the other part of me wants to keep shutting her out of my life.

She deserves it. The words almost run out of my mouth as I bite back a tear. They say what goes around comes back around and this is true in this situation. *She definitely deserves it.*

"Ask God to give you grace," the pastor says in his closing remark as I catch a tear sliding down my cheek. "Give grace to one another and show unconditional love, no matter how others treat you."

An uncomfortable feeling settles in my chest as I adjust in my seat. The fact that I'm hearing these words from the pastor for the first time shows how distracted I've been throughout the whole sermon.

"Grace, brothers and sisters," the pastor repeats. "Grace, to forgive those who have hurt you, even when they don't deserve it. For in the same way God has shown us mercy, let us all also show each other mercy. Amen."

"Amen." The congregation responds, and the pastor says a word of prayer. Everyone bows their head and closes their eyes, including Dad. Everyone except me.

Heather.

I can't do it. My thoughts trump the still voice as the pastor prays for God to help us extend grace to one another. The war between my head and my heart continues. I know what I need to do. I know what God wants me to do. But I can't do it.

"Amen," the congregation says before everyone stands up and starts clapping. I push myself up and wipe my tears again.

"I'll just go say hello to the pastor, honey. Do you want to come with me?" Dad says as the congregation disperses one by one. I shake my head and he squeezes my shoulder before leaving. It's enough torture that I didn't listen to the pastor's sermon and that I'm struggling to come to terms with the message. If I stand in front of the pastor, I'll feel even more guilty about not forgiving Mom as quickly as Dad has.

"Heather, dear, it's so good to see you." Mrs. Tanner, my favorite eighty-year-old, walks toward me, elegantly dressed as always. I stand up and hug her and she gives me some candy from her purse before reminding me to stop smoking even though I've told her a million times I've quit. When the elderly woman walks away, I lower myself back on the seat, tapping my foot and silently praying Dad doesn't take too long.

"Hi, honey." A familiar voice says and I ball my fists, wishing the voice to go away and hoping she's not standing behind me.

She steps closer and touches my arm, but I jerk it away. "Please don't call me that." My breath quickens as the same emotions from our lunch date two weeks ago come flooding back.

"Isn't it great to be back here?" she asks, and I say nothing. I slide further down the pew, but instead of taking the hint and leaving me alone, she takes a seat next to me. "How have you been? I..."

"Hey." Dad walks up to us, interrupting the conversation, and I stand up immediately. *Thank God.* "I see you guys have been catching up without me." He says with a broad smile and I shake my head. I don't understand why he ignores the fact that I'm obviously uncomfortable around her. "Honey, we were thinking of going for a walk and then getting pizza, just like old times. Would you like to join us?"

Just like old times? Is he being serious right now? I frown. "I'm good. You can go with her. I'm tired, so I'll walk home."

"Erm... there'll be no need for that," Mom says. "If you're tired, then your dad will take you home. I'll be on my way."

"You sure?" Dad asks and Mom nods.

"Yeah, don't worry about me. Bye, Heather," she says before walking away.

The ride home with Dad is quiet and I know he can sense my frustration now, but I don't care. This isn't easy for me and he should understand that.

"So... honey, you never told me how your lunch date with your mom went," Dad says as he hangs his jacket on the hook in the hallway.

I let out a deep sigh and turn to face him. "Really, Dad? I'm sure you've already spoken to her about it, so why are you asking me?" I take my shoes off and place them on the shoe stand before walking into the living room and plopping down on the sofa. Dad follows behind and sits on the sofa across from me.

I drop my gaze to the floor, fiddling with my thumbs, and chewing on my lip as the war between my heart and head continues—or shall I say, between my flesh and my spirit. I'm so focused on winning my internal battle, I don't even realize when the tears return and slide down my cheek. *The spirit is willing, but the body is weak.* The scripture I read last night comes to me, but I lock it out of my mind. *I can't do it.* My comfortable response returns.

"How do you do it, Dad?" I ask after five minutes of silence between us. "How can you just forgive and forget like that? How can you smile at her, hug her and... breathe the same air as her when she's hurt you so much?"

Dad stands up and sits on the arm of my sofa. "Honey, I haven't forgotten. I can never forget and I'm not saying that you should. I held on to the hurt and grudge for years, and it killed me. Holding on to anger is like drinking poison and expecting the person you hate to die. I couldn't do it anymore. It's never easy, but it's always worth it to extend grace to others. "

"Oh, please don't preach to me, Dad. Don't make me look like the bad guy here because you know we wouldn't be in this situation if Mom hadn't left."

"But, honey, she's a changed person."

I can't help but snort as I let my head fall into my hands.

"She is," Dad continues. "When she first called me from Beijing, I was very angry. I wanted nothing to do with her and I didn't want to help her at first. But she was stranded and you know she burned a lot of bridges with her family and friends when she made the move. I know she hurt me, but I wasn't going to let that be the reason I didn't help her when I could. If anything had happened to her—if that guy had killed her—that memory would have haunted me forever."

Dad runs his hands through his auburn hair and holds my hands. "She's still the only woman I've ever loved and I couldn't reject her when she needed me the most because God would never do that to me. She has made her peace with God and God has accepted her back. So why wouldn't we?"

I wipe my tears, waiting, hoping that I'll feel better, that I'll also have that overwhelming urge to run into her arms, hug her and accept her as my mom again. I wait earnestly, but the feeling doesn't come. Finally, I say to Dad, "I'm happy you have your wife back, Dad." I squeeze his hands. "But I'm sure you'll agree that everyone heals at a different pace. This is just too much for me to deal with. I need more time and I think it would be better if I keep my distance for now."

19

EMMANUEL

How do you label the dilemma of not being able to stop thinking about someone? Being a creep? A stalker? Catching feelings? Whatever it is, the dilemma remains that I can't get Heather Osborne out of my head. Why? Because the girl intrigues me.

She's so different from me—bolder, more direct, assertive,—and I'll be honest, I'm envious. My respect for her reached a new level after our talk on the balcony two weeks ago. I love how confident she is in her faith and how sure she is of her convictions.

It reminds me of Yin, and how encouraging he was when I wavered after Mom's death. Yin was the constant friend, reminding me it was never too late to come back to God. I need more people like this in my life.

"Everything okay, boss?" Yin's voice drags me out of my thoughts, but before I can peel my gaze away from the subject of my attention, he turns around to look at *her*—Heather Osborne. It's in times like this I question whether it was a good idea to have glass walls in this office.

"Erm... yeah." I clear my throat. "Everything is fine."

"Really?" Yin turns to look at me again, a grin plastered on his face.

"Why are you smiling like that?" I frown, but realize I have to pull out a believable explanation from my jumbled thoughts. "Listen, Olanna is coming home for the summer break next week, and I thought that she and Heather would make good friends."

"Mmm-hmm. Sure!" Yin crosses his arms against his chest and leans back in his chair.

"What? I'm serious. You don't think they would make good friends?"

"The real question is, are you asking for Olanna or are you asking for yourself, huh?" He pushes himself up and picks up the file he brought with him to our meeting.

"I don't know what you're talking about." I pretend to tidy up the stack of files on my desk and Yin suppresses a laugh.

"I think you know *exactly* what I'm talking about, boss," Yin says before taking backward steps toward the door. "But when you're ready to admit it, I'll be right here waiting to tell you 'I told you so.'" His laugh intensifies as he dodges the stress ball I launch at him.

"Hey, don't forget you owe me the report about the campaigns before lunch."

"Don't worry about me, boss. I'll do my work and I won't be getting in the way of you and your crush," he says and then bolts out the door before I get the chance to say anything.

When my gaze lands on her again, my smile finally breaks through. Could Yin's theories have some truth in them? No, Yin jokes around a lot, so I'm not giving him much thought. The morning hours pass by quickly with no more distractions and, like he promised, Yin drops off his report before he heads out for lunch. He is meeting up with Jess because they have a meeting with their wedding planner, so he'll be skipping lunch with me today.

Heather is no longer at her desk, so I pick up my lunch from the fridge and step out of my office to look for her. Let's hope she didn't catch me staring at her all morning and she'll agree to have lunch with me. I power walk up the stairs to the first floor communal area, but Heather is already sitting with Melissa and Neil. *Oh, no. I'm too late.*

This shouldn't be a big deal, but the disappointment twisting my stomach says otherwise. Like a child who has been scolded, I redirect my steps down the stairs to the communal area on the ground floor. It's busier, but it's not long before I find a table to sit with Ben, Adriana, and Carolina from the advertising team.

If Yin could notice me staring at Heather when we were in a meeting, then I don't trust myself to not do the same if I sit at another table on the second floor. After lunch and a good catch up with the advertising team about their families, I return to the office to find Heather and Melissa talking at her desk. *Sigh.* It doesn't look like I'll be speaking to Heather on her own today.

My plan is to walk past Heather's desk and straight into my office so I don't interrupt their conversation, but when Heather locks eyes with me, I can't help myself. "Hey." I stop in front of the ladies.

"Hey, boss." Heather turns her whole body to face me as a smile appears on her face.

"Sorry, I hope I'm not interrupting anything."

"Oh, no, no. I was just leaving," Melissa says before walking away.

Yes, I finally have my alone time, but now that I do, I don't even know what I've been dying to tell her all day. "How is everything going today?" I put one hand in my pocket. "Are you still enjoying it?"

She smiles. "Of course. I've made so much progress with Yin this week, and I'm sure he updated you this morning."

"Yeah, he did. I'm very impressed—as always."

"Thank you. Well, only a few hours to go and my energy is waning, so I'll get to work now. I don't want to stay late."

"Yeah... yeah, of course." What did I expect, that she'll spend her whole afternoon talking to me because I finally got to speak to her alone? *Get a grip on yourself, Emmanuel.* "That's a good idea. I shall... speak to you later."

She nods and turns back to her computer while I return to my office to get on with my own work. A few minutes later, I overhear Melissa saying she's going to get coffee, and an idea pops into my mind, so I call out to her as she walks past my office.

"Yes, can I help, boss?" Melissa pops her head in, but I beckon her to come inside.

"You're going to get coffee from Rosa's Café, right?"

She nods. "Mmm-hmm, do you want me to get you anything?"

"No, but I want you to get something for Heather, please?"

"Heather, huh?" Melissa raises her brows and tilts her head. She has the same sly grin Yin had on his face this morning. "That's very interesting," she sing-songs as I hand her some cash.

"Please add in some shortbread as well. I think she likes those, too."

"Of course she does. She hasn't stopped talking about them since I got her to try one a few weeks ago. Good choice, boss." Her voice gets louder with each word.

"Shh!" *This is what I get for involving people in my business.* "When you give her the coffee, tell her I hope it keeps her energy from waning, so she doesn't have to stay late."

"I sure will." Melissa smiles before she leaves, and ten minutes later, she returns and walks straight to Heather's desk.

My heart pounds against my ribcage as I watch Heather's facial expression when Melissa hands her the coffee and the shortbread. They talk and laugh for thirty seconds and Melissa walks away while Heather's gaze returns to her computer.

I'm not sure what I was expecting to happen, but she doesn't look at me at all and for the second time in a row today, my stomach twists tighter with disappointment. I return to my work and throw myself into my meetings with the other department managers.

The hours pass by so quickly that I don't even realize when Heather leaves. Well, I guess what today has taught me is that when you do something nice and expect to get something in return, you may end up with disappointment.

When I end up finishing half an hour early, I have to ask myself whether getting disappointed is all it'll take for me to go home on time every day. I stretch out the tension in my neck and fingers before carrying my files back to my bookshelf. After checking the plant babies once more, I carry my suitcase, turn off the lights in my office, and head out.

As I approach the reception area and my gaze lands on a familiar red-haired girl sitting in the waiting area, I stop in my tracks. "Heather? I thought you'd gone home."

She pushes herself up and walks toward me before swinging her backpack over her shoulder. "No, I was waiting to speak to you before leaving."

"Really?" I ask, surprise wrapped around my voice. "Is everything okay?" I have to ask that question because what if she didn't like the coffee and—

"Yeah, everything is great," Heather's response cuts through my line of thought. "I wanted to say thank you for the coffee, the shortbread... and the message too." She chuckles. "I didn't think you were paying attention to what I was saying."

Relief and satisfaction wash over me as a wide grin takes

over my face. "You're welcome. I think kindness is a virtue I want to foster in this workspace." The serious tone in my voice is unnecessary, but it's the best I can do to stop myself from literally patting myself on the back.

"Well, I appreciate your kindness, boss," she says with a playful nod as we walk to the door.

"Good to know. How are you getting home?" I ask when we step out of the building.

"I'll take the train. My car is not in great condition at the moment, so I'm saving up to buy a new one." She tucks a strand of her hair behind her ear.

"I see. Well, I don't live far from you, so I'm happy to drop you home, if you don't mind."

She shakes her head. "Thank you, but I don't want to inconvenience you. I'll be fine."

"You're not inconveniencing me at all. I just saw another opportunity to be kind and I'm grabbing it. Please?"

She pauses for a moment, looks toward the parking lot, and then nods. As she follows me toward my car, I mull over the events of today and I think it's safe to say now is the time where I get to pump my fists in the air for getting some victory. But of course, I'll save that energy for when I'm in the safety of my own home.

20

HEATHER

Two *months.* That's how long it took to become the boss's favorite employee. Yes, that's right. Emmanuel's favorite employee. Given how much attention he has been giving me the last month, that's the only title befitting of my status in this office.

Since the day we had our heart-to-heart talk on the balcony, it seems we now see each other in a different light. It's true what they say that pouring out your heart and being vulnerable with someone can build intimacy. That conversation on the balcony never felt awkward or inappropriate. It just felt like two friends talking and encouraging each other through challenges. Well, it was mostly Emmanuel sharing his challenges, but I related to them in a way I never thought I would.

The reckless lifestyle I lived during my teenage years meant I made no real friends, except for Teeyana and Amara. But with both girls being so far away and busy preparing for a wedding and a baby, it's been hard finding time to catch up.

I like the foundation of my friendship with Emmanuel. This is the kind of friendship I need to build. It's good for me and I hope the butterflies in my belly won't ruin it for me.

I've barely worked with Yin this week because Emmanuel has asked me to join him in meetings and run errands with him for the Long Term Health project. If it were any other boss, I would complain, but Emmanuel has bought me coffee every morning, bought me lunch whenever we spent our lunch hour out of the office, and he has driven me home on the evenings we've finished late.

I know I wanted to impress the bosses here at Madu Health, but I thought I would have to work extra hard to prove myself. It turns out all I had to do was to be myself and here we are—the boss's favorite employee.

Workload on the Long Term Health project has intensified over the last month and even though my never-ending tasks and to-do lists make me want to scream, Emmanuel has made things a lot more bearable. I have to be honest and say that his extra attention has been making me think about him a lot.

I always try to compose myself whenever he locks eyes with me or whenever he compliments my work, but then I play over the moments in my head when I get home from work or before I fall asleep. *Snap out of it, Heather. He's your boss.*

"Good morning." Just like that, my real life distraction is standing in front of me, dressed in gray trousers with a white shirt and tie. He smiles at me and the perfection of the curve of his mouth unsettles the butterflies in my stomach again.

"Morning, boss." My voice is croaky as I turn in my desk chair to face him. "You had a haircut?" I ask, my gaze lingering on his low fade haircut even though the real reason I noticed was because of how much neater his beard looks.

"Yeah, I did. Do you like it?" He smiles and turns his head from side to side, giving me a full view.

"Yeah, it's very nice." *Of course I like it. You're handsome.* "Your barber deserves an award."

"I know. You deserve one too, because you've been so helpful over the last few weeks. Here you go." He places a brown bag on my table. "We have a long day ahead of us, so I need to make sure you're getting all the energy you need."

The aroma from the bag is so strong, saliva wets my mouth and forces me to open up the bag to check out the contents. There's a breakfast burrito with avocado, cheese and eggs—just the way I like it. "Wow, thank you so much."

"You're welcome. Meeting is in thirty minutes. Please bring your notebook, as I'll need you to jot down some important points." He says as he walks backward toward his office.

"Sure. I'll be there in fifteen minutes."

He winks at me before turning around and entering his office and my heart skips a beat—literally. I lean back in my seat and try to suppress my smile, but can't stop myself from laughing when Melissa gives me a thumbs up and Neil makes kissing faces. If I didn't have twenty pairs of eyes staring at me right now, I would break out into a dance.

"Hey, what's this?" Yin says from beside me as he peeks inside the bag. "Wow. Emmanuel and I have been friends for the last two years and he has never bought me breakfast."

"Oh... you can share mine if you want." I push the bag close to him. "I had breakfast before leaving the house today, anyway," I lie. There's no way I'd eat when I know Emmanuel will get me breakfast.

"No, don't mind me. I'm only joking. I'm just glad you guys are getting along," Yin says before turning his head to look at Emmanuel in his office. He is now seated behind his desk, with his glasses on, and typing on his computer. That means he has already checked on his plant babies and sprayed them with water.

"There's something about him that has changed and I have a good feeling about it," Yin says, and I know exactly what he means.

I can feel what Yin feels, too. I can't explain it, but I know something good is about to happen. With the project deadlines being met and successful milestones being reached, I can't be grateful enough for being part of this wonderful company.

"Okay, have a nice day. I'll see you later," Yin says as he walks down the office to his desk.

Ignoring some of the watching eyes, I devour my burrito so I can satisfy my hunger pangs. The explosion of spices from the eggs blends in perfect harmony with the melting cheese and the subtle taste of the avocado. It's a food symphony—one I can't explain. One needs to experience it to know what I'm talking about. I don't know how Emmanuel found out that food is my love language, but he has officially won me over.

The day passes quickly and after a lot of meetings and me working on some blog content for LTH, the evening finally draws near. I watch from my desk as everyone leaves one by one, leaving me, Neil, and Emmanuel, who is still cooped up behind his desk. Neil joined us halfway through the day and had to complete some press releases and articles to prepare for the launch.

"See you tomorrow, Heather. Don't stay too late," Yin says as heads toward the exit. "I promised to take Jess and her little sister out to the movies tonight. I would have stayed and helped otherwise."

"Please, don't apologize. Go have fun and I'll see you on Monday." I shoo him away before returning to my work.

Another half hour passes and at six o'clock, Emmanuel bursts out of his office, shock on his face as he looks at me. "Heather? You're still here?"

I nod. "Yeah, just adding some finishing touches on these blog post drafts and—"

"Oh no, no. It's an hour after your finish time. You shouldn't be here. I'm sorry. I forgot to tell you both to leave," he says, turning to Neil at the other end of the office.

"It's okay, boss. I'll be done soon," Neil says, his eyes still glued to the computer screen in front of him.

Emmanuel turns to me as if expecting me to say otherwise, but of course I have to agree to stay. "I'm not complaining."

He chuckles, shakes his head, and rubs his eyes. He has now taken off his tie and unbuttoned the top button of his shirt. "You don't give up, do you?"

I only shrug and suppress a smile as I feel his gaze on me.

"Fine, give me a second." He disappears into his office and reappears five minutes later with his laptop. "Come on, let's all work together, so we can make sure we finish on time." He nods toward one of the round center tables at the far end of the open plan office. "Neil, are you coming?"

"No, I'm okay over here. Too much effort to move."

Well, that sounds great. More 1:1 time with the boss. I power walk behind Emmanuel and place my laptop on the table as he settles in a chair across from me.

Not long after logging on, an ache pierces through my eyes, radiating to the back of my head and then all around. I close my eyes for a few seconds before rubbing them until the ache subsides.

"You're getting eye strain, aren't you?"

I lift my head to find Emmanuel staring at me. "Huh?"

"Eye strain. From staring at the screens for too long." He nods toward the laptop. "You get sore eyes and headaches, right?"

"Yeah, all the time." I sigh and rub my forehead.

"One second." He scrambles in his backpack and takes out a glasses case. "These are blue-light blocking glasses. They'll help reduce the strain on your eyes. Trust me, they do the trick."

I take the case from him and immediately notice the logo on

it. No way. He wouldn't just give away his designer glasses to me, would he?

My jaw drops when I open the case. The branded name and colors are indeed embossed on the glasses frame. I lift my head to look at him again, waiting for him to change his mind and ask me to hand them back, but he doesn't. Instead, he sits there and smiles at me.

"Happy birthday." He flashes me a grin and I frown, confused.

"Erm... sorry to burst your bubble, boss, but my birthday was in February."

"Well then consider it a late birthday present," he says. "I'm Nigerian and we like to be extra." He winks at me again and my cheeks warm up. He needs to stop doing that before I melt. "Go on. Try it on and you'll see what I'm talking about."

I put on the glasses before staring at my screen again. The glasses block out the harsh light and I don't have to squint to type anymore. "This feels great. Thank you."

"You're welcome."

I try to focus on my work, but my silly thoughts keep pushing my gaze toward the handsome man sitting next to me. His closeness sends my heart racing and my stomach twisting into a knot as the butterfly feeling returns. I can't help but wonder what it would feel like if I just take one step back and dip my toes into those pleasures I used to enjoy and ... no, no, no.

Mortified by where my thoughts are taking me, I shake my head and push myself up, almost toppling my chair over.

Emmanuel looks at me, worry etched on his features. "Are you okay?" he asks and I nod.

"Yeah, sorry. I just need to use the restroom." I power walk out of the office without looking him in the eye.

In the restroom, I open the faucet and wash my face before

slapping my cheeks. *Snap out of it, Heather.* I stare at my reflection in the mirror. One moment, the reflection is a girl with auburn hair, soft green eyes and no make-up. But the next moment, it's flashing images of the girl with red-hair, thick black eyeliner, bright red lipstick, a nasal septal ring, and piercing green eyes.

Heather.

"No." I shake my head and turn away from the mirror before leaning against the sink and massaging my temples.

Speak the truth to yourself, Heather. Meredith's voice echoes in my mind, reminding me about what to do in situations like this. Remind yourself about who you are in Christ.

"I'm a new creation." I blurt out the words from the first Bible verse I ever memorized. I need it to be true—especially right now. I can't go back. I refuse to go back. "Anyone who belongs to Christ is a new person." I repeat the words to myself. "The old life has gone. A new life has begun."

My old life held no promise for me. All that waited for me at the end of that road was pain and heartbreak. This life is what I was created for. "I'm a new person. Saved. Redeemed. Sanctified." I repeat the words over and over again as my whole body sinks to the floor.

21

EMMANUEL

It's been twenty minutes (not that I've been counting) since Heather went to the restroom. I'm not sure if I should start worrying or if that's typically how long she takes. I tilt my head, trying to estimate how long I usually take.

Well, it's often a five-minute job and I'm out of there (that includes washing my hands, of course). Unless I'm doing a *number two,* then that would depend on what I've eaten because God knows I can spend a long time... *oh, come on, Emmanuel, are you seriously thinking about this right now?*

I shake my head and glance over my shoulder again, looking down the hallway where she went. Is she okay? Did I say something wrong? Was she offended by the gift? Was it the breakfast sandwich? "Oh, no." I gasp. It must be the breakfast sandwich. I hope she's okay.

When a further ten minutes pass, I glance at Neil, who is still engrossed in his work. He doesn't look concerned that Heather has been gone for that long. Well, of course he doesn't look concerned because he doesn't care about her the way I do.

As I push myself up to make my way down the hallway, Heather appears from behind me and I sit down again. "Oh, there you are." I give her a sheepish smile. "I was about to come check on you." My mouth betrays me before I can even consider my words.

But the smile on Heather's face makes the betrayal worth it. "Aww, you were worried about me? Sorry I took so long. I'm okay, it was just... just..."

"It's okay. You don't have to explain," I say, and my phone starts ringing. I pick it up and press it against my ear. "Hello? Cool, I'll be right down."

Heather frowns. "Is someone joining us?"

"No, I ordered Chinese while you were away. Since we decided to stay late, we might as well eat." I stand up, but pause when I remember that the breakfast sandwich might have poisoned her. "I'm sorry. I didn't ask if that's what you wanted before ordering. Is that okay with you?"

"Of course it's okay with me. Why would I turn down food from the world's best boss?" The sparkle in her eyes coupled with her smile makes my heart glad.

In a few minutes, I return with the food and after Neil collects his portion, Heather and I sit at the table, eating Kung Pao chicken and noodles. "I didn't know you liked spicy food," I say to her, surprised by how well she's taking the spice.

"My mom taught me how to cook when I was really young," she says after placing a forkful of noodles in her mouth. "As a teenager, I knew how to make quite a few cuisines and I love learning how to make more."

"Have you tried African food?"

She nods. "Yes, but mostly Nigerian cuisines. One of my close friends is Nigerian and I've tried some of her mom's jollof rice, which is delicious."

"That's amazing." I'm sure my smile is stretching from ear to ear now. "What's your friend's name?"

"Amara."

"Sounds like she's Igbo—she's from the same tribe as me."

"Really?" Heather's eyes sparkle. "You wait till I tell her my boss is from the same tribe as her. She would ask me to make sure you guys meet." Heather chuckles. "My other close friend is called Teeyana, but unfortunately, both girls don't live in New Jersey. Teeyana is expecting a baby and lives in Boston with her husband while Amara is engaged and planning her wedding in Atlanta, which is only two months away."

"That's amazing. Congratulations to them." I spin a few noodles around my fork while thinking about how to bring up her family again. I haven't stopped wondering about why she doesn't get along with her mom. "Sounds like your mom did a good job exposing you to all these different cuisines, then?"

Heather's jaw stiffens, and she doesn't respond. Instead, she dabs the corners of her mouth with her tissue and tucks a strand of her hair behind her ear.

"It's okay if you don't want to talk about your mom. I shouldn't have—"

"No, it's fine." She lifts her head to meet my gaze, and after another brief pause, she talks. "My mom abandoned me and my dad when I was eight years old. She ran off to China with another man and for the last sixteen years, I've gotten used to not having a mom in my life. Two months ago, she came back, and she wants me to forgive her. I know I once prayed for her to come back, but I'm still so angry. You know what I mean?" Tears line her eyes as she looks at me.

"Yeah. I know what you mean," I respond as I hand her some tissue paper. "When my mom died two years ago, I was angry at God. I knew it was all going to be fine, and I knew God had everything under control, but I couldn't bring myself to go back to church until recently. Letting go of anger is difficult, so I understand."

"I'm sorry about your mom," she says, dabbing the corners of her eyes with the tissue paper. "What happened to her?"

I brace myself for the conversation while thanking God that it has gotten easier to talk about her. "Car accident. In Nigeria."

"Aww, I'm so sorry." Heather's hand covers mine and I squeeze back, refusing to let go of the warmth it brings.

"It's okay. I'm glad I can remember her as the amazing woman she was. She founded a charity in Nigeria called A Widow's Comfort and it's dedicated to helping widows, single mothers and their children. She sponsored a lot of the children, sent them to school and also helped the women set up businesses so they could provide for their families."

"Wow, it sounds like she did amazing work. I've always wanted to be involved in charity work, but I've never made up my mind about which one."

"Me too. I went with her to Nigeria the summer before I started college and I enjoyed volunteering with all the members of her team. It's the one memory with her I would cherish forever."

"Aww. How is the charity doing now?"

I open my mouth to answer, but close it again after realizing I don't know the answer to her question. "Erm... I have no idea. I haven't been in touch with anyone from AWC since Mom died, and they called to offer their condolences."

"Do you know who is running it now?"

I shake my head again, leaving myself a mental note to do some research on AWC when I get home.

"Well, I'm sure your mom would be proud of everything you've accomplished." Heather changes the subject.

"Thanks, Heather."

"You're welcome, boss." We both chuckle and then Heather glances at her watch, gasping.

"What?" I ask.

She lets go of my hand and pushes her glasses to sit on top of her head. "I just realized I missed Bible study. They recently moved it from Wednesday to Friday and I forgot to set a reminder on my phone."

"Oh, no. I'm sorry. If I had insisted you go home early, then you probably would've remembered."

"It's okay." She shrugs, but I shake my head.

"No, it's not. Next week, I'll make sure we finish early. I'll move my meetings around, so I can drive you to Bible study and home after that."

She raises her brows. "Really? You'll come to Bible study with me?"

"If it's okay with you?"

"Of course. That would be great."

"Awesome. It's a date."

The redness that spreads across her cheeks after I mention the word "date" answers so many unspoken questions for me. I like those answers.

22

HEATHER

After Emmanuel drops me off at home, I wave at his car as he drives away and it takes five minutes of me staring down the road to realize I've been smiling the whole time. If someone was standing next to me right now, they'd think I'm a fool, smiling to myself like I'm crazy.

But you know what? It seems I've finally met a guy who likes me for me and not just how I look, how I dress, or whether I'm wearing make-up. If that's the only reason for my smile today, then I'll take it.

Emmanuel is different. He's nothing like Connor or any of those other guys who took advantage of my desperation and vulnerability in high school. Even if we only end up being friends, I'll still take it.

"It's a date." I repeat Emmanuel's words to myself as I recall how his eyes sparkled when he said them—a sparkle I'm trying not to read too much into. He's my boss and I'm his employee. I'm pretty sure we're not allowed to date. *Or are we?*

"Honey, are you okay?" Dad's voice rips me out of my thoughts and back to the present. I turn my head to face him, only now realizing I've been standing outside for ten minutes staring down the road, which is partially lit by street lamps.

"Hey, Dad." I walk toward him, still smiling.

"Are you okay?" he asks again, this time with a smirk.

"Yeah, why wouldn't I be?" I walk into the living room and plop down on the sofa, ignoring Dad's questioning looks as he walks in shortly after. "What?" I shrug, choosing to stay oblivious even though I know he saw everything. "It was just my boss dropping me off, that's all."

"I know *that*." Dad takes a seat across from me. "But what I don't know is why you're smiling like a Cheshire cat." He chuckles.

"*Ugh*, Dad." I whine and lean back on the sofa. "Nothing is going on. He's just a nice guy who cares enough to make sure I get home safe."

"Well, if you say so." He picks up the TV remote and changes the channel, leaving me disappointed at how easy it was for him to give up.

I want him to ask more questions about Emmanuel, so I can gush about how amazing he is, how I can't think about him without smiling and how much I like him. Of course, I won't tell him all that, but I need to tell someone something before my fragile heart bursts with excitement.

"He asked to go to Bible study with me next week," I blurt out, and Dad lowers the volume before turning to face me.

"So, like a date?" He grins and at the mention of that word again, the butterfly feeling in my stomach returns.

"Well, that's what he called it, so it must be a date, right?" As the question leaves my mouth, I realize how awkward it is to have this conversation with Dad. I've never spoken to him about boys before, never spoken to him about any crushes, and never spoken to him about all the boys I messed with in high school and college.

"It sounds like a date to me." Dad gives me his undivided attention and I can see he is enjoying this. "I like him already. Next time, invite him inside instead of—"

"Okay, I think it's time for me to go to bed." I push myself up and place a peck on Dad's cheek before power walking out of the living room.

"But honey, I thought you were going to tell me more about him," Dad's voice trails behind me.

"Not today, Dad." I respond as I make my way up the stairs. It's too soon. Maybe someday I'll tell him about my experiences with boys. Today is not that day.

"Are you hungry? There's some leftover meatloaf and mashed potatoes."

"No, I already ate at the office, but thanks. Good night, Dad." I quicken my steps, holding my squeal long enough for me to enter my room and shut the door. I'll talk to Teeyana and Amara about this tomorrow when we have our video call. Until then, all I can do now is throw myself on my bed and squeal into my pillow.

"He asked to go to Bible study with you? Girl, that's definitely a date. *Eeek!*" Amara's piercing scream fills my room and I have to lower the volume on my iPad so I don't wake Dad up. The only noise I can't stop is that of Phoebe running from one end of my room to the other as she plays with the new spring toy I bought for her.

Last night was a blur and I still can't believe there's a possibility that Emmanuel likes me, too. This is so surreal. The only way I can explain how I'm feeling right now is if I compare it to one of those many mornings when I woke up after a crazy night out feeling hungover and barely remembering what happened the night before. *I really don't miss those days.*

"Amara, you know I can hear you just fine, right? You don't have to scream." I laugh and Teeyana turns the phone camera toward her, so I can see her too.

"That's right," Teeyana says. "I've been trying to tell her that for the last eight years." She turns to Amara, who is pushing a shopping cart behind her. "You need to use your indoor voice."

Amara rolls her eyes and kisses her teeth. "Please, leave me alone. I'm Nigerian. This is my indoor voice." We all burst out laughing. Amara is in Boston, visiting Teeyana and helping her out with some shopping for the baby's nursery. Teeyana is fifteen weeks gone now and her twelve-week dating scan was normal. *Thank God.*

"No, seriously, girls. We're just two friends hanging out, that's all." I bring the girls' attention back to the issue at hand.

"Mmm-hmm. Girl, please." Amara jumps in. "Soon, you'll have sparks flying when your hands touch."

Who says we haven't had that already? I definitely felt the sparks flying when he passed me the glasses case at the office. I'm glad the girls think he likes me, too. At least now I'm sure I'm not imagining things.

"Soon, you'll break the news that you're getting married." Teeyana squeals and before I can put in another word, both of them start singing, "*Heather and Emmanuel sitting in a tree, K-I-S-S-I-N-G.*"

I roll my eyes at my friends, but I can't stop myself from smiling, and of course, my red cheeks throw me under the bus.

"Aww, look at you. Your cheeks are as red as the tomatoes I'll be using to cook my jollof rice this evening." Amara and Teeyana giggle as I cover my face again, imagining the taste of the delicious spicy jollof rice Amara's mom cooked for Teeyana's wedding.

"Aww, I miss your mom's food." I uncover my face as the girls pause and take a seat on a bench inside the mall.

"This is why you should come to my traditional wedding," Amara responds. "Come on, Heather. I'm only going to have this once, and I don't want you to miss it."

I chuckle. "But your church wedding is coming up in a few months."

Amara and Teeyana both shake their heads. "No, this is different," Amara answers for both of them.

"Yeah, we've spent hours watching Nigerian traditional weddings on YouTube and it's so interesting. It'll mean so much to both of us if you come. Please." Teeyana juts her bottom lip out and tilts her head. She knows I can't resist her pleading eyes.

"Okay, fine. I'll speak to Emmanuel and make sure I'm not too bogged down with work that week."

"Yay! You mentioned he's Igbo, right?" Amara points out. "You should invite him as your plus-one."

My heart flutters at the idea of Emmanuel and me taking a trip to Atlanta and spending a weekend away while getting to know each other. Then, reality kicks in and I shake my head. "Nah, I'm sure he'll be busy and he'll have other things to do."

Amara lifts a perfectly penciled eyebrow at me. "*Ahn, ahn.* How do you know if you haven't asked him? *Abeg*, ask him, *jor*." Amara exaggerates her "Nigerian accent," drawing giggles from me and Teeyana.

"Okay, okay. I'll see what I can do, but I'm not promising you he'll be there."

"Well, I'll be praying he comes, so we can sweet talk him into liking you even more," Teeyana says.

"Okay, bye. You girls need to return to your shopping because I'm clearly distracting you." I close my laptop slowly as the girls protest, but they squeeze in their goodbyes before I close the laptop shut.

Throwing myself back on my bed, I stare at the ceiling as Amara and Teeyana's words swirl around in my head. But soon, my thoughts are interrupted by the meowing Phoebe, who is now tired of playing with her spring, so she climbs on the bed and takes her favorite sleeping position on my tummy. I need to feed her soon, but after all the screaming Amara and Teeyana have subjected us to, I think a few more minutes of silence will do us both some good.

"I'm happy." My answer to Meredith's question during our virtual therapy session takes me by surprise and with Meredith's raised eyebrows, I can tell she's surprised, too.

"Wow, I haven't heard you say that in a long time," she says as she tucks her pen behind her ear.

"I know." I chuckle before pulling at the sleeve of my hoodie. The room, which was cold before, now feels ten times hotter as perspiration lines my underarms.

"Has anything happened recently that you can attribute this feeling to?" Meredith asks and I nod.

"I made a new friend. My boss Emmanuel, who I mentioned to you before."

"Oh, yes. Emmanuel." A small smile tugs at the corners of her lips as she retrieves her pen from behind her ear and starts scribbling on her notepad. "Care to tell me more?"

Like a fangirl gushing about her favorite artist, I spill all the reasons I think Emmanuel is cool and different. Meredith listens attentively, nodding here and there and adding in 'hmms' where necessary. Then when I'm done, she asks, "So you like him?"

I nod, finally feeling free enough to admit it.

"Okay, I'm going to play the devil's advocate here, as I always do."

"Okay?" I bite my bottom lip and let out a deep sigh, bracing myself for her questions.

"What if you find out he doesn't like you back? How would you feel then?"

Ugh, I was hoping she wouldn't ask me that. My shoulders slump as I shove away the possibility of that happening. She's asking me that question because in the past, I've turned the feeling of dealing with unmet expectations into anger. But the past is the past. This is now.

"I'd be very disappointed at first because I've talked it through with Teeyana and Amara, and they both think Emmanuel's actions suggest he likes me, too." I pause, considering my words some more. "But if he doesn't, I'd still be happy having him as my friend."

Then, just when I think I've gotten away with my answer, Meredith holds my gaze, in that way she normally does, which makes me believe she can see right through me. "Would you really?" Her question is simple, but between us, it carries a lot of weight. Meredith knows my past and only she knows how to help me challenge how I'm feeling.

I enter another spilling session where I tell Meredith about the mini bathroom breakdown I had when I couldn't control my thoughts toward Emmanuel. "It hasn't happened again since then." I smile, choosing to stay positive.

"But... what if it does?" Meredith asks, and my smile fades. "How will you deal with it?"

I swallow to wet my dry mouth before speaking again. "I'm trying to stay positive here, but these questions are making me feel a sense of dread."

Meredith closes her notebook and leans forward as she rests her head on her cupped hand. This is the part of the session where she'll tell me the hard truth, the bitter truth, all the truth pills that are good for me, but difficult to swallow.

"Heather, in life, there are two ways in which we can learn—through knowledge and through experience. It's always safer and less painful to learn through knowledge because even though experience is a good teacher, she's a very hard one because she *always* gives her test before the lesson.

"You might not want to admit it to yourself, but you and I know that the battle to protect your purity is going to be a constant one," she continues. "Yesterday's episode wasn't the first and it won't be the last because you're human. My job is not to make you feel bad about liking someone. I'm happy that you're happy and I want you to find love. But I also want you to remember that God not only freed you from a life of sin, He gave you the freedom to live a righteous life."

That's exactly what pastor Samuel said during Bible study two months ago. I think to myself as Meredith continues.

"The Old Heather is gone and you are now committed to a life of purity. In order to live out this testimony, you *need* to set boundaries from the beginning. A Christ-centered relationship is very different from what you had with Connor. It's a blessing and a beautiful thing, but it's also a battlefield filled with a lot of temptation. The enemy will wage a war against the purity of the heart God has given you, so you need to be ready to fight. The battle starts with what you know about God, because knowing God means knowing wisdom and understanding. Knowing God helps you learn how to have a relationship that honors him."

Hearing Meredith refer to a relationship as a battlefield wells up some anxiety in my heart, but I talk myself out of it. *I can do this.*

"Heather, you're not doing this alone," Meredith continues, as if she's able to hear my thoughts. "Your entire experience will change when you learn how to depend on God alone. Never stop praying, keep on studying His Word, and make sure you have accountability. God is roaring behind you, ahead of you and all around you. It will be hard. You may get hurt, but keep fighting and don't give up."

23

EMMANUEL

"I told you your old man still has it in him," Dad gloats, pointing his golf club at me and I laugh as he walks back to stand next to our bag of golf clubs.

"Yeah, not a terrible start." I pick up a ball from the tray and walk to the green mat. "But let's see how that shot will compare to mine–the Madu Family Golf Champion." I lift both arms up, flexing my biceps one after the other, and a belly laugh erupts from Dad, drawing stares from the golfers in the other hitting bays.

"Son, I've been playing golf since before you were born and experience is always the best teacher," he says as he leans on the metal barrier of our hitting bay.

"Hmm, you're right. Experience is the best teacher and I have experience in beating you, so today won't be any different." I smirk before placing the ball on the tee. Adjusting my stance, I lean forward and place my golf club next to the ball.

After a quick glance between the target and the ball, I lift the golf club and swing, twisting my upper body. The ball soars over the fairway and hits the target, so I turn to Dad and flex my muscles at him again.

Since Mom died, Dad has been intentional about allocating "family time" where we choose an activity to do together once a month. Most times, we have lunch or dinner together, but when we're less busy, we do an outdoor activity. With the warm June weather setting in and the sun showing its face more often, a trip to the driving range today was inevitable.

Olanna is back home for her summer break and she has been staying with Dad, but she'll be staying with me from next week until the end of her break. I need to think of fun activities to do with her, so I don't bore her to death.

"That was a good one," Dad says with a grudge. "But this is only the beginning. Let's see how far you'll keep up." He switches his club and walks over to the mat.

The rays of sunlight hitting the golf course make the green pop more and the view of the blue sky hanging above us puts me in a much happier mood. Given the mounting pressure and stress at work, I'm finding beating Dad at golf to be more therapeutic than ever. It's rare that we spend time together without him bringing up work, so this is nice.

"I've been wanting to ask you something." Dad looks at me. "How is Heather really doing as an intern?"

I spoke too soon. He really can't help himself. "She's doing great, actually. She's carrying her weight and meeting all her deadlines, so I'm very happy with her progress. I was hoping we would have a fun day without talking about work, though."

Dad lifts a shoulder before adjusting his stance. "How do you expect me not to talk about work when it's all I think about these days?" he says before hitting the ball and it lands left of the fairway. "I see Heather is very involved with the LTH project. Do you trust her enough to handle all that responsibility?"

I switch places with Dad before responding. "Myself and Yin strictly supervise her work. So far, she has been an asset to the team, and she's very determined."

"Is she? *Chai, inu kwa m.* Can you imagine you wanted to bite my head off when I hired her?" A wide grin spreads across Dad's face. "So are you going to thank me for making you a better leader?"

I roll my eyes and mutter a thank you, causing Dad to laugh even more. "You should give her a permanent position when her internship is over." I swing my club and hit the ball, also making it land left of the fairway. *I hope Dad didn't see that.*

"Well, if you think she's that good, then you can give her the permanent position yourself, you know, when you become C.E.O."

I knew he would bring this up again. Sighing, I choose not to respond, but to focus on my shot, so I can beat him while he's not paying attention. But as suspected, my silence doesn't put Dad off as he carries on.

"You're awfully silent, son. *Bia*, have you changed your mind about taking over the company? Our agreement was to start the transfer paperwork when…"

"Yes, I know what our agreement was, Dad," I cut him off, praying he would take the hint and change the subject.

"Okay, I'm just checking. If you change your mind, let me know because I need to be sure this company is in good hands before I retire."

Really? He wouldn't mind me declining his offer? I open my mouth to give him a hint about my doubts, but he cuts me off. "Your mother would have been so proud of you, Akachukwu. How I wish she was here to see our legacy passed down to you. It would have made her the happiest woman in the world."

And there he goes again. Although he says I should tell him if I've changed my mind, I know he doesn't mean that. All my life I've had to face moments like this—when I feel like I have a choice (in fact, he'll say something that'll make me feel like I have a choice) then in the next sentence, he'll make it clear it's my duty and I can't refuse.

If I don't do what he says (after all, parents know best), then there's always someone I'm disappointing. If I'm not disappointing him, or my mom, then I'm disappointing Olanna. I've grown to accept that in this world of mine, I can never win.

Obligation or conviction? Heather's words press into my thoughts as Dad continues to ramble on about how Mom would be so proud of me. If Heather was here, she would have stopped him at his first sentence, pinned her green gaze on me, and then perhaps flipped her red hair, before placing one hand on her hip and reprimanding me for not speaking up.

What does this situation make me? A coward? Of course it does. No one needs a coward to lead a company.

You're the world's best boss. Heather's laugh and giggle fill my thoughts again. Every time I try to focus on what Dad is saying, images of Heather's smile press in even further. I shake my head, surprised at the direction of my thoughts and wondering why I enjoy thinking about her.

"Emmanuel, Madu Health is yours," Dad's voice finally dispels all thoughts of Heather, and I lift my head to find him looking directly at me. "You can have it whenever you want it." He squeezes my shoulders before changing his clubs and returning to the mat.

"Speaking of Heather," Dad continues. "I'd like to say this in the most polite way possible, but please stay focused."

I frown. "What do you mean?" My words falter, guilt creeping up my chest and my mind fathoming the possibility of Dad reading my thoughts and finding out that I was thinking about Heather while he was talking to me.

"I've been watching the way you interact with her recently. Now is not the time for distractions."

"So you're saying I can't be friends with my co-workers?"

Dad straightens his back before looking at me again. "I'm your father and you can't fool me, Emmanuel. I used to be as young as you, and I know when a man is interested in a woman. I see it in the way you look at her and I hear it in the way you talk about her. All I'm saying is that you have a huge task ahead of you, so please don't throw that away for some temporary feeling."

Temporarily feeling? Who says it has to be temporary? I pinch my lips together to stop the words from coming out. Knowing Dad, he'll make a big deal out of this if I challenge him and this peaceful outing might turn sour, so yet again, I choose to be silent as we continue our game.

I may have let so many aspects of my life revolve around Dad's decisions, but I'll never let him into my love life. Something about this conversation feels like he's asking me not to eat a forbidden fruit—except there's nothing forbidden about Heather Osborne.

He's right. I like her. That's why I keep thinking about her and why I can't get her smile out of my head. That's why I now look forward to seeing her at the office every day and why I miss having her around on the days when she's not working with me. I like her. That makes sense.

She has turned my life on its head since the day she walked into it and her friendship has been nothing but a breath of fresh air—as if God planned it all along (and of course He did, because He is omniscient). So of course I'll live to fight another day, but as long as God is in it, no one will stop me from getting close to Heather Osborne—not even Mr. Chijioke Madu.

24

EMMANUEL

T his was a great idea. I applaud myself in my head as Heather and I sit next to each other in her church Bible study group. The conference room we're sitting in has beige-colored walls with Bible verse posters stuck on them.

The delicious smell coming from the dozen pizza boxes on the table at the back of the room teases my nostrils and makes my mouth water. It reminds me of the time after Mom's death when I ate pizza all day, every day. If Olanna hadn't talked me out of it, I would've eaten myself into obesity, high blood pressure, and diabetes for sure. But given that it's been six months since I had pizza, I think it's safe to have a celebratory slice today.

There are approximately thirty twenty-something year olds sitting in the chairs arranged in a crescent shape across the room. The group is smaller compared to the Bible study group at my church (at least from what I remember), but I never knew I preferred an intimate setting until now.

The pastor (who Heather mentioned is called Samuel) is sitting at the front facing us and judging from his jeans, t-shirt, sneakers, and overall youthful exuberance, he doesn't look a day over thirty, but he mentioned earlier he is actually forty-four years old.

Pastor Samuel has been teaching from the book of Galatians and I joined at the perfect time because they just started chapter one today. The title of his message is *An Audience Of One* and for the last twenty minutes, I've been listening and meditating on the tenth verse, which Heather read out loud for the group earlier.

"Am I now trying to win the approval of human beings, or of God? Or am I trying to please people? If I were still trying to please people, I would not be a servant of Christ."

Okay, this verse hits me hard. The more I listen to the pastor's words, the more my mind drifts to that one time I attended Bible study with Mom in Bende, Abia state during our stay in Nigeria. Apart from helping the widows and children financially, Mom centered the core of her charity on spreading the gospel, so she sat in with the widows for their weekly Bible study sessions sometimes.

That day, the sun was high in the sky and the scalding heat prevented the women from having the Bible study at their usual spot at the center of the church compound, so Mom moved the women inside the church building where it was cooler. She enjoyed doing the Bible study outside as she loved nature, but she didn't want to give the women a heat stroke.

I remember sitting at the back and watching Mom reading from different passages of scripture as she explained the words to them in both Igbo and pidgin English. As I watched Mom teach that day, one thing was clear in her voice—passion. She had a passion for her work and she always put God first.

"So seek ye first the kingdom of God," Pastor Samuel's voice pulls me out of my thoughts as he closes his Bible. "He is your audience of One. He is all that matters. Seek Him first and all other things will be added onto you. Anyone have any questions?"

A couple of people raise their hands and the pastor spends the next fifteen minutes answering their questions before he closes with a word of prayer. In less than five minutes, everyone huddles around the tables at the back, which now have the open pizza boxes, revealing the different flavors.

Heather introduces me to Pastor Samuel and a few others before we grab a couple of slices of the barbecue chicken pizza and head out the door. As we make our way down the stairs and out the church building, the words *audience of One* make a home in my thoughts, poking and prodding so much that I start mentally kicking myself for not having the guts to just tell Dad how I feel.

"So?" Heather looks at me as she takes another bite of her pizza. "What did you think?" she asks as we stroll toward the parking lot.

"Huh?" I turn to face her while trying to figure out what we were talking about before I zoned out.

"The Bible study," she clarifies, with a mouth full of pizza. "What did you think of it?"

"Oh. Right. I enjoyed it and I'm glad I came."

"That's great." The sparkle in her green eyes returns, complementing the freckles on her cheeks. "I'm glad you came too. I haven't had a Bible study partner since Teeyana and Amara in college."

"Really? In that case, we should definitely do this again sometime."

Her smile broadens. "That would be great." When she takes another bite of her pizza, she smudges barbecue sauce on the corner of her mouth.

"You've got barbecue sauce right here." I touch the corner of my mouth and after her attempt to lick it off fails, we burst out laughing before I remember I grabbed some tissues from inside the church. "I'll get it." I take out some tissue paper and wipe the sauce off.

A moment of silence passes between us as we stare into each other's eyes.

"Thank you." Heather clears her throat and we continue walking to my car. "Emmanuel, this might be none of my business, but I've noticed you've been quiet for most of the evening. Is everything okay?"

I nod. "Yeah, everything is fine, it's just that... the Bible study was very convicting and I've been thinking about a lot of things and re-evaluating my life, you know?"

She walks over to a nearby concrete bench and takes a seat before tapping the space next to her. "Care to tell me more? Maybe I can help."

I pause for a few seconds, trying to decide whether to go for it. I can't resist pulling down my defenses around Heather, especially since God continues to use her to encourage me. If I feel so strongly about her, then I might as well let her into my world.

The starry sky stretches above us, accompanied by the full moon, which is glowing. Apart from the sound of cars entering and leaving the parking lot and from the coffee shop a hundred yards away, the well-lit space provides a safe atmosphere to share secrets. "You remember when I told you my mom used to work for a charity back in Nigeria, right?"

"Mm-hmm." Heather nods as she sips on her bottle of water.

"As I listened to Pastor Samuel's message tonight, I realized why I used to admire her work so much."

"Oh?" Heather twists the bottle lid back on and then folds her arms. "Tell me."

I turn to face her and start spilling. "Working with my mom in Nigeria was the closest I ever got to experiencing what it's like to love others genuinely. I watched her show kindness and sacrifice for those women and children who weren't even her family.

"They all loved and appreciated her, but she always remained humble and gave all glory to God. Her life challenged me and made me want to be a better man. I was sure I would follow in her footsteps and live a life only driven by my obedience to God, but all of that changed when she died and I've retreated to letting others' opinions be my motivation." I pause as the wound in my heart reopens.

Tears blur my vision and I quickly wipe them away, embarrassed that I've let my emotions overwhelm me outside the four walls of my bedroom. When Heather reaches for my hand and squeezes it, I look up to find not judgment or sympathy, but kindness in her eyes, and this encourages me to keep talking.

"Aspiring to be a better man for God was an easier goal when my mom was here. Her life was evidence that it's possible to serve God joyfully and feel fulfilled while doing it. But when she died, I lost all hope, and that dream became long forgotten."

A few moments pass before Heather speaks again. "My dad once told me that there's no such thing as *too late* when it comes to serving God. If you want to work with your mom's charity, I'm sure it's not too late."

How did she know that's what I want to do? Lord, is this You speaking through her? Is this the answer to my prayer? Is this—

"No." I push the thoughts aside and turn my head away. "Too much time has passed, and it doesn't matter anymore."

"But it clearly does." She cups my face in her hands and turns my head so I can look her in the eye. "If it didn't matter, we wouldn't be sitting out here in a parking lot at nine pm talking about it. If it didn't matter, then you wouldn't be thinking about it two years down the line." She pauses before continuing. "If it didn't matter, then you would be satisfied with taking over Madu Health."

I let out a heavy sigh as Dad's voice pokes at me. I know he would be fuming if he were listening to this conversation right now. *"Akachukwu, you will be whatever God has decided that you will be."* Mom's voice overpowers Dad's and I rub my forehead. "I know you're right, but there's nothing I can do about it now. What's the difference between working for Madu Health and my mom's charity? Both jobs involve helping people and whether it's helping people grow their businesses or helping people improve their quality of life, helping is still helping."

"Yeah, but the difference is passion," Heather responds. "Everyone knows you're hardworking and you have a gift for serving others. That's why you're the world's best boss. But throw passion in there and you'll find your work rewarding—even with the mundane aspects of it."

Heather's words are thawing at the frozen ball of doubt in my heart. I've been refusing to accept this for so long, but tonight's message was my confirmation that I can't keep running away. "Okay, let's say hypothetically, I wanted to accept this and work for my mom's charity. I can't do what she did. I don't have the same skills she had; her easy-going way with the women, the way she showered motherly love on the children, and her charisma. She was Amarachi Madu and I can never be her—the same way I can never be my dad."

"Then don't be," Heather says. "You don't have to help the charity the same way your mom did. You just have to do it the way you know how to, with the talents and gifts God has given you. How is the charity doing in terms of marketing?"

I pause to think about her question. "Erm...I haven't had the chance to look them up after we spoke about them last time, but

I remember my mom mentioning once that they were struggling to get people to donate."

"Well, there you go." Heather claps her hands. "You have the experience, you have the skills and you are a professional. You can help them. That way, more people will know about the amazing work they're doing?"

I sit upright as the idea becomes more appealing. "Yeah... yeah, I guess I can try."

"Of course you can. You can even help them out with their next fund-raising campaign. You can reach out to the organizer and give them some ideas to help them reach their target audience." Heather's voice rises with every word as she flashes me a wide grin.

"Yeah... I think they'll appreciate that." I chuckle, unable to resist Heather's infectious excitement. "But what if it doesn't work out?"

Heather tilts her head, still smiling. "Then it doesn't work out. But at least you won't go on wondering about what could have been." She nods before standing up and I follow her to the car.

The idea of helping AWC in my own way already sounds fulfilling. But as a million and one ideas push their way into my mind, the one thing I can't ignore is how blessed I am to have Heather in my life.

25

EMMANUEL

The talk I had with Heather tonight has sparked a new fire in me. As soon as I got home, I jumped on social media and went to the AWC page. I've spent the last hour perusing through it and checking out all the campaigns they have done in the past.

The last update on the page was a year ago and my heart sinks at the possibility that they might not be running the charity anymore. Since the charity doesn't have an official website, I don't have direct access to the team members, so social media is my only option. The easiest way to go about this is to ask Dad for the contacts, but I'm not ready for the questions that will follow.

I click on the followers icon and scroll through the names and faces, praying I can recognize at least one person who works for the charity. Mom introduced me to a few members of her team when I went with her to Nigeria. From what I remember, there were a maximum of five members and they didn't have distinct roles. They all helped each other do everything and anything.

I pause my scrolling after spotting a familiar face—Mr.

Dennis Nwaeze. The name doesn't ring a bell, but the face does. I met him once when Mom took me to their office in Lagos. He took me out for lunch and I had the tastiest *abacha* and stewed chicken I have ever had in my entire life. Ignoring my now watery mouth and hunger pangs, I click on the man's name and open the message chat. He's not online, so I type a quick message.

Good evening, sir.

I hope this message finds you well. I'm not sure if you remember me, but my name is Emmanuel Madu—the son of the late Mrs. Amarachi Madu, your founder. We met briefly eight years ago in Lagos when my mom and I visited Nigeria. It would be nice to catch up with you. Please let me know when you're free to talk.

I press send and put my phone away. I'm not expecting him to respond in the next twenty-four hours, so I have time to do more research about charity marketing. I open my laptop and start searching, watching videos, reading articles, looking at different charity websites and making notes as I go.

The more I read about charity marketing, the more excited I get about it because it's a combination of using the skills I have and actively showing love by touching the lives of others and spreading the gospel. Another hour passes by before my phone pings, taking my attention away from my laptop. When I unlock it, there's a message notification from Mr. Nwaeze. *Wow, that was quick.*

Good evening Emmanuel,

Wow, this is a very pleasant surprise. Of course I remember you.

Your mom always talked about you and your sister and she showed us many photos of your achievements. I'm very happy to hear from you. It's been a long time. Things have not been the same without your mom here with us, but we thank God all the same. It will be nice to chat with you. I'm free tomorrow after 5pm. We can have a phone call then if you are free, too. God bless you and have a good night.

I stare at the message for a few minutes before reality hits that this is really happening. I could stop right here and turn back, but I'll never know until I try. Excitement wells up in my chest again as I respond to his message to let him know I'll be free at that time.

Then I return to my research and stay up well into the night, cruising through website after website, notes after notes and videos after videos. When my eyes start aching, I take off my blue-light blocking glasses and rub them. It's only then that I notice it's past two am. *Wow, how time flies.*

The next morning, I wake up early again, do my devotions, shower, have my quick porridge breakfast and return to my desk. I'm glad it's a Saturday, so I don't have to worry about work (at least not for a few hours). A text pings into my phone from Heather and I swipe up to read it. She was online when I was going to bed last night, so I updated her about the email from Mr. Nwaeze.

Heather: Morning, boss. I just wanted to check that the research black hole hasn't sucked you in again this morning 😄

Me: Morning 😊 *Haha nah, I woke up not too long ago, but I'm back at my desk now. We move* 💪

Heather: Aww look at you go. I'm so excited for you. Need my help?

Me: Is that even a question? 😊 *Of course, I'll be needing lots of your help. But I'll call you tonight after my meeting with Mr. Nwaeze. Is that okay?*

Heather: Of course it is. I'm at your service, boss. 😎

After messaging Heather, I call Olanna to check up on her. I don't know how long my meeting with Mr. Nwaeze will take, so I suggest we postpone our Bible study to tomorrow after church. She appreciates me for letting her know so she can spend more time catching up with Dad. She'll start living with me next week until the end of her summer break, so I still need to find some fun things we can do together.

As the time draws near, my heart thumps faster as I tap my foot on the floor. My mouth feels so dry and my tongue keeps sticking to the roof of my mouth, so I've been making trips to the kitchen to refill my water bottle. I just hope my meeting with Mr. Nwaeze doesn't become interrupted with trips to the bathroom because of all this water I'm drinking.

"Lord, please... all I ask is that you tell me what to say because I don't know what I'm doing," I pray out loud before unlocking my phone. Mr. Nwaeze and I exchanged numbers earlier today, but the easiest way to call him would be to use one of the social media apps. I start typing a message to let him know I'm ready for our phone call when he starts video calling me instead.

It's a good thing I thought about this as a possibility and tidied my room. After fixing the collar of my shirt, I swipe left on his call and balance my phone against the stack of books on my desk, so I can fit in the frame. "Good evening, sir," I say to the older man when an up close view of his familiar face appears on my screen.

One look at him and memories from our first encounter

come flashing back into my mind. I still remember his character-
istic mustache (which made me so envious I wanted to grow my
own) and his glasses, which have frames that occupy almost half
of his face.

"Wow, Emmanuel. *Nke a bu gi n'ezie? Is this really you?"* His
grin is so wide it spreads his mustache across his face.

"Yes, uncle Dennis. *O bu m.*"

"The last time I saw you, you were only a boy and now look
at you—a full grown man with a full grown beard." We both
laugh before he continues. "It's so good to see you, my son."

"It's so good to see you too, Uncle. How are you and your
family?"

"We are doing fine. This country and its government keep
trying to frustrate us, but God has continued to keep us healthy
and strong. *Las las we go be alright.*"

I smile and nod at his hopeful stance. "That's great to hear.
How is everything going with AWC?" I ask, hoping to get to the
crook of the matter.

His smile slowly fades, and he lets out a heavy sigh. "Well...
it's going okay, but I have to be honest with you, things haven't
been the same since your mom died. She was the brain and the
heart behind the charity and we are struggling to keep it
running. We care about these women and children, but we don't
have enough funds coming in, so we can't provide for all the
people who have come to us for help. We've even had to turn
away some women and their children, which has been heart-
breaking to do, but that's the reality of the situation now."

"How long have you been struggling with funds?"

"Erm..." The older man rubs his mustache before continuing. "The last five years, I would say. Our annual campaign day
has always been our biggest source of funds and the highest
we've ever raised from this event is five-hundred thousand naira,
but after taking out the costs of organizing the event, we're left

with barely enough to last the whole year. Our staff are all volunteers, but with the increasing number of women and children joining us, we don't have enough to accommodate everyone.

"The donations help to pay the children's school fees and also to help the mothers set up businesses, so they can continue taking care of themselves and their children. Your mom built a shelter home in Lagos where we accommodate some women and children. We also provide food and water for them until they have enough to provide for themselves."

"Wow." I rub the back of my neck as I take in all the information. "You do a lot for these women and children. What about regular donations throughout the year? You don't have many of those?"

"We have some regular donations from our locals, which is good, but it doesn't add up to a surplus. Sometimes, we have one time big donations from good Samaritans and we've had a few from your father over the last five years, but once we use up those funds, we are back to where we started."

Hearing this makes my heart sad. I can't believe I put this off for so long. I can't believe I claim to care for this charity and I've never even donated. This has to change. "Mr. Nwaeze, I'm not sure if you know this, but I'm now the managing director of my dad's company and I have experience in marketing. God has been prodding me to help this charity for the last two years, so I want to set up a robust marketing strategy that will help bring in consistent donations throughout the year." I pause. "And before you ask, I'm going to do this for free."

His eyes widen at my last sentence. "Really? Oh, God bless you, my son. This is the best news I've heard in a long time. Please, just tell us what we have to do to get started. We are at your service."

"Okay, we have to start by creating an official website for the organization and we have to set up an engaging social media platform..." We spend the next half hour talking about my drawn up plan to reach the target audience and get more donors. "Just let me know by the end of the week when it'll be good to speak to the rest of your team and we can start."

"I will update you," Mr. Nwaeze says as we say our goodbyes. "Thank you so much, Emmanuel. Have a good weekend."

When we end the call, satisfaction and excitement settle in my chest and after saying a quick prayer of thanks, I pick up my phone and dial the only person who would understand how amazing this feels.

"I'm so excited. This is going to be great," Heather says and I can hear the smile in her voice as I press my phone against my ear. "God needs you there. You're going to help change the lives of all those women and children."

I smile, my heart liking the idea that I'm going to be spending more time with Heather doing this. "Heather, I understand that this is my cross to bear and you're not being paid to do this, so please tell me you don't want to get involved and I promise I won't take offense."

"*Pfft*, what, and miss all the fun? Heck no. I'm serious. I'm excited to do this with you."

"Okay, good. I also wanted to ask you something, if you don't mind."

"Sure."

I hesitate for a second, but then it comes rushing out of me. "My sister Olanna is home for the summer break and she'll be staying with me from next week until she goes back to college at the end of August. She wants to go shopping next Saturday, but I'm not into all that. I'll probably annoy her the whole time, so I thought it'd be good to have someone else come with us... if that's okay with you?"

"Aww, of course. That would be great. I'd love to meet your sister... on one condition, though."

"Oh, yeah?" I chuckle. "Come on then. Name your price."

"I'll agree to come with you on Saturday if... you come with me to Amara's traditional wedding in Atlanta next month."

"Wow, seriously? Of course, I'd love that." My voice comes out louder than I intended, but I can't help myself.

"Really?"

"Yes. I haven't been to a Nigerian wedding in so long. I miss the food, the dancing, the colors... everything. I can't wait."

Heather chuckles, leaving me only with imaginations of what her smile is like right now. "That's great. It's a date," she says and I love how comfortably those words rolled off her tongue.

26

HEATHER

"Honey, can I come in?" Dad knocks on my bedroom door, which I've left ajar. He wasn't home when I got back from work, so I've been working in my room while waiting for him.

"Yes, you can." I turn my chair away from my desk as he walks into the room and gives me a hug. "Hmm, you're looking nice," I say when he sits on my bed. Then I sniff the air as I wheel my chair close to him. "Are you wearing perfume? You smell good."

"Thank you." He smiles and takes off his cap, alerting me to something else that's different about him.

"Wow, you had a haircut?"

Dad smiles again and nods. "I thought I'd do something different."

I open my mouth to say something, but pause when all the puzzle pieces fit together in my brain. The new cap, the perfume, the haircut? "You went out with Mom today, didn't you?"

He doesn't need to answer the question because it's written all over his face and body language. "I should have known," I shake my head while turning to face my desk again. "Could you please tell me next time, so I don't stay up worrying about you?"

"Honey, I'm sorry. I should have mentioned I was going out. Your mom and I are giving our relationship another shot and we've been seeing a marriage counselor to address all the issues we had before the divorce."

Wow. So they're really getting back together. "It's okay. I mean, whatever." I shrug as I scroll aimlessly through my AWC marketing notes. He can do whatever he wants. He's a grown man, and she's still the love of his life. I can't change the way he feels about her. But my feelings toward her are still the same.

I don't care if they go on dates, have fancy dinners or watch movies together. I'll just patiently wait for the day I can move out of this house and get my own apartment, so she can move back in. Dad knows better than to ask her to move in now. He'll never do that to me. *Or will he?*

"Heather?" Dad's voice breaks into my thoughts. He's now looking over my shoulder at my laptop screen. "What's this?"

"It's a side project Emmanuel and I are working on." I explain about Emmanuel's mom, her charity, and his dad.

"I think it's amazing that Emmanuel is doing this. It's also great that you're helping him, but isn't this going to be too much work for you?"

I shake my head without even thinking about it. "No, it's fine." Spending one-on-one time with Emmanuel can never become too much—even when we're working. But of course, Dad doesn't need to know all that.

"Hmm. You like him that much, don't you?"

"Huh?" I lift my head, realizing I might have missed the last thing he said. "Well, we're still just friends."

"Friendship is a good foundation for any relationship, but I don't want you to get hurt. Please don't make any assumptions if he hasn't clearly defined his feelings for you," Dad says, echoing Meredith's thoughts, and I nod.

Emmanuel and I have a lot in common and we get along well, but I still don't know how he feels about me. "Thanks, Dad. I'll be careful."

"If you need any advice, I'm right here." He stands and kisses me on the cheek. "Good night, honey."

"Good night, Dad." I watch him walk out the door and close it behind him. He seems so much happier now. Both of us were heartbroken after Mom left and for many years, we were shadows of ourselves—well, mostly me, but God delivered us from that.

I feel betrayed that even though we started this journey together, Dad has moved on without me. I want to be happy for him, but how can I be when I can't forget the past? This is so much harder than I thought. *Lord, please help me.*

The last time I felt this nervous was six years ago on my college move-in day at St. John's University in New York. You would think that for a rebellious eighteen-year-old who was so excited to leave home, I would've been ecstatic and ready to embrace my freedom.

But I was dreading the entire experience of making new friends. Mom's sudden departure left me with the false belief that no relationship was worth building because they were all going to end up leaving.

That day, I was a total mess. Dad took away all my cigarettes, so I couldn't smoke for the entire two-hour drive to New York. By the time we got to Queens, my heart was beating erratically. I was restless, hungry, and couldn't concentrate on anything Dad was saying.

To top it off, rage and envy bubbled inside me as I walked past the moms and dads helping their children move in. I should have been one of them. I could have been one of them if Mom didn't leave.

Everything and everyone around me irritated me and I was so absorbed in my thoughts that when I bumped into Teeyana on the stairs leading up to our dorm, even her kind offer to help me carry my bags didn't stop me from blowing up.

After pouring out my frustrations on Teeyana, I headed straight for Dad, who was my next target. He was always at the receiving end of my temper and I blamed him for not going after mom.

I still remember the scene I created and how I drove my poor dad to his wit's end when I left him with all my bags and went for a walk on my own. Dad kept calling me, but I switched off my phone and wandered the streets of Queens until I found the closest bar next to my dorm.

That's where I met Connor. He was standing outside, smoking, and he sensed I needed one. When he offered to share one with me, I jumped at the chance and he sneaked me into the bar, so I could get access to more alcohol and cigarettes.

I shake my head to discard the memories before folding my arms as I wait for Olanna to pick the dress she wants to try on. The Old Heather is long gone now. We have nothing in common anymore. I now have friends. I don't run after boys begging them to sleep with me. I don't smoke or drink anymore and I wouldn't intentionally hurt my dad.

"Heather, what do you think about this one?" Olanna picks out a floral dress from the hanger and places it across her body before turning to face the full-length mirror. "It's nice, isn't it?"

"Yeah, I think it'll be perfect for your picnic date. You should try it on," I say, encouraging my new friend as she tilts her head and scrunches her nose. She will be celebrating her six monthiversary with her boyfriend Alex, and she has been trying to pick out an outfit for the last half hour.

"Hmm, I don't know. I already own too many floral dresses. Maybe I should go for something different." She turns to Emmanuel. "Manny, what do you think?"

"Huh?" Emmanuel lifts his head from his phone, his gaze darting between me and his sister.

Olanna rolls her eyes and steps away from the mirror, walking toward him. She hands me the dress before folding her arms and tapping her foot until Emmanuel stops typing, his gaze sliding up from her comfy pair of heeled sandals to her unimpressed facial expression.

Emmanuel flashes her a sheepish smile and opens his mouth to say something, but she lifts one hand up and silences him. "Nuh-uh. Hand it over, please." She stretches out her hand and much to my amusement, he hands over his phone to Olanna, who then switches it off and places it inside her bag. "Thank you very much."

I can't help but clap as I approach the siblings, smirking. "Now that's how you know who's the boss." I give Olanna a high-five.

"Wait a minute," Emmanuel interjects. "I'm still the boss here. I just... I just made a promise to Olanna I would stay off my phone and be more present during this trip. That's the only reason I let her have the phone. It's because I'm a man of my word."

I shrug and walk up to Emmanuel. "Well, it doesn't matter why you did it. The only thing that matters is that she has your phone now, and she's the boss."

"Whatever." Emmanuel rolls his eyes as Olanna and I break into laughter. "I see what's going on here. You girls are ganging up on me."

"*Ugh*, please. The world doesn't revolve around you, Manny.

But I would love to get you to try on this outfit I saw on the mannequin." Olanna leads us across the sea of colors that is the women's section, and up the stairs to the men's section.

She speaks to one of the store assistants to take out the outfit from the mannequin and hands it to him. "Go on then. Try it on, please." Olanna smiles as he walks away, and then she turns to me. "It's so easy to tease him, isn't it?" she asks, linking her arm with mine as we walk over to the nearby bench, the latest pop song blasting from the overhead speakers.

We lower ourselves on the seat and she continues talking about how much she admires and loves her brother. She's so laid-back and fun to talk to, which is great because all my nerves are gone now. Olanna could pass off as Emmanuel's twin— except she has burgundy locs which graze her shoulders with such elegance. I can't help but wonder how I would look if I had locs too. Her hoop earrings hang on so gracefully to her ears and her nose piercing reminds me about my septal nasal ring.

"I'm glad I finally got the chance to meet you," Olanna says, bringing me back to our present conversation. "He always talks about you."

My stomach leaps to my throat, making me taste some of the burgers we had for lunch. "Really? What does he say about me?" I usually wouldn't care if I heard that someone has been talking about me. But this is Emmanuel—the first guy I've liked in five years. I have to know.

"He says you're going to help him out with marketing for my mom's charity," Olanna responds and my shoulders slump.

"Oh." Of course that's what he'll talk about. I'm not sure what I was expecting to hear, but either way, I try to hide my disappointment.

"He misses her a lot, you know?" Olanna continues. "What you're doing means a lot to him." Her eyes become wet with tears as she places one hand on my shoulder. "Heather, you have no idea how happy I am to see him happy again. He was a shadow of himself after Mom died. Her death hit him the hardest, and he buried himself in work and stopped going to church.

"It's only in the last two months that I've noticed a significant change in him." A tear slides down her cheek and she palms it away. "Thank you from the bottom of my heart." To my surprise, she pulls me in for a hug.

When she breaks the hug, her voice drops to a whisper as she says, "I think Manny likes you."

It takes a lot of strength in me not to start squealing and doing a dance. Instead, I shake my head calmly while my heart does all the dancing. "What? Me? *Pfft*, no way."

"Yes, way." She nods vigorously.

"And you know this because..." I raise a brow at her, waiting for evidence—some tangible evidence.

"He told me."

Ah, there it is. "He did?" I ask, disbelief etched in my voice.

"Yeah." Olanna gently pokes my shoulder and then looks around before lowering her voice again. "Last night when we were having dinner, I asked him why he chose you to come out with us today. The last girl he introduced me to was his last girlfriend, who he broke up with after Mom died. You need to hear how he praises you, how he calls you hardworking and ambitious and God-fearing. He even said he admires you and—in his own words—he said 'I really like her.'"

Words elude from me as I try to take in the news. So he likes me and I haven't been making assumptions in my head. "Wow."

"I know, right? You two would make such a cute couple and I can already imagine all the fun double dates you'll have with me and Alex. I know Manny still has his reservations about Alex, but I'm sure they'll get along well when they finally meet," she says, her excitement evident in the way she's dancing around in her seat.

I open my mouth to say more, but stop myself when Emmanuel approaches us. When he realizes that we're both looking at him, he pauses in his tracks, fixes the collar and sleeves of his shirt and starts walking as if he's a model on a runway. Olanna and I burst out laughing when he does a spin and a dramatic skip to the full-length mirror.

"Okay, calm down, Michael Jackson. Who you trying to impress?" Olanna teases as he turns around to look at us.

"So..." He opens his arms wide, so we can take in his moss-green shirt and black trousers. The green looks so good on him and I like what I'm seeing. "How handsome do I look?"

"Very handsome," Olanna responds. "Right, Heather?" She asks and as they both fix their gazes on me, my words catch in my throat for a few seconds.

But as I stare into Emmanuel's eyes, his loving smile coupled with everything Olanna has told me today boosts my confidence. "Of course he does," I say and Emmanuel's smile broadens.

Olanna starts talking about what events she thinks would be good for him to wear the outfit to, but her words become background noise as the intense gaze that Emmanuel and I share continues. I probably look as red as a tomato, as Amara would say, and I might, in fact, look like a fool, just staring at him and smiling. But it doesn't matter because Emmanuel Madu likes me and I can't wait to tell him I like him, too.

27

EMMANUEL

Two *minutes.* That's how long it's been since I last glanced at Heather. I literally have to force my gaze to stay on my laptop screen instead of it wandering across the table to the girl who has successfully opened my heart up to love again. What if I tell her right now that I like her? Would she say she likes me back, or would she think I'm trying to take advantage of her? If she doesn't like me back, will our friendship become strained or will she keep working with me? *Lord, please help me.*

"Done." Heather lifts her head and locks eyes with me. I didn't even realize when I started staring at her again.

I quickly avert my gaze and try to act casual, but it's too late.

"Were you staring at me again?" She squints and tilts her head.

I clear my throat and rub the back of my neck. "Erm... no? I was... trying to check out the progress you were making." After my meeting with Mr. Nwaeze last weekend, Heather and I decided to meet this weekend at my house to finalize the details of the marketing plan.

Heather leans her head on her cupped hand. "Unless you're

Mr. Fantastic, there's no way you can see my laptop screen from across the table."

Olanna's giggle comes in from behind us as she puts down her plate of *Indomie* and turns to look at us. "Manny, I didn't know you have the power of elasticity that you can stretch to look at her laptop from where you are," she says before putting a forkful of noodles in her mouth.

You would think she is engrossed in her Netflix show, but she keeps eavesdropping and butting into our conversations. I shouldn't have told her I like Heather because now she keeps teasing me about it with every opportunity she gets.

I roll my eyes at her before turning to face Heather again. "Let's see what you have," I change the subject, hoping to expel the awkward atmosphere.

To my relief, Heather asks no more questions, but instead of turning her laptop screen to show me from across the table, she stands up and takes a seat next to me, so we can look at the screen together. I don't know why I didn't just sit next to her from the start.

"So these are all the ideas we've put together." She scrolls through our comprehensive marketing plan, which I'm going to go over with the AWC team. "On our to-do list, we have to make the website, create interactive social media pages, create a banner for their upcoming fundraising campaign, make flyers, set up a mailing list and organize a bake sale."

"That's a good list." I lean back in my chair. "But bake sales aren't very common in Nigeria. We love food, so I think we'll be more likely to attract people if we organize something like a food and craft fair. If the women are into crafts, they can sell some of their work at the fair, and we can also raise money from raffle tickets and stall fees from vendors."

"That's a brilliant idea." Heather types the extras into the document.

"I would definitely go to a food and craft fair." Olanna takes a seat across the table from us while still working her way through her *Indomie*. "That's a long to-do list, though. Do you think you'd be able to keep on top of everything?"

"Yeah, we work well together, and I'm sure we can pull it off," Heather responds before looking at me. "Right, boss?"

Her confidence in me is so reassuring it expels all the doubts trying to claw at my heart. "Of course we can." I turn to Olanna, who is grinning at us. "And we will."

Heather's phone vibrates on the table and when she picks it up, a message pops up on the screen. "Look, Amara finally sent the photo of the fabric we will use for the as...as..." She brings her phone close to her face before showing it to me. "How do you pronounce this?"

"*Asho-ey-bee.*" I help her out. "It's like a uniform dress code Nigerians typically wear to ceremonies as a sign of solidarity. Most people buy the same fabric and then find a designer to sew their own style."

"The fabric is beautiful. I love the teal color," Olanna adds as she zooms in on the photo on Heather's phone. "Have you ordered yours yet?"

Heather shakes her head. "Nah, I don't know any designers, so I'll pass."

Olanna and I gasp at the same time as we stare at Heather.

"You have to wear the *asoebi*. Amara is your friend. I'm sure she'll love to see you in it," Olanna says.

"Yeah, we have a family designer here in Jersey City," I add. "Tell Amara you're going to order the *asoebi*. I'll give our family designer a call and book us a slot to go see him when the fabric arrives." I pick up my phone and start scrolling through my contact list.

"But the wedding is only three weeks away. You think he'll be able to finish it in time?"

"I'm positive. Just tell Amara to save your own *asoebi* and leave the rest to me."

"Aww, thank you," Heather says. "This is so exciting. My very first *asoebi*."

Her excitement is infectious, and it makes my heart glad. Here's my chance to impress and go above and beyond for her.

A week later, when the fabric arrives, I drive Heather down to our family designer's shop, so we can get our measurements done. We arrive early for our appointment, so we take a seat in the waiting room. "This man makes eighty percent of the cultural outfits my dad wears, so I can confirm he's great at what he does." I try my best to reassure Heather, who seems a little nervous.

She nods. "Okay. I'll take your word for it."

"Emmanuel." Mr. Adebisi walks toward us. "It's so good to see you again." He shakes my hand and turns to Heather.

"This is Heather. We work together." I place my hand on the small of Heather's back and she leans in close to me as Mr. Adebisi and I continue to exchange pleasantries.

"I can promise that when we're done with your dress, you will keep coming back for more," Mr. Adebisi tells Heather as we make our way into the shop.

On the left, there are fabrics stacked on shelves and finished outfits hanging from rails on the right. The rattling sound of a sewing machine fills the air as one of Mr. Adebisi's employers works at the back of the shop. One woman is cutting into a piece of fabric, another is placing a finished dress on a mannequin, and another is taking measurements for another customer who is standing on a small pedestal.

"Have you decided what styles you want?" Mr. Adebisi asks us.

"Well, I'll go for a teal green *Isi Agu* top with a matching hat, since that's the color of the *asoebi*. Heather hasn't decided yet, so I was hoping you could show her a catalog for inspiration?"

"Of course." The older man pulls out a few catalogs and spreads them out in front of Heather. Her face lights up and she pulls herself to the edge of her seat as she scans the pages.

"Wow, these all look so elegant." She tucks a strand of her hair behind her ear before pointing at one. "I love this one. Do you think it'll suit me?" She asks Mr. Adebisi, her voice almost dropping to a whisper.

"I don't see why not," he responds. "You have the confidence to own any style you wear. Right, Emmanuel?"

I nod at her. "I couldn't agree more."

Heather's cheeks grow pink and a smile forms on her lips. She agrees to go for the style she chose and as Mr. Adebisi leads her to the pedestal for her measurements, she turns back to me and mouths the words, "thank you."

"So when are you going to tell her you like her?" Yin says as we walk out of church. "You know you have to tell her at some point, right?"

"Shh!" I lower my voice before looking over my shoulder at Jess and Olanna, who are chatting behind us. "I'll tell her soon. I just need to find the right time."

"Why do I have the feeling that time is not the issue?" Yin raises his eyebrows at me. "You guys have been spending a lot of time together at the office and outside the office. You have lots of opportunities and reasons to tell her how you feel."

And lots of reasons to wait. I still don't know how Dad will react if he finds out how I feel about Heather. I certainly don't want to start any drama at the moment, so maybe it's best if I tell her after I've come clean to Dad about my interest in charity marketing.

"I'm just treading with caution, that's all." I pat Yin's shoulder when we get to the car. "Like I said, I'll tell her when the time is right."

"Okay, boss. If you say so."

"Manny." Olanna runs to my side, holding Jess's hand. "Jess thinks it'll be cool to have a triple date when Alex visits during fall break. What do you think?"

I frown before crossing my arms against my chest. "So the young man thinks he's ready to meet your big bro, huh? I like his confidence. Just tell him to get ready for some grilling."

Olanna rolls her eyes, and Yin chuckles. "Come on, boss. Take it easy on the poor guy," Yin says as we get into the car.

"Yeah, he seems nice," Jess adds. "I think a triple date will be fun."

"See, I told you. I promise you'll like Alex when you meet him," Olanna says.

"Yeah, yeah, whatever." I laugh as Olanna sticks her tongue out at me.

28

HEATHER

Not only is a Nigerian traditional wedding an experience, but the prep leading up to it is also an experience. Now I understand to some degree when Amara keeps saying the wedding planning is stressing her out. But at least she was happy when I told her Emmanuel agreed to come to the wedding as my plus-one.

The last week has been extremely busy for myself and Emmanuel. We finally met with the AWC team and we've been using our weekends to get through our to-do list while also getting ourselves ready for this wedding.

I knew the wedding would differ from what I'm used to, but I didn't expect two hundred guests, lots of music, dancing, and also a live band. If I didn't have Emmanuel here with me, God knows I would have been like a lost puppy who is trying to find its way around New York's Times Square.

Not only did Emmanuel find me a designer, he covered all the costs for the outfits, including accessories. So as I sit here, adorned in this beautiful dress made of this teal green fabric with colorful beads around my neck and earrings, it's all thanks to the handsome man sitting next to me.

I turn to look at him again as the Nigerian music plays from the speakers on the opposite ends of the hall. He is wearing a top made from beautiful teal velvet fabric and I remember him calling it an *Isi Agu*. I know the groom looks good, but in my eyes, Emmanuel beats every man in this room when it comes to how well he's slaying his outfit.

I smile as my gaze drops to our hands on the table. They're so close together and I'm tempted to reach out and hold his, but Emmanuel's attention is on the live band playing on stage as he bops his head to the loud music.

The music is amazing, but I have no idea what they are saying, as a lot of it is in Amara's native language—Igbo. Emmanuel clearly knows the words because he's singing along and, as if he can read my mind, he leans close and explains the meaning of the song. "*Igwe* means king," he says, as his warm breath tickles my neck and sets off the butterflies in my stomach again. "This song is all about hailing Jesus as the King of kings."

"That's beautiful," I respond as we continue watching the band, who are very entertaining with their unique style of playing the guitar and the drums. I love this. I could get used to this. Me sitting here and learning from him, assimilating into his culture and being a part of his world. I could really get used to this.

When the live band finishes their last song, the master of ceremony, who is also adorned in a red *Isi Agu* top and a matching red hat, chants a greeting into the microphone. "*Igbo Kwenu. Kwenu. Kwezi Onu oh.*"

"Ouohhh." The crowd chants back in response before the MC continues.

"It is time for us to welcome for the second time the wonderful and beautiful bride, who is none other than Amara-chukwu Ifeoma Ikezie." The MC makes a gesture toward the double entrance doors.

The crowd cheers as the music resumes, this time playing from the loudspeakers in the corners of the room. The doors open up to reveal Teeyana dancing and leading a group of girls into the hall. The girls' dresses are made from the same fabric, but different styles, with matching head wraps tied in an exquisite pattern.

I remember Emmanuel referring to the head wraps as *geles* —another word I've noted down for my ever-growing dictionary. The girls dance out in twos, holding feathered fans and shaking their waists in ways I would never know how to.

Teeyana sticks out like a sore thumb with her round twenty-one week baby bump and her 'catching-up' dance moves. I teased Teeyana about that when she and Amara showed me the dance moves on video call, but the girl couldn't care less. You can tell she would do anything for her best friend, so it doesn't matter if it's obvious she can't dance like the other girls.

Behind the bridal train is Amara, the queen herself, in all her glory. Her dress is made from burgundy fabric and it has rhinestones and skillful embroidery all over it. She also has coral beads around her neck, her feathered fan is bigger, her *gele* is broader and her exquisite dance moves will make her groom impressed.

I turn my head to look at Raymond—the groom, who is sitting at the far end of the hall in a three-piece outfit Emmanuel referred to as an *agbada*. Emmanuel also mentioned that Raymond is not sitting on the stage meant for the bride and groom, because Amara will have to find him later. The smirk on Raymond's face is priceless. His gaze is trained on Amara and there could be a nuclear bomb explosion right now or a meteor heading for earth and his eyes would not leave his bride.

The one word I pick out from the song playing is *Ada,* and Emmanuel explains that it's the way the Igbo people refer to the first daughter. In Amara's case, she's the only child, so the praises are all for her.

When the music stops, Amara walks up to her mom and dad and kneels in front of them. I can't help but notice Mrs. Ikezie's dress. While her husband has a simple white *agbada* and red cap, Mrs. Ikezie went all out. Her green blouse and wrap skirt also have rhinestones, and she has an orange fabric draped over her left shoulder, which also has rhinestones. Here *gele* is also orange but not as big as Amara's and her matching gold jewelry is the icing on the cake. I can see where Amara got her love for fashion from.

Mr. Ikezie stands and leans on his gold-tipped decorated walking stick as he greets everyone in Igbo. After a brief speech welcoming everyone again, he hands Amara palm wine poured out from a calabash and into a cup made from wood—I think. The music resumes and Amara dances around the room, looking for her groom.

The bridesmaids follow her closely, dancing as some men in the crowd reach out, asking Amara to choose them, but she turns them down respectfully. After dancing to almost every corner of the room, Amara finally finds her man—the one with the biggest smile on his face and the only one whose outfit matches hers.

She kneels in front of him and takes a sip from the cup before handing it to Raymond. He drinks the rest of the wine and then takes out some cash from his pocket, places it in the cup and gives it back to her.

After helping Amara to her feet, the couple dances over to Amara's parents and kneel in front of them. Mr. Ikezie prays for them and then they both move their bodies to the music without any effort as they travel to the dance floor.

An older woman who seems to be Raymond's mom—because they look so much alike—joins them on the dance floor and starts throwing cash on the couple as they dance. Then Amara's parents join them and more people from the crowd join in, everyone spraying cash on the couple. One guy even brings out a spray gun, spraying money on the dance floor without a care in the world.

"Is that real money?" I ask, shocked—in a good way—by the entire display.

Emmanuel laughs. "Of course it is." He stands and extends his hand. "Come on, we need to dance."

I shake my head. "Oh, no, no. You want me to embarrass myself?"

"Come on. No one cares. If you support your friend, you have to dance with her. You can't come to a Nigerian wedding and sit down the whole time. That's just impossible."

"But I didn't bring any cash with me."

A smirk appears on his face. "That's not a problem. I've got you." He hands me a stack of one-dollar bills and I follow his lead, trying my best to dance to the beat. We dance with the bride and groom as Emmanuel and Raymond hit it off as if they are long-lost brothers.

"Girl, I'm so glad you made it here on time. You look so beautiful." Amara pulls me in for a hug after I spray her with the dollar bills Emmanuel gave me. Her energy seeps through me, throwing any reservations I had out of the window. "So is this him? Hmm?" Amara wiggles her eyebrows at me.

I send her a sheepish smile and nod. "Amara, this is Emmanuel and Emmanuel, of course you know the bride." I make the introductions before hugging Raymond.

"It's so good to finally meet you, Emmanuel." Amara gives him a side hug before saying something in Igbo and when he responds, they both burst out laughing. "She has told me amazing things about you. Thank you for treating her well. She's very special to me, you know?" The tone in her voice is pleasant, but also holds an underlying message—as if to say *don't break her heart or else.*

"Don't worry, she's in safe hands." Emmanuel gives my shoulder a gentle squeeze before going over to speak with Raymond and Jayden, Teeyana's husband.

Amara pulls me to the side, away from the dancing crowd so we can talk a bit more.

"Heather." A voice calls out and we turn around to find Teeyana waddling toward us. She wraps me up in a warm hug and my heart melts at the sight of her glow. She looks so beautiful.

"Where did you go?" Amara asks as Teeyana blows out a breath.

"Listen, I'm convinced this child is jumping on my bladder because I've been going to the toilet every twenty minutes."

Teeyana had another scan last week and found out she'll be having a baby boy.

"Oh, no, does it hurt when you pee?" Amara jumps in. "Do you have any pain in your tummy? Do you have a fever?" She places the back of her hand on Teeyana's forehead.

"Whoa, calm down, Missy. I already tested for a urinary tract infection and it was negative."

"Good." Amara exhales. "Sorry, that's what happens when you marry a doctor." She smiles and nods toward her groom, who is engrossed in a conversation with Emmanuel.

"Hey, babe." Jayden sneaks in from behind Teeyana and gives her a hug. "I brought your water."

"Thanks, my love." Teeyana smiles and takes the bottle of water from him. Even Jayden is wearing a two piece African print Kaftan—the first time I've seen him in one. I love how we've all embraced each other's cultures.

"Boy, this girl has been peeing every twenty minutes. You going to give her more water?" Amara asks, and we all laugh.

"I know. But she also needs to stay hydrated." He smiles at us. "Are you girls okay?"

"Yes, we are," Amara responds. "Thanks for looking after our friend."

"You're welcome. Now, if you'll excuse me, I have to get back to the guys. Let me know if you need anything else, okay?" He plants a kiss on Teeyana's cheek and slips away.

"So?" Amara and Teeyana lean close to me when Jayden is out of sight. "Is it official between you and Emmanuel yet?"

My gaze darts between the two of them as I hide my face with my small feathered fan. "No, it's not. But I met his younger sister recently, and said that Emmanuel told her he likes me."

"Oooh," the girls say before breaking out into a song. "*Heather and Emmanuel, sitting in a tree. K-I-S-S-I-I-N-G.*"

"Girls, please, stop. He could hear, you know?"

Amara rolls her eyes. "I don't care. Just let me know when the wedding is and I will be your makeup artist. You will make a wonderful Igbo bride, I know it. I can already picture you with a *gele* and the beads around your neck." Amara squeals.

"Girls, let's not jump ahead of ourselves." I hold their hands as we walk back to the dance floor. "I will let you know if he makes things official."

Emmanuel returns to dancing by my side and he teaches me more dance moves as the music continues. I love this carefree side of him.

Amara's mom walks onto the dance floor with a group of middle-aged women surrounding her. The women also have outfits made from the same fabric but different from everyone else's. Again, there's more spraying of money on Amara and Raymond and lots of dancing, cheering, and hailing from the women.

"Welcome, Heather. I'm glad you could make it." Mrs. Ikezie hugs me before turning to Emmanuel.

"Thank you. This is my boss." I point to Emmanuel.

"Welcome, my son," she says. "Thank you for coming all the way from New Jersey to celebrate with my daughter. God will bless you both abundantly."

"Amen." Emmanuel bows and she touches his shoulder. "Thank you, Aunty."

"What's your name?" Mrs. Ikezie asks, craning her neck to look at him as he towers over her.

"Emmanuel Madu."

Her eyes light up. "*Ibu onye ala Igbo?*"

Emmanuel smiles. "Yes, Aunty. I'm Igbo."

"That's wonderful. Are you married?"

I almost choke on my saliva because of the directness of her question, but thank God my mouth is dry from the shock of how this conversation has changed trajectory.

"No, I'm not," he responds, still smiling.

"Oh, that is very good. You see my friends over there?" She points to the group of women who were dancing with her. "They are from the Boston Igbo Women Society. Very good Christian women with good Christian grown-up daughters who will make wonderful wives. Marriage material—the whole hundred yards. *I ghotara?*" She grabs his hand. "Come, let me introduce you to one of them. I know the perfect girl for you."

A mixture of jealousy and shock bubbles in my chest as my brain tries to make sense of what is going on.

"No, Aunty, sorry that won't be necessary." Emmanuel resists her pull and my heart rate slows down.

"Ah, ah, why *nau*? Are you shy? I will hype you up, don't worry. I can tell you are a good boy and well trained. Listen, all you need is the phone number and when you talk, you will see if you like each other."

He laughs again and says, "I'm seeing someone, Aunty. Sorry."

What? My eyes widen at the revelation, and I stand there, too stunned to speak.

Mrs. Ikezie's shoulders drop. "Aww, that's too bad. The good ones are always taken. Well, she's a blessed woman. I pray you marry and have many fine children, *n'aha Jisos.*"

Emmanuel laughs and replies, "Amen."

When Mrs. Ikezie finally leaves, Emmanuel returns to my side, grooving and dancing as if nothing happened.

He's seeing someone? Who is this someone? If he is, then why am I here? What are we?

"Heather, are you okay?" He places his hand on the small of my back, bringing me out of my thoughts.

I nod and force a smile, refusing to let him see how bewildered I am. "Yeah, I just feel a little dizzy, that's all."

"Oh, okay. Let me take you back to your seat and I'll get you some water."

As he leads me back to our table, the music becomes background noise as my thoughts run wild with lots of unanswered questions.

29

HEATHER

"I can't believe you still have your jollof rice. I finished mine two days after the wedding," Emmanuel says as he takes out a sandwich from his lunchbox. We took two chairs out of one of the conference rooms and we're having lunch at our favorite balcony spot. Enjoying the view of the Hudson River and inhaling the cool air as the sun's rays warm my skin is the perfect way to spend my lunch break.

"How did you finish three Tupperwares of jollof rice in two days? Were you having it for breakfast, lunch, and dinner?" I chuckle as Emmanuel struggles to talk with the sandwich he has stuffed his mouth with. "Authentic jollof rice doesn't come by easily for me, so I can't eat it all in one day," I continue. "I have to make sure it lasts a long time because I don't know when next I'll be able to get some."

Emmanuel swallows the last bit of sandwich in his mouth before saying, "Well, if you don't finish the rice soon, I'll have no choice but to turn up to your house and finish it for you."

We both laugh as I open my Tupperware and the aroma of Amara's mom's spicy jollof rice teases my nostrils. Mrs. Ikezie refused to let us leave the wedding empty-handed, so she stuffed plastic bags with lots of jollof rice and now I don't have to cook for a week.

"Okay, stay out of my freezer. If not, I might just fight you." I point my fork at Emmanuel, but my threat doesn't scare him as he laughs again.

"Don't worry, Olanna cooks delicious jollof rice, so I'll bribe her into making some for you."

"Do you think she'll mind teaching me how to make it?"

"I'm sure she'll be happy to teach you. Leave that to me." Emmanuel smiles as we continue eating.

I'm still riding on cloud nine after celebrating with the girls last weekend, but as Emmanuel returns to talking about how cool it was to meet Raymond and Jayden, one question keeps lingering at the back of my mind, begging for an answer. *"Who is he seeing?"*

I've replayed the conversation between Emmanuel and Mrs. Ikezie in my head at least a thousand times, and each time, it hurts more than the last. Does Olanna know he is seeing someone else? If she knows, why didn't she tell me? Why hasn't Emmanuel told me about this girl? How can he be seeing someone else when he spends so much time at the office? *It doesn't make sense.*

"Heather?" Emmanuel's voice pulls me out of my thoughts. "Are you okay?"

"No... I mean, yes." I close my eyes and shake my head. "Yeah, I'm fine. Sorry, what were you saying?"

"I said Jayden and Raymond forgot to give me their numbers. Do you have them?"

"Yeah, I'll send them to you now." I pick up my phone and scroll through my contacts. After sending the numbers to Emmanuel, we finish our lunch in silence before Emmanuel walks up to the metal bar and I join him.

We lean against the bar for a few minutes as we admire the

view. Emmanuel takes a deep breath and exhales and I can't help but wonder what he's thinking about. Is he thinking about her? If he is, then what am I doing here with him?

"What are you thinking about right now?" Emmanuel breaks into my thoughts and I bite down the words from leaping out of my mouth.

Is it wise to open up to him right now? What if he only likes me as a friend? Wouldn't that make me a desperate employee trying to hit on her boss? Meredith was right. I can't handle being just his friend. This is too much.

"Heather?" Emmanuel steps forward and his hands slowly graze my folded arms, concern etched across his face. "Is everything alright?"

I want to tell him. I want to tell him I like him. But I've replayed the scenario in my head a million times and it always ends badly. If he's seeing someone else, then I shouldn't be here. "I'm sorry, I have to go." I turn to pick up my bag, but Emmanuel's grip on me tightens.

"Hey, hey, hey." He lowers his head so he can meet my gaze. "You know you can talk to me, right?"

I lift my head slowly to look at him. "It doesn't matter."

"Of course it does," he says. "If it makes you look this worried, then I'm sure it matters. Look, if it's about the job, then you don't have to worry because I talked to my dad and we are going to be keeping you on the team."

"Really?"

"Yeah, the job is all yours if you want to stay." He lets go of my arms. "I'm hoping you'll stay."

If he had told me this before Amara's wedding, I would've been jumping for joy and celebrating that he wants me to stay. But why should I stay when he is seeing someone else? I can't stay around for that.

"So what's truly on your mind?" He leads me back to the

table and takes a seat across from me. As he stares straight at me, my head and my heart wage war against each other. Instead of giving in to my heart, I stall and ask him the first random question that pops into my head. "Do you think people can genuinely change for the better?" I ask, partly referring to mom, but also partly referring to myself.

He tilts his head, confusion written all over his face. "Erm... yes? I believe God is still in the business of changing lives," he responds and then continues. "I remember how my mom used to drag Olanna and I to church every Sunday when we were teenagers. She didn't care if we didn't feel like it, as all she wanted was to show us the Way. What I've learned, though, is that God Himself was the one who worked on my heart and transformed it. The last four months have been a turning point for me."

I smile at him, loving that he trusts me enough to be all kinds of vulnerable with me.

"What about you?" he asks. "What was the turning point for you?"

"Well..." I start, "You won't believe it when I say that I used to be a rebellious and manipulative teenager. I smoked, drank alcohol and did drugs too." I avert my gaze, dreading his reaction and praying that when I look at him again, he won't have a look of disgust on his face.

"Really?" Emmanuel chuckles. "You? Who looks like you've never hurt a fly in your life?"

"Looks can be deceptive." I join him in laughing. "I'm serious. After my mom abandoned us, I spent my entire teenage years trying to fill the void she left behind. I used to sleep around with any boy who showed me any kind of attention, and that's how I got this tattoo." I pull up the sleeve of my blouse to expose my wrist and Emmanuel takes my hand in his.

He leans close to me as he examines the tattoo and my gaze

slides up to his face, his neck, and his lips. His sweet cologne smell wraps around me like a hug and all I want to do is bury my face in his neck and stay there forever.

"That's a really cool tattoo. What's the story behind it?"

"Well, I was drunk that day and the reason I got it was because I knew my dad would hate it, so I did it to annoy him. When the tattoo artist asked me what I wanted my tattoo to be, I blurted out the word 'beloved' without knowing why. So here you go, the word beloved in cursive writing with a small cross next to it. I was angry at God, but I still told the artist to add a cross. That's ironic, isn't it?" I laugh at how ridiculous it sounds.

"No, I think that was God still working through you, even when you disobeyed."

"You got that right." I take out my phone and swipe through some old photos. "I deleted most of my old photos from my phone, but for some reason, I kept this one." I turn my phone around so he can see.

"Wow, what's with the red hair and the blinding red jacket?" Emmanuel asks and we both laugh.

"I used to dye my hair red and wear thick eyeliner with choker necklaces and bright colors, so I could give my dad a hard time."

"The poor guy has been through a lot."

I nod, a surge of guilt resurfacing in my chest as I wonder how he could accept me back into his life so easily. "He really has."

"So, what was the turning point for you?" Emmanuel asks again.

I sigh before putting my phone back in my pocket. "I met Teeyana. We were college roommates, and I bullied her because I thought she had an easy life. I didn't know she was also going through some tough times. I kinda hated her for most of freshman year, but after my ex-boyfriend Connor dumped me, Teeyana showed me what it's like to have a true friend. She comforted me when I was feeling low, told me about Jesus, and encouraged me to mend my relationship with my dad. I don't know where I would be today if Teeyana hadn't obeyed God and spoken to me that night. It would not have ended well."

"Wow." Emmanuel rests his elbows on the table. "That's an amazing testimony. It's mind-blowing to think that if these things hadn't happened, then I wouldn't have met you." He takes my hand in his and I meet his gaze.

My breath catches in my throat as he brushes my hair away from my face, but the wind keeps blowing it straight back into my eyes. "Yeah, right." I pull my hands away from his before standing up and picking up my lunch box. I still don't know where this is going and I can't let him get close and personal if he is seeing someone else.

He stands up too and I think he has noticed the shift in my mood again, but this one-on-one time has to end right now.

"So you want to have lunch again here tomorrow?"

"*Pfft.* No, thank you. I don't want to get in trouble with your girlfriend." The words are snarky, but I don't care. I'm done trying to pretend it doesn't bother me anymore.

"Wait, what?" Emmanuel pulls his eyebrows together as I walk past him, heading for the door.

"Heather, wait." He runs after me, but I don't stop. "What are you talking about?"

"The girl you told Mrs. Ikezie you're seeing. I don't want to get in trouble with her, so I think I'll have lunch with Yin and Melissa from now on."

"No, Heather, wait." He holds my hand and stops me from opening the door. "You're getting it all wrong. I thought you knew who I was talking about."

"Well, you didn't tell me, so how would I know?" I stop

myself from raising my voice. *Calm down, Heather. He's still your boss.*

Emmanuel tilts my chin up with one finger, so I can look at him. "You really don't know who I was talking about?" He asks as he leans closer, his intense gaze making it difficult to answer the question. Warmth floods through my body and the butterfly feeling in my stomach returns with a vengeance. "It's you, Heather." His voice reduces to a whisper as his face stops a few inches away from mine.

Before I can process his response, his hand slides up my neck and he closes the gap between us. I close my eyes and lean into him until our lips touch for the first time. He wraps his other arm around my waist and pulls me close as I savor every moment, in case it's a dream I have to wake up from.

"It's no one else but you." His voice pulls me out of cloud nine, and I open my eyes to see him staring at me.

No, it's not a dream. Emmanuel just kissed me. I exhale, stunned for words. "I didn't know." My words stumble out of my mouth as I regain my bearings. Olanna was right. He likes me and... wait a minute. "But if it is me, why didn't you just tell Mrs. Ikezie?"

"I didn't want that to be the first time you were hearing about it."

"So you just let me believe this whole time you had a girlfriend?"

"No, it wasn't intentional. I was only..." He pauses, takes a step back, and raises one eyebrow. "Wait...are you jealous?"

"Oh, please." I roll my eyes and turn my back to him, but he wraps his arms around my waist and plants a kiss on my temple, which turns my insides into mush.

"I'm sorry I made you feel that way. I was waiting for the right time and I also didn't know whether you liked me back."

Aww, he was nervous to tell me how he feels? That's adorable.

My smile returns as my skin melts under his touch. "You're forgiven." I turn around and lean close enough to inhale his sweet cologne. I can't believe this is happening. I could stay here all day getting lost in his gaze and praying he never lets go of me. "Please, kiss me again," I say and a smirk appears on his face as he pulls me close and claims my lips once more.

30

EMMANUEL

"I kissed her." The words come out of my mouth in a hushed tone and Yin's eyes widen as he pushes himself away from his desk. If we were characters in one of those animated movies I watched as a kid, this would be the part where Yin's eyes pop out of his head for a second—except it won't be in horror, but in excitement.

"You go, boss man." Yin raises his voice as he gives me a handshake, followed by a loud pat on my back. A dozen heads turn in our direction as employees strain their necks to listen in to our conversation.

Conscious of the disruption we're causing, Yin and I walk away from the open-plan office and when we're inside my office, I shut the door behind us. Yin hugs me again and from the corner of my eye, I catch a glimpse of the employees, especially Melissa, staring at us through the glass walls.

"I'm so excited for you," Yin says as he takes a seat across from me.

"Honestly, I'm excited too and the funny thing is, I never saw this coming. If someone had told me that when Heather walked in through that door four months ago, I'd feel this way about her, I would have laughed at how ridiculous it all sounds."

"Yeah, I'm glad you *finally* told her how you feel. I always knew she liked you back."

"You did? How?"

Yin shrugs. "I sensed it. Plus, Olanna confirmed it."

I chuckle as I imagine what Olanna's response will be when I tell her about me and Heather. "That girl is something else."

"She always knew you two would end up together. God knows how to have His way." Yin adds and I nod.

"He really does." Something else catches my attention in the corner of my vision and when I turn my head, it's Heather waving at me from outside my door.

My day was already going well, but seeing her smile has made it even better. She opens the door and pops her head in. "Are you busy?"

"No, please come in." I stand up and gesture for Yin to stand, too.

"Look who we have here." Yin grins at Heather and her cheeks go red as she tucks a strand of her hair behind her ear.

"Okay, playtime's over. I think it's time for you to get back to work." I step in to stop Yin from embarrassing my woman. *Hmm. My woman. I like the sound of that.*

"But, but I want to hear everything..." Yin protests as I guide him toward the door.

"Yeah, we'll catch up during lunch. Remember, you still owe me a report before noon."

"Yeah, yeah, yeah. I always owe you a report." Yin grumbles as he steps out of my office, and I close the door behind him.

Exhaling, I turn around to look at the only person occupying my thoughts right now. "Hey." I take her hand in mine and plant kisses on her freckled cheeks.

"Hey." She hugs me for a few seconds before pushing me away and holding me at arm's length. "Should we be displaying this much affection when everyone's watching?" She asks as we turn to look at them on the other side of the glass walls.

Melissa and Ava are pretending to engage in conversation, while Neil is writing on a notepad even though I know he hates writing and has always preferred typing. Heather and I chuckle as we turn to each other again. "Maybe we shouldn't, but you look so beautiful and I can't help myself." My words don't do justice to the view she's gracing me with.

She presses her lips together and covers her face to hide her smile. "Stop, you're making me blush."

"Stop doing what? Telling my girlfriend she's beautiful? Never."

She laughs and pushes my arm gently. "Thank you. You're handsome. You should have seen all the looks I was getting as I walked into work this morning."

"Why won't they look at you? Do you know what a privilege it is to be the boss' girlfriend?" I wink at her and she pushes my arm again for the umpteenth time.

"I don't know what you're talking about. Anyway, I just came here to tell you I completed all the AWC tasks you sent me for the week."

I blink back in surprise. "Really? That was quick."

"Yeah, I shared the folder with you. It has all the information you asked for. I just came to tell you so it won't get lost in the thousands of emails you have."

I walk over to my desk and log onto my computer. When I open my email, the folder is sitting there with all the drafts of social media posts and links to the social media accounts she has created. There's also a link to the finished website and lots of videos she has put together from previous campaigns, which are ready to go up on the social media accounts. "Wow."

"So, what do you think?" She bites her bottom lip when I look at her.

"Heather, these are great. I'll save them and then you can present them to Mr. Nwaeze tonight. Thank you so much. I owe you big time."

"Yeah, you do." She chuckles. "Okay, I better get back to work before people start talking."

"Do you have to go?" I groan, holding her hand.

"Yes, I do. I've got work to do. LTH launch day is only eight weeks away and I have lots of tasks waiting for me to complete, remember?" She sends me a smile before letting go of my hand and heading for the door. "Oh, by the way." She turns back. "Did you tell your dad yet?"

My smile fades as I lower my gaze and clear my throat. "Errm… no, not yet. I'll tell him when the launch is over." I promised her I'd tell Dad yesterday about our relationship, but when I got home, I couldn't bring myself to call him. Every time I dialed his number, I kept thinking about how unimpressed he'd be, and his look of disapproval taunted me.

"Oh… okay." The disappointment in her voice is so obvious it sends daggers straight to my heart. "So, that is even more reason why we need to be careful. I don't want to make a bad impression." She opens the door.

"Heather, wait." I inch closer to her. "I think it'll be better to tell him when he's not so stressed about the LTH project. So I'll tell him after the launch. We'll be fine. You have nothing to worry about. Trust me." To be honest, those words are more for me than they are for her.

"Okay," she says simply before opening the door and I know she's not convinced, but I need time to figure out how to tell him.

"So, I'll see you at lunch?" I ask, holding the door open for her.

"Yeah," she says as she walks out without looking at me.

As soon as I close the door, I lean against it and let my head collapse into my hands before resisting the urge to kick myself. *Come on, Emmanuel. Do something or you'll ruin this and lose her.*

31

HEATHER

"**G**irl, what did I say about you wearing that *gele*?" Amara squeals on one corner of my laptop screen and Teeyana follows suit in the other corner.

"Yes, I can already picture you on your wedding day," Teeyana adds. "This is amazing news. I told you he liked you, but you chose to keep lying to yourself about him being just your friend."

"Okay, fine. You girls were right. There, I said it. Are you happy now?" I roll my eyes at my friends, but can't hide the smile that breaks through.

"God has been so good to you this year." Teeyana leans forward. "You've almost finished your successful internship with a job offer pending, God has sent an amazing man of God your way and someday, you'll launch your business again. I'm so excited for you."

"Girl, I'm more excited about the wedding," Amara chimes in and we all laugh.

"I don't know why you're talking about a wedding. We've only been dating for two weeks. He hasn't proposed yet." I cover my face to hide my blush. Maybe today Amara won't notice my tomato red cheeks.

"True, but the intention is to one day get married, right?" Teeyana asks.

I place my hands down and shuffle into a butterfly pose to make room for Phoebe, who has now climbed on my bed. She snuggles next to me into her favorite curveball pose and meows. It's almost time to feed her, so she'll keep meowing until I get the message.

"Yeah, of course," I respond to Teeyana's question. "Marriage is the goal, but we're taking things slow and I'm trusting God all the way." I let out a sigh, hoping that the tone of my voice wasn't as heavy as my heart, but my friends are smarter than that.

"Heather, is everything okay?" Amara asks, and from the look on Teeyana's face, I can only assume that she, too, wants to know the answer to that question.

I lower my head and pet Phoebe. "You know what? I think I'm just over-analyzing things and trying to sabotage this before it even starts. Let's forget about it, please."

"No, no, no. Heather, your concerns are important, so don't brush them away," Amara says. "What's wrong? Did Emmanuel do or say something bad? I know where he lives and I'm about to fly down to New Jersey and—"

"Okay, calm down, *Mom*." I laugh. "He didn't do anything, but..." I sigh again, a very exaggerated one this time. "We've been dating for two weeks now and even though his sister likes me and practically calls me her sister-in-law, Emmanuel hasn't told his dad yet."

Amara frowns and tilts her head. "Okay? Did he say why?"

I nod. "He said he's waiting for the right time, but I don't believe him. He has also spent two years waiting for the right time to tell his dad that he doesn't want to take over the company. Emmanuel is amazing and I really like him, but... if he can't stand up for himself, then I don't know if he'll ever stand up for me."

"Have you spoken to him about it?" Amara asks.

"Yeah, we've talked about it briefly and he knows that sometimes he can let his dad's opinion of him influence what he does. I hope we'll be fine, but I don't know whether he'll ever have the courage to stand up to his dad and choose the path God has called him to take."

The girls are quiet for almost a minute before Amara speaks again. "Yeah, we need to pray about this."

"You got that right." I nod.

"Hey, don't worry about it," Teeyana says. "Keep counting your blessings and remain positive. Hand over all your uncertainties to God. I'm sure He'll work it all out. He's very capable."

"Yaas Jesus," Amara hollers.

"Hmm. Preach it, sister," I shout out before our giggles fill the room.

"You never told me you had a cat," Emmanuel says while holding my hand as we meander through the passing buyers at the garden center. I know nothing about plants, but when he asked me to help him choose the twelfth plant for his plant sanctuary, I couldn't say no to spending more time with him.

"Yeah, I do. Her name is Phoebe," I respond, squeezing his hand tighter as I get used to his warmth against my skin. "She was a stray and used to turn up to our house every day when I was in my senior year in high school. I used to feed her all the time and after my dad and I couldn't find her owner, we adopted her and she became part of the family."

I stop in my tracks and awkwardly try to use my left hand to take my phone out of my right pocket so I wouldn't have to let go of Emmanuel's hand. He laughs at my misery for a few seconds before helping me out and handing me my phone.

"There she is," I say, scrolling through the hundreds of photos and videos of Phoebe on my phone—mostly ones of her carrying out her shenanigans—like the one I took after she wrecked my room because she was trying to bounce like the ball she was playing with. "She's hilarious. You need to meet her. I'm sure you'll love her."

Emmanuel shakes his head before I even finish my sentence. "That would be a no from me," he says casually as we resume our walk.

I frown. "Why not?"

"Errm... because she sounds like she would wreck my plants and also... I don't do cats."

I squint at him. "What do you mean you don't *do* cats? Phoebe is fun. What did the innocent creature ever do to you?"

He stops in front of a shelf filled with ceramic-potted plants and inspects their green leaves as he continues talking. "When I was younger, Olanna and I used to watch Nigerian movies with my mom and some of those movies portrayed cats as the home of... evil spirits. I also read *Animal Farm* by George Orwell and there was a cat in that book who sunk his claws into a man's neck."

I burst out laughing, drawing the attention of other customers. "So you're saying you're scared of cats?"

"It's not funny." Emmanuel tries to suppress his laugh. "I'm saying that cats are not for me."

"Phoebe is not like that."

"Oh, yeah? So what are those scratch marks on your arm then? Did the *innocent* Phoebe give you those?"

"Oh, please." I roll my eyes and walk across the aisle to the other shelf of potted plants. "She was only playing with me and it was my fault for not cutting her nails." It's my turn to inspect the plants' leaves, although I have no idea what I'm supposed to be looking out for.

"Yeah, right!" Emmanuel scoffs as he stands next to me. "I'm not about to get claws in my neck, so I'll pass."

"Well, too bad because Olanna loves Phoebe, and she always gushes over photos of her, so I'll bring Phoebe over one of these days."

"Not in my house, you won't." His smile disappears, and it's my turn to snort.

"Yeah, I will." I stick out my tongue at him and retrace my steps, but he grabs me and pulls me close before I can get away from him. Laughter escapes my lips as he turns me around in one swift motion, wraps his arms around me and plants a kiss on my temple.

A few heads turn in our direction and others send side glances our way, but I don't care. If only they knew the blessing I've found, they would join me in laughing. Emmanuel and I have been praying about our relationship and in my quiet time, I've also been praying that God helps him to learn how to stay true to his purpose.

After my talk with Teeyana and Amara last week, I took their advice and stopped worrying. Emmanuel still hasn't told his dad about us, but I'm not letting that bother me. I'll keep counting my blessings while I wait patiently for the right time.

"This is pretty." I point to a plant on the shelf further down the aisle. Its bright green leaves have a red rim around their perimeter, making them stand out from the sea of green.

"That's an Aglaonema Red Lipstick," he says without even looking at the card hanging from the pot. "I've always wanted one, so I guess now's the time to get it."

"Well, there you go." I clap my hands together. "I vote for her because she looks so... fiery, like she's commanding attention to all the passing buyers."

"Yeah, like you."

"Like me?" I take a step back, my head tilting to one side. "You think I'm fiery?"

"Hmm... yeah, but not in a bad way." He shakes his head. "I mean fiery in terms of being assertive, passionate, and proactive."

"Yeah, but also easily angered." I sigh and turn away from him. It took a lot of willpower to open up to Emmanuel about Mom, Dad, my anger issues, and the fact that I'm still going to therapy to deal with these emotions.

"Hey." He walks ahead and stands in front of me. "I'm sorry I offended you. I didn't mean to."

"No, it's okay." I force a smile. "It's just that... sometimes I wish I could dial it down a little."

"Dial it down?" Emmanuel frowns. "No, that's one thing I love about you."

"Really?"

"Yeah, I love a woman who knows her worth in Christ and lives it out unashamedly. I think it's very attractive." He winks at me before going back to pick up the plant from the shelf.

My cheeks warm up and my smile returns. *Did he just say love?* "Okay, when you put it like that, it actually sounds like a compliment," I say when he returns.

"Believe me when I say it is a compliment. You're a blessing to me, and I mean it." He kisses my cheek. "Now, your last assignment is to help me name this plant." He holds my hand again as we head to the cash register.

"Don't worry, I already have some ideas."

If someone had told me five months ago that I would be picking out plants, naming them, and learning how to take care of them, I would have never believed that. But it's not the plants themselves that have captured my heart. It's the man walking beside me right now, the one who makes me believe every day that God has indeed smiled on me.

32

EMMANUEL

"Ladies and gentlemen, it's an honor to announce that our marketing strategies have brought Long Term Health a two-hundred and twenty-five percent increase in profit for the launch of their newest product compared to their last launch," I conclude my speech as loud cheers erupt from everyone sitting in the conference room.

Dad's clapping is the loudest, followed by Yin and then the Long Term Health representatives Mr. Chen and Mr. Brown. My gaze sweeps through the room as everyone stands up and the lights come back on, allowing me to appreciate the expressions on their faces.

There's only one smile I want to see, though, and that's from the beautiful redhead sitting at the back in her cute white blouse and black trousers. When I lock eyes with her, she smiles at me as I place my pointer on the table and walk back to my seat.

Mr. Chen and Mr. Brown shake hands with me and Dad hugs me briefly and returns to the front of the room. "Wow, look at all those numbers?" Dad says when the crowd quiets down again. He turns to the colorful graphs and bar charts on my presentation slides and says, "I have never been so proud of anyone else like I am of this boy right here." He points at me.

Ugh, trust Dad to call me a boy in front of everyone.

I smile at him as I accept his compliment, but when he takes his attention away from me; I glance at Heather again. God knows that the last six weeks wouldn't have been the same without her. We know how to work hard and play even harder. Balancing a new budding relationship and our LTH deadline wasn't easy at first, but Olanna organized creative date nights for Heather and me, which helped us unwind after our long and tiring work days.

After Olanna went back to college last month, Heather and I decided it would be wise not to hang out at my place anymore, so we've been working at the office and having dates in public places. She has been vulnerable enough to open up to me about her past and the last thing I want to do is ruin this beautiful journey God has put her on.

I need to show her I'm different from all those guys who treated her badly. I want to do this right, and I want our relationship to glorify God. My feelings for her deepen every day and there's no doubt in my heart that this is it. She's the woman for me.

"Thank you again to Long Term Health for choosing us," Dad says to the gentlemen as he places one hand in his pocket. As usual, he's wearing a gray native Nigerian outfit today, an *agbada* complete with a hat and his stick. He has never been one to wear a suit and I don't think he'll be changing that soon.

"I'm sure you're now convinced that you didn't make a mistake choosing us," Dad continues. "We're looking forward to working with you again. There's food and drinks in the cafeteria for us to celebrate."

Everyone applauds again as we stand up. Mr. Chen and Mr.

Brown follow everyone else out of the room while Dad and Heather stay behind.

"Akachukwu," Dad calls out and with that name, every guilt I've felt the last six months comes flooding back. "I am so proud of you, my son." He squeezes my shoulder and, as he stares straight into my eyes, I spot the tears forming in his.

"This company will be in good hands and the Madu legacy will live on. Thank you, *nwa m nwoke.*" He hugs me tight and I can feel his emotions through the hug. "*Daalu o,*" he thanks me again in Igbo and I fight back the tears blurring my vision.

I thought that when this time came, I'd be strong enough and more prepared to not give in to his words. But this is getting harder every day. *Lord, please help me.*

Dad finally breaks the hug and pats my back. "When you're ready, come and join us." He wipes the tears under his eyes and walks out of the room after greeting Heather briefly.

I stand still, unable to move from the table as a tear slides down my cheek. I can feel Heather's gaze on me and I can imagine what she's thinking. That was yet another opportunity I let pass me by without telling Dad.

Her warm hand rubs the top of my back as I turn around to look at her. But instead of disappointment or anger in her eyes, she flashes me her gorgeous smile. "I'm so proud of you, Manny." She hugs me and lets me rest my heavy head on her shoulder. In this moment, nothing else matters and I just want to stay there for as long as I can.

Later in the evening, Heather and I take a stroll on the Hudson River Waterfront Walkway. She previously mentioned that she loved looking at the skyline of New York, so I knew she would love this. The road stretches for miles as we walk on the concrete and cyclists ride past us occasionally.

We walk past several couples sitting on benches, talking, chatting and taking photos. To the right of us is a black metal barrier and on the horizon is the beautiful skyline Heather and I love watching from our favorite balcony spot—especially the reflection of the lights from the skyscrapers on the water.

Holding her hand and talking with her for over an hour about everything and anything is a blessing I can't fathom. I've never been so happy and I can't thank God enough for it. That's why I need to move my feet and act to protect not just myself, but also my relationship with Heather.

"What are you thinking about?" Heather's voice breaks into my thoughts and I look down at her, her fringe flying upward under the influence of the wind.

"You." I kiss her forehead and she frowns.

"Really?" She chuckles. "Speak the truth."

I pause in my tracks before holding her hand and leading her to the barrier. "I am speaking the truth. You're a blessing to me." I pull her close and lean my back against the barrier.

She smiles and is about to hug me when a passerby takes her attention away. I follow her intense gaze to a man smoking a cigarette and strolling past us. A few feet away from us, he takes his last smoke and throws the cigarette on the sidewalk.

Heather's countenance changes as she stares at the used cigarette and I release my hold of her. She sighs before walking over to a bench and sitting down. I lower myself next to her, dreading the answer to the question I'm about to ask her. "Babe, what's wrong?"

She fiddles with the hem of her jacket before speaking. "Manny, before we move forward with this relationship, I need to be honest with you."

Uh oh. I swallow to wet my dry mouth. This is it. She's going to call me out for what I did today (or shall I say, what I didn't do). "Okay."

"I've been a Christian for five years now, but I'm still a work in progress. Sometimes I struggle with cravings to smoke and drink. I'm still seeing a therapist who is helping me work through my feelings, especially the anger and frustrations I've kept bottled up inside me since I was a child." She sniffles. "And the worst of all is that.. I still haven't forgiven my mom." Her tears slide down her cheeks. "I've been trying so hard the last six months, but I can't do it. It's too hard."

"God knows it's hard, babe. He sees your struggles and He doesn't want you to struggle on your own." I cup her face in my hand and wipe her tears with my thumb. "You remember that verse that says to cast your cares and burdens on the Lord? Seems like the perfect one for this scenario."

"Yeah, I know." She wipes her nose with the sleeve of her jacket. "But how do I cast my burdens on Him?"

"Go to Him, trust Him, have faith that He will help you forgive." I wrap my arms around her, letting my warmth bring her some comfort. "Go to Him and He will show you how."

"You think so?" Her voice cracks.

"I know so." I hug her and time passes until my phone rings in my pocket. When I take it out, it's Mr. Nwaeze calling with an update from the AWC campaign day. "Sorry, babe. I have to take this." I swipe right on my screen and bring the phone up to my ear. "Hello?"

"Emmanuel. Good evening. I hope I'm not disturbing you." Mr. Nwaeze's voice comes through the other end of the line. The background noise of honking cars and voices is so loud I can barely make out what he's saying. "I wanted to call you and share the good news."

"Oh? What happened?" Heather lifts her head and looks at me as I put the call on speakerphone.

"Your marketing strategies worked. Since we started raising awareness of the charity on social media and posting more about our projects, we have been getting a steady stream of donations."

"Oh wow, really?"

"Yes, and this morning I got a phone call from *Wake Up Nigeria* TV show to come on and talk about the charity. We will air it in two weeks and I'm sure that will raise more awareness because, from my research, they have over 3.5 million daily viewers. The food and craft fair was a hit and in one week we have raised over eight hundred thousand naira, which is way more than what used to be our yearly donations."

"Wow." *Thank You Jesus.* "That is amazing."

"Indeed." The older man continues. "Thank you so much for making this happen. You mom would be so proud of you. God will bless you, my son."

When I end the call with Mr. Nwaeze, I turn around to find the sadness in Heather's eyes replaced with new joy—the same joy in my heart now. "Congratulations, Manny. You did it." She wraps her arms around my neck and leans close.

"We did it." I lift her off the ground, spinning her around as laughter escapes her lips. "God did it." I set her safely on the ground and naturally, our lips find their way back to each other.

33

HEATHER

"Then he kissed me... again." I whisper to Olanna and shush her to stay calm, but instead of holding back her squeal like we agreed, she goes all out, stomping her feet on the ground and flailing her arms around like a little girl.

The same day Emmanuel kissed me, Olanna squeezed the information out of him when he went home after work. I even remember her calling me that evening and we spent an hour talking about it. But that was over two months ago, so when Olanna told me she would come home this weekend to celebrate the LTH launch with us, she made me promise to fill her in on everything that has been going on between the two of us while she was away.

"So what happened next?" Olanna asks when she finally stops squealing. I've been telling her about our last dinner date while Emmanuel takes a toilet break.

"Shh! I'll tell you later. You know boys pee fast." I look over my shoulder, expecting Emmanuel to appear behind us and catch us talking about him.

"Don't worry. He's probably doing a *number two* or something." Olanna chuckles and then pauses. "Aww, you look so happy."

"I am. I can't stop smiling." My cheeks and face hurt as I talk.

"We're going to be sisters. This is so amazing." She pulls me in for a hug and squeezes me tight. It's good to have Olanna back, even if it's only for a few days, because Emmanuel and I can hang out at home again. I was so glad to find out that Emmanuel and I are on the same page about saving ourselves for marriage.

When I opened up to him about my past life, he never judged me. Instead, he has been intentional about us setting boundaries and making sure that we don't taint this beautiful bond God has blessed us with. Every day, I find new reasons to love him.

Olanna has also been supportive of our journey since the first day she met me. She's also an amazing cook, and she was kind enough to teach me how to make Nigerian jollof rice today. What more can I ask for? Well, it'll be nice if the third member of the Madu family also likes me, but that's a worry for another day.

"Aww, look at you girls bonding," Emmanuel says in a mocking voice as he walks back in. "So, this is what you do when you spend time alone, huh? Gossip about me?" He smirks and lowers himself on the sofa next to me.

Olanna feigns a gasp. "You were eavesdropping on us? I wondered what was taking you so long in the bathroom."

I chuckle as he wraps his arm around me and plants a kiss on my forehead. "We were having a girls-only conversation, and you weren't supposed to be eavesdropping."

"Listen, as long as it concerns me, I'll eavesdrop for as long as I like." He laughs before catching the throw pillow Olanna has flung at him.

"Hey, I just realized you two even own the same pair of glasses," Olanna points out. "Was that planned?"

"Yeah, that's his fault." I nod toward Emmanuel. "He insisted on giving me this as a *very* late birthday present."

"Aww, that's so cute. How do you know which one is yours?"

"I had my initials engraved on the side. See?" I take the glasses off and show them.

"Hmm, that's smart and fancy," Emmanuel says.

"I learn from the best." I smile as he leans over and kisses me.

"Okay, people, back to the movie because at this rate, I'll be watching you guys snuggle all night."

Our laughter quiets down when the doorbell rings and after a brief pause, Emmanuel stands. "Are you guys expecting anyone?"

Olanna and I look at each other before shaking our heads. "It's your house. Shouldn't we be asking you that question?" Olanna laughs before catching the pillow Emmanuel throws at her.

He walks to the door and looks through the peephole. "Oh, it's Dad," he says, the tension in his voice apparent. His head drops for a second as he places his hand on the door handle.

I sit up and tuck my glasses in so they hang out from the front of my shirt. "Do you want Olanna and I to leave?"

"No, no. Please stay," he responds before letting out a sigh and opening the door. "Hey Dad. I wasn't expecting you today." He opens his arms wide as he gives the older man a hug.

"Do I always have to ask for permission before visiting my children?" Mr. Madu's deep voice comes through when he lets go of his son. "Besides, we have important matters to discuss." He pats Emmanuel's shoulder before stepping into the room and pausing at the sight of me. "What are we having here? A party?" His gaze sweeps over our plates of leftover jollof rice and chicken bones on the table.

"Good evening, sir." I bow my head respectfully, like I've seen Emmanuel do a few times, but Mr. Madu only gives me a stiff smile in return. He is wearing his usual African print attire with his hat and stick. He must have a ton of these in his closet because I've never seen him wear an outfit twice.

"Daddy!" Olanna throws herself at him, sending him into a fit of laughter.

"Hello, my princess." He hugs her back. "One of these days, you'll have to remember that your old man is not as agile as he used to be, so *biko,* slow down your velocity when you give me a hug before I end up on the floor."

"Dad, stop. You'll always have the energy to handle my hugs."

"Amen to that prayer," he says before focusing on Emmanuel, whose demeanor has now changed.

When he locks eyes with me, I mouth, "Are you okay?" and he nods, but he can't deceive me. I know he feels as nervous as I do. No matter how hard I try to stay relaxed, I can't shake away the sense of dread building in my chest.

"Can you girls excuse us for a moment? Emmanuel and I need to talk."

Uh oh. The seriousness in Mr. Madu's voice doesn't do much to calm my nerves..

I pick my bag up from the floor, getting ready to leave, but before I can open my mouth, Olanna jumps in. "Sure. Heather and I will be in the kitchen." She picks up the dirty plates from the table and leads me away from the men. *Okay, that wasn't what I wanted to do, but this works too.*

When we get to the kitchen, Olanna, who is oblivious to how tense my insides are, starts going on about the movie we were watching as she washes the plates in the sink, but my mind wanders off to the planet of worries drawing closer and closer to my brain.

Is Emmanuel finally going to tell his dad about us? What if Mr. Madu doesn't like the idea? Will Emmanuel stop seeing me if his dad tells him to? Will I lose my job at Madu Health?

"Heather?" Olanna clicks her fingers in front of my face, bringing me back to the current conversation.

"Huh?" I glance at the door before focusing on her again.

Her worried look slowly turns into a smile. "Do you want to eavesdrop on their conversation?"

"Is that okay?"

"Of course it is. It's a free country. Come on."

I swing my bag over my shoulder as we tiptoe to the door, and Olanna opens it slowly. Walking down the hallway, we stop next to the living room and Olanna chuckles silently as we press our ears against the wall.

"You're slacking, Emmanuel." Mr. Madu's irritated voice comes through. "We made a deal six months ago and there's no time to waste. I've already spoken to my lawyers and set up a meeting with them on Monday. We have to begin the process of passing this company down to you."

"Dad, actually... I..." Emmanuel hesitates and my heart races for him as I squeeze Olanna's hand.

Come on, Manny. You can do this. Tell him the truth.

"I don't think..." Emmanuel continues stuttering.

"You don't think what, son? You have to speak up. Come on."

"Dad, I don't... want to take over the company."

The silence that slashes through the air is so thick, it weighs heavily on my chest, and I forget to breathe.

"What was that?" Mr. Madu asks, first quietly and then again in a loud voice. "What did you just say?"

Olanna and I flinch at the same time, still holding on to each other.

"This must be a joke, right? No, clearly it is because I don't understand how we've been talking about this for the last twenty-six years, and this is the first time I've ever heard you say that."

"Dad, I wanted to tell you. I've been waiting for the right moment, but you never let me."

"*Chineke m.* I never let you? Akachukwu, are you being serious right now?" His stick hits the floor repeatedly as he talks. "Is this how you have chosen to bring disgrace to this family? Is this how you want to drag the Madu name in the mud? You want to give me high blood pressure, don't you?" Mr. Madu's voice rises with every question.

Olanna turns to me, concern etched in her features. "Did you know about this?" she whispers and I'm sure the look in my eyes gives away my answer.

"All I want to know is why?" Mr. Madu continues. "Why would you ever indulge in such foolery?" he asks, but Emmanuel stays silent.

Speak up, Manny. Please.

Emmanuel's continuous silence spurs a new determination in me and without thinking about the consequences of my actions, I let go of Olanna's hand and walk into the living room. "Because God has been leading him to charity marketing instead."

Emmanuel's eyes widen as he shakes his head at me while Mr. Madu frowns, his gaze darting between me and Emmanuel. "What is this?" the older man asks. "Why is she talking, and what is she talking about?" He turns back to his son.

I stare at Emmanuel, giving him an encouraging nod. I thought starting the process would spur him on and encourage him to talk. But unfortunately, my plan backfires when Emmanuel remains silent.

A lump builds in my throat as tears blur my vision. I make a step toward the door, but Mr. Madu's voice stops me. "So, this is the reason you want to throw everything away?" He gestures toward me. "This is the reason you have lost your senses?"

"Dad, Heather had nothing to do with this. It's my decision."

"Is it really?" He snorts. "Because all I see here is a son who has chosen to be foolish and let a woman control him."

"With all due respect sir," I start, anger now rising in my chest. "I take offense to your accusations because you don't know me."

"Keep your respect to yourself," he shouts at me. "I know enough to make my conclusions about you being a home breaker."

"Dad!" Emmanuel and Olanna say at the same time as Olanna steps out from behind the wall, sniffling.

I have nothing to lose, so I continue talking, spilling everything from my chest without giving second thoughts to my words. "You're so blind, aren't you?" I look Mr. Madu straight in the eyes. "All you think about are your ambitions and you've failed to see how unhappy your son has been for the last two years. You've been so sucked into your own world that you have no idea what your son *actually* wants."

"How dare you?" He narrows his eyes and starts walking toward me. Emmanuel steps forward and holds his arm, but the older man shakes it free. "What gives you the right to stand here and utter such rubbish?"

"Dad, please..."

"You keep quiet, son. I will not stand here and let her disrespect me." He turns back to me, his gaze now piercing through me. "Get out of my presence and I don't want to ever see you in my company again."

"Dad, please calm down, so we can talk about this," Emmanuel starts, but Mr. Madu raises a hand and silences his son.

The older man walks up to me again, looking me dead in the eye, and my stomach jumps to my throat as I grip the handle of my bag tighter. "Get out," he says through gritted teeth and all the anger in my chest turns into the energy that fuels my legs as I bolt out the door.

"Heather, wait." Emmanuel's voice trails behind me, followed by Mr. Madu calling after him.

My sneakers slap against the concrete as I run down the sidewalk, the chilly evening air blowing against my face and drying out the tears on my face.

"Heather..." Emmanuel shouts out, but I don't stop. His steps get louder as I slow my walk to catch my breath and he finally catches up to me. "Heather, please don't leave like this. I'm sorry. My dad didn't mean any of those words." He steps in front of me and places his hands on my shoulders.

"Let go of me." I jerk my shoulders out of his grip. "How would you know he didn't mean what he said?" The anger in my voice is obvious and I can't stop myself from shaking.

Ten. Practice relaxation techniques. I inhale sharply, but my breath catches in my throat and I release sobs instead.

Nine... nine... I try to recall my techniques, but I can't concentrate. Pain muddles my thoughts and heat flashes through my body, so I give in to my anger once again.

"Manny, you had two months to tell him about us and about AWC. I thought now that you had your confirmation from God, you would finally do something about it, but I thought wrong. You just made me out to be the villain in there and your dad hates me."

"No, he doesn't hate you." Emmanuel cups my face in his hands. "He's just shocked right now, but I promise, he'll come around when I explain everything to him."

"Are you *really* going to explain?" I sniffle as I push my fringe away from my face. "Olanna and I were listening. You could barely form a sentence when he asked you a question."

"Heather, this is hard for me. I thought you understood that." He straightens his back and rubs his forehead.

"You're right. I understand perfectly well. That's why I'm about to make it really easy for you," I say before walking away.

"What... what do you mean? What are you saying?" He power walks beside me.

"This will not work out, Manny. This..." I gesture between the two of us, "will never work until you learn how to speak up for yourself. If you can't speak up for yourself, then how can I ever trust that you'll speak up for me? I'm not a home breaker, and it'll kill me to drive a wedge between you and your family. I've had enough experience from my own dysfunctional family, and I would never wish that on anyone."

"But Heather..." He holds my hand and brings it up to his chest before running his thumb down the side of my face. "I want to be with you. I need you here with me. Please, don't leave." His voice breaks.

My heart wants to believe everything will be okay. But my head knows that this relationship will never work unless Emmanuel learns how to do this on his own. "Speak to your dad, Manny. He deserves to know the truth." I touch his face, his beard soft and warm against my palm.

"Tell him about everything God has placed in your heart and tell him why you're so passionate about AWC. You'll be fine without me, and you'll be *exactly* who God wants you to be." I take a step back and hold my bag tight again. "Goodbye, Manny." With that, I continue running down the sidewalk without once looking at him again.

34

EMMANUEL

I *failed her.* Regret weighs heavily on my shoulders, resentment for myself claws at my heart and disappointment pulls at my legs as I push through the hesitant strides leading me back to my house. All I had to do was speak up, push away my excessive compulsion to please my dad, and choose God.

But I stood there, numb like a helpless puppy, waiting for someone to swoop in and rescue me. I failed her and now Dad hates her because of me. How am I ever going to prove to Heather that she is important to me? How am I ever going to make her believe I haven't been living a lie and I'm convinced that this is what God wants me to do?

I stop outside my door and lean against the wall, my chest filling up with dread about my confrontation with Dad. Then Pastor Samuel's words come flooding back into my memory. *An audience of One.*

Heather told me this months ago, and I knew this day was coming, but I never prepared myself for it. I have to choose between my convictions and guilt. There's no other way to go about it.

Feeling defeated and not knowing what to do, I clasp my hands together and whisper the words. "Lord, please help me." I lift my head to stare at the black sky, the blanket of stars spread across it. Then, as if providing an instant response to my prayer, the scripture from Exodus chapter four presses into my heart loud and clear.

"Who makes a person's mouth? Who decides whether people speak or do not speak? Hear or do not hear? See or do not see? Is it not I, the LORD?"

I push myself away from the wall as my breathing slows. "Lord?" My voice is a whisper. "Is that You?" I ask as I remember the next verse in that chapter.

"Now go! I will be with you as you speak and I will instruct you in what to say."

When I open my eyes again, the dread and anxiety I had before dissipates and with renewed strength to my limbs and bones, I turn around and head for the door.

As I enter the house, Olanna, who is sitting next to Dad, stands and walks up to me. "Manny, what's going on? Where's Heather?" Dried tears have marred her cheeks and the concern in her eyes pulls at my heartstrings. She lowers her voice. "Dad is upset. Please promise me you won't do anything to upset him more."

I pull her in for a hug and kiss her temple. "It's going to be okay. Don't worry about it." I wipe her face. "Go to your room and wait for me. When I finish with Dad, I'll come and explain everything to you, okay?"

She glances over at Dad, who is sitting with his head bowed, hands clasped and foot tapping the floor. "Okay." She squeezes my arm and leaves the room.

"You have some explaining to do, young man," Dad says as I lower myself on the sofa opposite him.

"Dad, I'm sorry you had to find out like this, but... I still stand by what I said earlier."

If looks could kill, then I would be dead right now. "Emmanuel Akachukwu Madu." He stands and I spring to my feet as well, refusing to let him tower over me. "After everything I've done for you, this is how you choose to repay me?"

"Dad, I–"

"Wait, let me finish." He holds up his hand again. I hate it when he does that. "I have worked for many years to build a future for you and your sister in this country. My only priority is to make sure that when I leave this earth, you and your sister will be comfortable. So you're telling me you're just going to let all my hard work go to waste by walking away from your family?"

"Dad, you're getting this all wrong. I'm not walking away from my family. I don't want to take over the company because I want to open up a charity marketing agency that will help charities like A Widow's Comfort."

Dad frowns. "Charity marketing? Akachukwu, you know nothing about charity marketing. That's a waste of your skills and your potential. You'll be taking a big risk."

"I know that, but I'm willing to take that risk because God is in this."

Dad steps back, holding his head and shaking it as he paces

the length of the room. "Oh, Amarachi, my dear wife. I wish you were here, so you can see what your son is doing to me."

"I think she would have been proud of me." I stand my ground. "Her last words to me that day at the airport before she left were to let no one stand in the way of God's purpose for my life."

"This is madness. This is absolute madness. I don't see how any son of mine, in the right sense of mind, would ever do such a thing. How could you let that girl brainwash you?"

I ball my hands into fists. "I'm not doing this because of Heather, Dad. God used her to help me see the vision clearly because I've been fighting the conviction for two years."

Dad bursts out laughing, leaving me confused. He laughs so much that tears roll out of his eyes. I'm not sure if he's laughing because of pain or because he finds this amusing. "God told you to do this?" He asks, looking me straight in the eyes.

I swallow to wet my dry mouth. "Yes, Dad. He did."

"Then you go ahead, son." He waves his hand. "Go ahead and do whatever you want." He turns and heads for the door.

"Dad, please wait." I step in front of him. "I never wanted to do it like this. I want your blessing."

For the first time in forever, anger flashes across Dad's eyes as he looks at me. "I will never give my blessing to support such insolence. When you come back to your senses, you know where to find me."

His words pierce through my heart like sharp daggers and as I take a step aside, he brushes past me before slamming the door on his way out, leaving me alone in the room to wonder whether I've just made the biggest mistake of my life.

35

HEATHER

I'm a failure. The words pierce into my thoughts as I take slow steps up the stairs, barely able to pull myself up. My joints ache, my muscles are tired, my throat hurts from trying to suppress my sobs, and my eyes are sore from the tears that have escaped, anyway.

Today has topped my list as the worst day I've ever lived through. How can anything be worse than losing my job and the man I love on the same day? I vaguely remember the day Dad told me Mom had left us. I was eight years old and didn't understand the gravity of the situation.

The resentment only grew as the days turned into weeks and weeks turned into years. The pain reached its peak when I gave up on praying for her to come back and instead turned my frustration into living a reckless life. After all, if my own mom didn't care enough to stay with me, then why did I need to care about myself?

But the hurt and frustration I've carried inside for sixteen years is nothing compared to the fresh wound I've gained today. Everything about this day sucks. I woke up with a job, a man who loves me, and hope that one day I'll launch my business again. But here I am, standing outside my house with nothing left but pain.

When I reach our white front door, I take out my keys from my bag and turn it in the lock before opening the door. The warm air welcomes me and a small smile forms on my lips. I might have lost everything, but I still have my dad. I know he'll never judge me and I know he'll encourage me until I can get back on my feet again.

The sound of the TV grows louder as I trod toward the living room. The thought of eating Dad's delicious chili and crying in his arms as we binge-watch movies is already making me feel better.

I take off my jacket and hang it on the clothing hook before opening the door of the living room. "Hey Dad." I step inside, but immediately stop in my tracks when my gaze falls on her. It's not that her green eyes are locked with mine, or that she takes on an innocent look when she sees me. It's the fact that she looks cozy leaning into Dad, who has his arm around her shoulder. It's the pretense that everything can be the way they used to be that ticks me off.

"What is she doing here?" I ask Dad, who takes his arm off her and stands. She follows too and stands behind Dad as he speaks.

"Hi, honey. Your mom and I were catching up on some old movies while waiting for you to come back," Dad tries to explain as my irritation grows.

"Waiting for me?" I scoff and turn to the one person I believe deserves the short end of the stick. "So now you care enough to wait for me, huh?" I stare straight into her green eyes. "You think this is how you're going to make up for all the damage you've done? By worming your way back into Dad's life and then getting him to convince me to like you again?"

"Honey, please, can we talk about this like a family?"

"We're not a family, Dad," I say through gritted teeth. "This woman doesn't care about me."

"That's not true, honey." Her small voice comes out as she takes two steps toward me. "I love you."

I burst into laughter, the foolishness of her words refusing to register in my mind. "Love?" I look at her again. "You call what you're doing right now, love? Well, I'm sorry, I feel the opposite. I hate you, *Mom*."

"Heather Mae Osborne, stop this right now." Dad steps in between me and Mom, but my gaze stays on her. "What is wrong with you?"

"She's what's wrong with me." I glance at Dad briefly before pointing at her. "It's your fault I turned out like this. Were you expecting to come back and meet your sweet little eight-year-old daughter? Well, I've got bad news for you. I'm no longer the innocent girl you left behind, and it's all your fault. You ruined my life the day you abandoned me and it was because of you I stopped believing in God."

My voice cracks, my throat burns and my eyes sting, but I don't care. I have to get it all off my chest. "You're the reason I started sleeping around in high school and you're the reason I started smoking, drinking, and taking drugs. I was trying to fill the void you left in my life. I hate you and I wish your beast of a Chinese lover had finished the job he started."

Mom's face goes pale as Dad drags me away from the living room. The pulse in my head drowns out his stern shouts and Mom sobs as she staggers back and lowers herself to the floor.

"You can't say this to your mom, Heather. I will not let you disrespect her." Dad tries to get me to listen, but in the same way I entered the house, I free myself from his grip, grab my jacket, and run out again.

Heather. The still voice presses in as I stare at the colorful lights from Ignacio's Bar across the street. Once. Twice. Thrice it calls out, but my heart stays locked, my lips stay shut and my mind stays resistant, pushing the voice out and choosing to cling to the poison I've given myself.

She deserves it.

Heather.

She hurt me.

Heather.

She has to pay for what she did.

With determined strides, I force myself to cross the road to the other side. A car honks at me, with the driver urging me to walk faster, but I only fix my gaze on the door, my taste buds already anticipating what a drink would taste like.

Alarm bells go off in my head, but the louder they ring, the faster my legs carry me to the door. I show my ID to the bouncer and walk into the bar, where the music drowns out my hesitancy. My gaze sweeps through the room as I try to find a place to sit, and my eyes adjust to the warm yellow light.

The round glass tables on the far left are surrounded by men and women sitting on red tub chairs, laughing, clinking their glasses and emptying whatever liquid is in there into their mouths. I spot an empty table at the center of the room, but I don't want to sit at the center where everyone's eyes will be on me.

As I mull over my decision, a gray-suited, mohawked, middle-aged man, who is sitting alone at the center locks eyes with me and his toothy smile makes me so uncomfortable, I turn away and head for the high chairs at the counter.

The bartender smiles at me when I settle in a chair and drop my cross-body bag on the counter. "Good evening, ma'am. Can I get you anything?" Another smile follows his question, but I want some time alone to think about the decision I'm about to make.

What am I doing? I've stayed away from alcohol for four years. Is my anger toward her worth me going back to this?

"Ma'am, are you okay?" The bartender's voice brings me out of my thoughts and I nod.

I want to tell him to give me one of my favorites—rum, beer, or even lager, but I stop myself. *This isn't worth it.* "You know what, never mind." The man's shoulders slump when I reply. "I shouldn't be here." I step down from the chair, but as I reach to grab my bag, a deep voice stops me.

"Are you sure you want to leave so early?" It's the mohawked gentleman from earlier who is now standing in front of me.

"Yes." I bring my bag close to my chest as my gaze slides from the tip of his mohawk to his smart, shiny shoes.

"But why so soon, *Princessa*? The night is still young." He sits on the high chair next to me. "Come on, live a little. Bars aren't for entering and leaving in five minutes. They're for de-stressing, making new friendships, having fun and distracting yourself from all your problems." He moves his arms as he talks and his whole body ebbs and flows with his Spanish accent.

Yeah, except bars don't take away your problems. Only Jesus can. The words leap to the edge of my tongue, but I don't have the strength to say them out loud. "I'm sorry, sir, but I need to..."

"Come on. Have one drink." He insists. "It'll be on me. I'm Ignacio, the owner of this place, and today, I choose you to be our special guest." He flashes me another smile, and I cringe. *Why does everything about this man give me chills?*

"Well, I guess one free drink wouldn't hurt," I say, not wanting to seem rude. The man is right, though. Maybe I need to relax and forget about my problems, even if it's just for half an hour. Then I can get out of here and figure out what I'm going to do next.

"That's the spirit." He taps the chair I just vacated before calling out to the bartender. "Roy, get the lady whatever she wants, *rápidemante.*"

The twenty-something year old bartender, who is shaking a cocktail for another customer, pours out the drink and serves the customer before returning to me. "What can I get you, ma'am?"

"I'll just have a piña colada. Not strong, please," I respond, satisfied with my choice. I won't get drunk, so there's no problem. When Roy walks away, I adjust the neckline of my shirt, then realize my blue-light blocking glasses are still hanging out from the front of my shirt. I'm surprised they haven't fallen off after all the running I've done this evening.

Sighing, I take the glasses off and place them on the counter before lifting my head to find Ignacio looking at me. Uneasiness wiggles in my middle, but I wrap my arms around myself to suppress the feeling. *Let's give him the benefit of the doubt.*

"Excuse my bad manners. I never asked for your name."

"Oh, my name is Heather." I'm pretty sure I shouldn't be giving out my name to a complete stranger, but oh well.

"Heather. An evergreen flowering plant, is that right?" He rests his elbows on the counter.

I frown, wondering why he knows what the Google definition of my name is. "Erm... yes?"

"So why have such a beautiful name and then look all dark and gloomy?"

I scoff. "Excuse me?"

"Oh, no, no, please excuse my bluntness." He raises both hands. "What I'm trying to say is that it's obvious there's a lot on your mind, and I wouldn't mind if you share. After all, a problem shared is a problem half-solved."

I'm not sure about that, buddy. The words ring in my head as my gaze drifts away to the shelf of alcoholic drinks sitting behind the counter. Meredith would flip if she ever finds out I came here. She'll probably go on and on about how she told me to be careful about Emmanuel and I don't need that right now.

Emmanuel is the only one I want to talk to, but things are not the same. He has his own problems to deal with and no one likes an extra burden when they've got theirs already weighing them down.

This wasn't how things were supposed to turn out. I was hopeful when I moved back here. I thought things would be different, that God would, for once, give me a break. But I'm practically drowning in every aspect of my life and I've messed everything up.

I'm a failure. I bite down my bottom lip to fight back the tears, but they break through my defense wall again and without caring about the eyes watching me, I throw my head in my hands and sob.

After a few minutes of embarrassing myself, I lift my head to find a box of tissues next to me with Ignacio nodding toward it. I grab one and dab my cheeks before blowing my nose. "I'm sorry you had to see that."

He shakes his head. "No judgment here, *Princessa*. That's what bars are for—to let out your frustrations, okay?"

I nod, agreeing that releasing those tears felt therapeutic.

"You should try the piña colada. I'm sure it'll make you feel better." He pushes the cream-colored drink toward me. "My customers say that Roy makes the best piña colada in all of Jersey City."

I drag the glass close to me. Apart from the pineapple slice and cherry topping which makes it aesthetically pleasing, the coconut smell awakens my senses and without thinking about it, I swirl the pink straw a few times and taste the drink.

The explosion of pineapple and coconut produces a beautiful flavor coupled with the perfectly blended texture. "Wow, this is great."

"I told you." Ignacio smiles before turning to Roy. "You have another one sold, eh?"

Roy puts his hands together, makes a quick bow, and then turns away to serve the next customer.

"So if you're not willing to share, that's not a problem. I'll go first." Ignacio explains how his ex-wife married him because of his money, cheated on him, then divorced him. "But you see, I was a fool for love and instead of learning my lesson, I went back and begged her to come back to me. She came back, but this time, she stole my money and ran away. I've not set my eyes on her again since."

"Wow, that's awful," I say, now realizing that my drink is half gone. My vision becomes blurry for a second, but I rub my eyes and it returns to normal.

"I know. Never trust anyone. *Nunca*. You just have to look out for yourself, live your life the way you want, and make yourself happy while doing that."

Yeah, I used to think like that until I surrendered my life to Jesus and realized how flawed that kind of thinking is.

"Actually, I disagree with you." The words I've been holding back for the last ten minutes come to the forefront of my brain and push themselves out of my mouth. "I don't believe we can give ourselves happiness that lasts forever. There'll always be something disappointing us and we'll always want more, which will always leave us dissatisfied."

The man cocks his brow and leans back. "You think so?"

"Yes, I know so." I slurp the last bit of my drink and burp before continuing. "Happiness that lasts forever can't be found within ourselves, our goals, our ambitions, or our relationships. People will fail us and we will even fail ourselves. I've done that so many times. But do you ever wonder whether there's something more, something better, and someone greater looking out for us?"

Ignacio laughs. "Aye, *Princessa*, if you're talking about God, then you're talking to the wrong person. This guy right here wants nothing to do with Him."

"I figured that part out, but it doesn't change the fact that He's real. Well, at least He is to me. If I believe my problems are real, then God is even more real, and He is able. If I believe He is able, then He can help me do hard things—even something as hard as forgiving Mom. If I believe He can help me forgive Mom, then what am I doing here crying like all is lost?"

I turn to face Ignacio, who is staring at me like I'm speaking gibberish. There's a renewed hope stirring in my heart and I can't leave without sharing it with him. "God loves you, Ignacio. He can heal every hurt and pain others have caused you and He can give you joy that lasts forever if you believe Jesus saves. It's been nice talking to you, but I have to go." I push myself up and stagger as a wave of nausea rises to my chest.

"Whoa, are you okay?" Ignacio stands and holds my elbow to keep me up.

I wrap my arm around my middle as I shake my head. "It's been so long since I had alcohol that it doesn't agree with my stomach anymore." I burp before looking up at Ignacio again. "Where's your restroom, please?"

The man points over my shoulder and I grab my bag, pushing my pair of glasses off the table by accident. They drop to the floor, sliding underneath my chair and I should make sure they're not broken, but that's the least of my worries right now. The room spins around me as I make my way to the restroom, so I hold the wall to steady myself.

My knees knock together as I move forward, and my brain refuses to cooperate with my legs. My heart pounds against my rib cage, and each step I take makes it more difficult to breathe.

Oh, no. This can't be happening. I stumble into a restroom stall and open my bag to find my phone, but my jumbled thoughts and shaking hands make it difficult to turn my phone on.

My heart rate quickens as tears slide down my cheeks. "Lord, please help me," I whisper as my whole body sinks to the cold floor and my strength dissipates. My vision blurs again, and I close my eyes just as the restroom door flies open.

The click-clack of his shoes against the tiled floor is the only thing I can hear for a minute, but when I open my eyes again, my gaze lands on the same gray-suited, mohawked, middle-aged man. He is laughing, but it's not the same laughter we shared a few moments ago. This time, I can only liken it to that of a spotted hyena who has finally caught his prey.

36

EMMANUEL

I've spent the last half hour explaining the whole situation to Olanna. She understood, just like I thought she would. I know Mom would have understood if she was here, so why can't Dad be more open-minded and hear me out? I've done things his way all my life and this one time, he accuses me of walking away from my family? *Ridiculous.*

I rub my temples and pace the living room, making sure not to knock over my plants as I swing my arms out to release the tension and frustration in my body. Olanna had an early night, and I don't blame the poor girl. It's already hard enough that we're still trying to deal with the grief of losing Mom. If my relationship with Dad is severed, this will crush Olanna.

Not knowing what else to do, I plop down on the sofa and let my head fall in my hands. I need to clear my mind. "Lord, if this is what you've wanted me to do all along, then why does it have to cost me my relationship with Dad? I spent the last two years avoiding this. I spent the last six months praying against this. Why did You let it happen, anyway?"

An audience of One. The words play out in my brain as well as other Bible passages, but one of them stands out clearly.

.   .   .

"Seek the Kingdom of God above all else and live righteously, and He will give you everything you need."

A sigh escapes my lips as I lean back on the sofa. My gaze follows the lines on my ceiling to the chandelier. "Lord, You know I love Heather. Apart from me returning to You, she's the best thing that has happened to me since Mom died. Why would you let me lose her like this?"

I push myself up and pace the room again. "I've always known Dad would react like this, but Lord, You never told me I was going to lose Heather too. If she wasn't meant to be here, then why did you bring her into my life in the first place?"

I shake my head as a tear falls. "Please, show me how to fix this. That's all I ask." I swipe the tear away and lift my head to find Olanna leaning against the door with her arms crossed.

"Call her, Manny," she says, and I shake my head.

"You should have seen the look of disappointment in her eyes earlier. I failed her. Dad wasn't supposed to find out about our relationship like this. I promised Heather I would tell Dad, but I was too afraid of how he would react and I ruined everything."

Olanna walks up to me and leads me to sit on the sofa. "Yes, you could have told Dad about how you felt earlier, and yes, you could have handled things differently with Heather. But that's all in the past. Let's be honest, keeping your mouth shut hasn't done very much for you the past two years. So, are you going to sit here and let Heather slip away?"

"But..."

Olanna holds up a hand before speaking again. "No buts,

Manny. Call her. Fight for her. Nothing will happen until you speak up. Speak up, Manny. *Soro Soke.*"

I frown and lean my head back. "*Soro Soke*? When did you start speaking Yoruba?" I chuckle, but Olanna folds her arms and raises one eyebrow at me as she maintains her serious expression. "Okay, okay. I'll call her." I lift my hands up in surrender before picking up my phone from the table.

I dial Heather's number and bring it up to my ear. The first two times, it rings and she doesn't pick up. Then when I try the third time, it goes straight to voicemail.

"She must have switched it off," Olanna says, squeezing my hand. "Maybe she went to bed early. You can try again in the morning?"

I want to say yes, but the uneasiness in my chest is not settling. Why do I have the sudden urge to make sure she's alright? Surely she would have gone home to her dad, but I don't have her dad's number to confirm.

"Listen, I'm just going to drive to her house quickly to check she's alright."

Olanna glances at the clock before looking at me. "Now? Manny, it's 10:30pm. Don't you think it's late to show up at her house?"

"Yeah, it is," I say, already grabbing my jacket and my keys, "but I know I won't sleep tonight until I know she's home safe and sound." I bend over and kiss her cheek. "Don't wait up."

"Heck no, I'll stay up and watch Netflix until you come back, so you can tell me all about it."

I smile. "Alright then." I head for the door before turning to look at her again. "Thank you for being so supportive. You're the best sister anyone could ever ask for."

"I know." She giggles before adjusting her satin hair bonnet. "Now forget about me and go get your woman."

~

Standing in front of Heather's house, I press the doorbell next to the white front door and it rings a few times before stopping. I always imagined that the first time I'd come to her house would be to have dinner with her and her dad, so I could finally taste all the amazing food she has been telling me about.

I never thought the first time I'd be coming here would be to make sure she's not crushed by how much I've disappointed her. I place my hands by my side and wait for someone to open the door. It'll probably be her dad and I'm sure Heather has told him about tonight, so I'm bracing myself for a protective father lashing out at me for hurting his daughter.

"Who is it?" A man's voice comes through from the other side of the door.

"Good evening, sir. I'm sorry to disturb you. My name is Emmanuel. Heather's friend. I know it's late, but I just came to check on her."

The door opens slightly and a red-haired man peeks through. "Emmanuel?"

I straighten my back and look him in the eye. "Yes, sir."

"Heather's boss?"

"Yes." I nod.

He opens the door even wider, revealing his t-shirt and shorts. "Heather's boyfriend?"

Oh, that's right. I forgot Heather had told him about us. "Yes, sir. Again, I'm sorry to bother you. Heather and I had a misunderstanding earlier today and I've not been able to reach her by phone. I just wanted to make sure she got home safely and I'll be on my way."

"Jack, is that Heather?" A voice interrupts Mr. Osborne's response, followed by loud approaching footsteps in the hallway. A middle-aged brunette woman appears next to Mr. Osborne, and her shoulders slump when she sees me. "Oh," she says, as she takes a step back and wraps her black cardigan around herself.

Her watery green eyes and pale complexion can't be mistaken, but it's the pain in her voice that's more concerning for me. "Is... is Heather not here?" My gaze darts between the older man and woman as worry replaces the nerves in my chest.

Mr. Osborne sighs and then opens the door. "Please come in, Emmanuel. I don't believe this is something we can discuss at the door."

"Thank you, sir."

"Please, call me Jack."

I nod and follow them down the hallway and into their living room, which has photos of Heather and Mr. Osborne hanging on the mauve-colored walls. The woman takes a seat next to Mr. Osborne before wiping her nose with tissue paper.

"This is Heather's mom, Erica. Honey, this is Emmanuel."

"Heather's boyfriend, Emmanuel?" she asks, and Mr. Osborne nods.

"It's nice to meet you, Emmanuel. Jack told me that Heather is very fond of you. Thank you for being good to her." The woman sniffles. "She has been through a lot and she needs someone who treats her right." Her voice shakes as Mr. Osborne wraps his arm around her.

Guilt pierces its way into my heart as I remember how hurt Heather was when she left earlier today. *I failed her.*

"I'm not sure how much Heather has told you about her mom, but..." Mr. Osborne's voice trails off as he looks at Erica.

I clear my throat to expel the awkwardness. "She has filled me in on the details."

"Okay." He sighs before continuing. "You mentioned you and Heather had a misunderstanding earlier? What was that about?"

I spend the next ten minutes explaining what happened

between myself, Dad, and Heather. "All she did was look out for me and I failed her. I know it'll take a while for us to work through this, but I had the urge to come and check on her tonight. Do you know where she is?"

The woman wraps her arm around Mr. Osborne as he speaks again. "Well, Heather came home a few hours ago, but unfortunately she didn't like the fact that Erica was here. We got into an argument and she left in a hurry. We thought she'd cool off and come back, but it's been three hours and her phone is switched off now."

Oh, no. Panic settles in my chest as I ball my hands into fists to stop them from shaking. "She didn't take her car, right? So, she must be close. I'll drive around the block and bring her back home as soon as I find her."

"You would do that?" Erica asks, nothing but hope radiating from her voice.

"Of course, I will. I love your daughter, and I regret not standing up for her. I need to win back her trust and I'll do everything I can to bring her back home safely." I push myself up and Heather's parents follow me to the door.

"Thank you so much, Emmanuel." Erica hugs me. "Please let us know when you find her and tell her we love her. Tell her I love her."

"I'll do just that." I shake Mr. Osborne's hand before opening the door. That's two more people counting on me. I can't disappoint them.

"Oh, and Emmanuel?" Mr. Osborne calls out when I step outside. "Don't worry about what happened between you and Heather. I trust God. Everything will be okay."

I smile and nod at them before running down the stairs. When I get to my car, my thoughts are running at a thousand miles a second, so I stop to pray, but the only words that come out of my mouth are, "Lord, please help me."

37

EMMANUEL

I've been driving around the block for the last half hour and there are no signs of Heather. On these Friday night streets, men and women are chatting and laughing, while others are driving around playing loud music.

Every time I see someone on the sidewalk, I hold my breath, hoping, praying that I'll spot her red hair—that those waves will still shine through even in the dark. But my hope continues to be crushed, leaving me more and more frustrated.

I drive into a parking space on the street and, after turning off the engine, I place both hands on the steering wheel and rest my head on it. What am I going to tell her parents? What has happened to her? I close my eyes and utter the same prayer I've been sending up for the last half hour. "Lord, please help me. Where do I find her? Where do I look?"

Now Go!

The words drop in my heart again from that verse in Exodus, but I'm not sure what to make of them. "Go? Go where?" I whisper.

A loud crashing sound forces me to lift my head and when I look out the window, I find a drunk man and woman who have dropped a bottle on the sidewalk, but instead of picking it up, they laugh and walk away without any care in the world.

I shake my head and turn to face the front when my gaze lands on the flashing lights of a bar across the road.

Go!

The voice presses in again, this time much stronger than the last.

"Go in there? No." I shake my head. "Heather has gone way past that. Why would she be in there? I don't think—" I start, but stop myself, realizing that if Heather is in fact there, then I'm wasting time asking questions. One thing I've learned about God in the last few months is that I won't always understand and sometimes I just have to obey. Now is one of those times.

I step out of the car and close the door before running across the street to this place, which is called Ignacio's Bar. Making a note of the street name, I walk into the bar just as two girls are heading out in the opposite direction.

Inside the bar, I glance around, letting my gaze linger for a few seconds on each face, but Heather is not among the group of men and women sitting on the sofas and chairs. Soft music is playing from the overhead speakers and the further I walk into the bar, the stronger the smell of alcohol gets.

I head to the counter where the bartender is mixing a drink for a man sitting in one of the high chairs. After he serves the customer, I raise my hand to get the bartender's attention. "Excuse me?"

"Yes, sir. Can I get you anything?" He flashes me a bright smile before throwing a small white towel over his shoulder.

"No, erm... I'm supposed to be meeting someone here and I'm wondering if you've seen her?"

"Okay. What does this person look like?"

"She's an inch shorter than me, red shoulder-length hair with bangs, and she has a tattoo right here." I point to the inner part of my wrist and watch the smile fade from the bartender's face.

"Erm..." The man averts his gaze and stutters. "No, I haven't seen anyone like that."

I tilt my head, studying his body language as he returns to serving two women waiting at the counter. Normally, I would walk away. I like to give people the benefit of the doubt, take their yes for yes and their no for no. But God wouldn't have brought me here if Heather wasn't here.

So when the two women walk away with their drinks, I sit in one of the high chairs. "I'm sorry. Are you sure you haven't seen anyone here who fits that description? She looks like this." I take out my phone and show him my wallpaper, which is a photo of Heather and I holding Anaiah—the Aglaonema Red Lipstick plant we bought together (and the one she named).

The man glances at the photo and then shakes his head so vigorously I'm surprised it doesn't fall off his neck. "I already told you, I haven't seen her, man," he says with agitation in his voice. "I'd like to be excused if you're not going to buy anything." He takes two steps forward and freezes as he looks straight ahead.

I turn my head to meet the object of his attention—a gray-suited, mohawked, middle-aged man walking toward us from the back. "Roy, *está todo bien?* Is everything alright?" The man asks as he walks toward us, his shiny black shoes catching my attention from afar.

The bartender nods and starts wiping the counter. Some-thing catches my eye in the left-corner of my vision—a pair of glasses lying on the floor under the high chair.

"Can I help you, sir?" I lift my head back up to meet the older man's gaze. His smile seems forced, fake, as if he's hiding the world's biggest secret behind it, but what proof do I have of that?

"No, I was just asking... Roy here, to make me a drink, that's all." I lie, buying myself time to check out the glasses under the chair.

"Okay. I'm Ignacio, the owner. If there's any problem, you ask for me. Roy, give the man what he wants," he says to the bartender before heading back down the hallway the same way he came.

"Give me any of your specials. I don't mind," I say and as Roy turns away to pick out some bottles from the shelf, I go down on one knee and pretend to tie my shoelaces. That's when I notice the HO initials on the glasses. *She's here.* After tucking the glasses in the back pocket of my jeans, I take out my phone and send a quick text message to Olanna.

Me: *Call the police now and ask them to come down to Ignacio's Bar for kidnapping. Don't ask questions.*

Olanna: *The police?* 😶 *Kidnapping?* 🤐 *Is Heather okay?* 😟

Me: *I said, don't ask questions. Call 911. Now! I'm sending you the address.*

"Here's your drink, sir," Roy says above me and I tighten my shoelaces before standing. Taking the drink from his hand, I place it in front of me even though I have no intention of drinking it. "Roy, where is the restroom?"

The man points over my shoulder and without hesitating, I power walk to the women's restroom first, knocking before entering and checking every stall. "Heather?" I call out, but she's nowhere to be found.

After checking the men's restroom, I step out, but instead of returning out front, I walk up the stairs leading to the first floor.

At the top of the stairs is a dimly lit corridor with a lot of rooms on either side. I'm about to walk down the corridor when a door flings open and someone walks out of a room, speaking on the phone. I retreat my steps and hide behind the long blue curtains round the corner.

Peeping from a tiny opening between the curtains, I spot the owner Ignacio walking past, still speaking on the phone, but now alternating between English and Spanish. "No, I'm a businessman. I don't like delays, so if you don't come on time and get the cargo as agreed, I will sell her off to the next highest bidder."

Her? The next highest bidder? This is worse than I thought. Oh, no. Human trafficking?

When the man's voice disappears down the hallway, I tiptoe from behind the curtain and walk to the room he just vacated. I twist the door handle, but it doesn't open. *Just great!*

"Heather?" I whisper through the door cracks, but there's no response. After a few seconds, I hear a groan coming from the other side of the door. "Heather?" I wiggle the handle and the groan continues, this time mixed with whimpers.

My phone pings and I take it out of my pocket, reading Olanna's message to say the police are on their way. Yeah, but how long? I can't just sit around and wait for them. Time is of the essence.

If I break down the door (that's if I know how to), then I will draw attention and I won't be surprised if the man has a gun. I stick my hand in my pocket and take out my wallet, which is the only other thing I have on me. Then I remember I didn't hear Ignacio lock the door with a key, which means I just need to get the latch out of the way. There has to be a way of opening the door without a key.

I take out my credit card and place it in between the door and the latch. I'm not entirely sure what I'm doing, but the card meets some resistance, so I wiggle it and it slides in some more. The more I wiggle, the more it slides in and then... *pop*, the door opens.

"Thank You, Jesus." I push open the door and find her laid out across the bed, hands and feet tied and scotch tape over her mouth. "Heather?" I rush to her side, kneeling next to her to check for any signs of life. Her chest is still rising and falling, tears are running down the sides of her face and she is letting out steady whimpers even though her eyes are closed.

"I thought I lost you." I brush her hair away from her face before kissing her forehead and then her cheeks. "Baby, the police are on their way. I'm going to get you out of here, I promise." When I stand up, the sound of approaching footsteps fills the air as Ignacio continues talking on the phone, this time shouting.

For a moment, my feet stay pinned to the floor as I try to figure out my next move. Then I search the room for a bat, a vase, or anything I can use to strike, but there's nothing. With no time left, I run to the side of the door and when he opens it, I swing a balled fist at him as hard as I can, smacking his jaw with so much force. His head makes a swift turn to the left, and he staggers back before going down to the floor with a loud thump.

My heart pounds against my rib cage as I kneel next to him, searching for a gun or any weapon he might be carrying. There are no weapons, so I run back to Heather's side and lift her into my arms, ignoring the sharp pain in my hand. "Come on, baby, I'm going to get you out of here."

As my vision adjusts again to the dark lighting in the hallway, I make careful steps down the stairs because if I miss one, I'll get both of us tumbling down and Roy will catch us. I pause mid-way down the staircase, wondering whether there is a back door we could escape from. I can't go back out front because Roy is still there. *Lord, what do I do? Please help me.*

With a grunt, I adjust Heather in my arms as she groans softly. The pain in my hand flares up, reminding me about how I just punched someone for the first time in my life. I've probably sustained a fracture, but I don't care about that right now. I need to get us somewhere safe until the police get here.

Please, Lord. Let the police get here on time. My silent pleas continue as beads of sweat pour down my face and drip onto Heather's semi-conscious body. Bile leaps to my throat, drying my mouth and constricting my chest as I fight to catch my breath.

Relief washes over me when I finally reach the bottom of the stairs, but the relief is short-lived when Roy appears in front of me and blocks my way. My stomach twists into knots and I stagger backward, almost dropping Heather.

"Where do you think you're going?" The supposed bartender crosses his arms against his chest and frowns. "I tried to warn you, man, but you didn't listen. Now give me the girl and I'll let you get out of here alive."

I stand tall, refusing to let him see the fear in my heart. "No," I say out loud. *Please, Lord. Save us.*

He lifts an eyebrow. "No?"

"Not without a fight."

"Okay, then. You asked for it." He flashes me a smile again before reaching into his back pocket and...

"Freeze!" Two police officers run in from behind Roy. "JCPD. Drop your weapon and put your hands where I can see them."

Roy's eyes widen, and the color drains from his face. With much hesitation, he drops his gun and the police officers place his hands in a cuff and lead him away.

"There's another man upstairs, officer." My voice comes out shaky as I lower myself to the floor and hold Heather against my chest.

The officer nods at me before sending two more officers up the stairs. I drop my gaze to Heather and hug her tight. "Everything will be okay. You're safe now."

38

HEATHER

My eyes flutter open, but a flicker of white light forces me to close them again. I wince as a sharp pain pierces into the back of my hand and a tight pressure squeezes at my left bicep. Muffled voices float around me and when I open my eyes again, my gaze lands on blue scrubs, white coats and medical equipment being passed over and around me.

I groan as I try to sit up, but there's no strength in my hands or legs. Memories of the last few hours trickle into my mind and panic sets in. "Emmanuel?" My voice comes out croaky, but I don't care. "Emmanuel?"

"Yes, baby, I'm here." His soothing voice rises above the ringing in my ears and then his face appears above me, blurry, but clear enough for me to recognize. "I'm here." He touches my face and kisses my forehead. "You're going to be okay. The doctors and nurses are going to take good care of you," he says and before I can open my mouth to say something, his face drifts away and is replaced by Dad's.

"Honey, I'm here." He squeezes my hand. "We're praying for you. You'll get through this." He leans his head on mine and the warmth of his touch calms me down. Then Dad's face too drifts away and is replaced by hers.

"Honey, I'm here too." She sniffles and wipes her eyes, but she doesn't touch me. "I love you."

A lump builds in my throat as all the voices become muffled and distant again. Tears run down my cheeks and my vision goes black, even though I'm still awake. Then all the noise and chaos around me ceases, leaving me in complete silence.

Lord, are You there? Please help me. I'm sorry. Please speak to me again.

Heather.

Lord, is that You?

Heather, my beloved.

Yes, Lord, I'm right here. They've hurt me, Lord.

I see you, Heather. I see your tears. I see your pain.

Please help me, Lord.

I have heard your prayers. I will heal you.

But how, Lord? I'm a mess. I'm only a sinner.

A sinner whom I have saved, redeemed, and sanctified. You are my beloved and I have forgiven you.

But why would You forgive someone like me?

Because I love you. So forgive as I have forgiven you. Love as I have loved you. Let go, my beloved. Let go and rest in Me.

Beep. Beep. Beep. My eyes stir open again and I'm lying on a bed in a quiet room with no one poking my arm or shouting over me. I rub my eyes and exhale deeply before pushing myself up to absorb my surroundings.

The view from the window on my left is of the hospital parking lot and the warmth of the sun's rays on my skin makes me feel more alive. I look down at my green hospital gown and sigh. I don't even remember when they took my clothes off.

There's a blood pressure machine next to the bed and what looks like an EKG machine with wires that have been attached to my chest with stickers. I have no idea what the wiggly lines on the machine are saying about my heart, but they're all green and... I'm alive.

I can't believe I'm alive. I don't have chest pains anymore; I don't feel dizzy, I can see clearly, I can lift my legs, wiggle my toes, and I can breathe. Turning to the table next to my bed, there are pink roses in a vase and notes folded up in pieces of paper all addressed to me.

Honey, we've gone home to eat, shower, and change our clothes. We'll be right back and hopefully before you wake up. We love you and can't wait to see you.

Love, Dad x

-

I'm so happy you're doing okay. I had to go home to take care of some client issues, but I'll come back as soon as I'm done.

I love you so much.

-Emmanuel

Happiness fills my heart as I bring the notes close to my chest and exhale. God saved me. I don't know what that evil man would have done to me if Emmanuel hadn't shown up. I prayed and begged God to help me, and He did. He sent Emmanuel when I got myself into that mess.

I see you, Heather. The words come back to me as I remember what God said. This must be what Hagar meant in the book of Genesis when she called God *El Roi*—the God who sees me. In that room where I felt helpless and almost gave up, He saw me. When temptation knocks at my door, He sees me then too and He *always* keeps me from falling.

A warm presence washes over me as tears leak out of my eyes and I bring my wrist up to look at the word tattooed on it. He calls me His beloved, so I truly must be. Instead of living every day doubting whether I'm loved by Him, I'll embrace the truth and live out my identity. I am His beloved and nothing or no one can take that away from me.

My phone rings on the table and when I grab it, Teeyana's name flashes on the caller ID. "Hello?" I clear my throat and wipe my tear-stained face.

"Oh, my goodness. Heather, are you okay?" Her panicky voice comes through the phone.

"Yeah. I'm okay now," I respond, wondering whether Emmanuel has told her.

"Thank God. I've been worried sick about you. I was praying last night and had this unexplainable urge to pray for you. I tried calling you, but your phone was off. I was so worried I got Jayden to pray with me, too."

"Wow." My voice comes out low as more tears slide down my face. "Teeyana, you have no idea the crazy night I had. I'll explain everything to you later, but I just want you to know that God heard all your prayers. Thank you so much for loving me this way."

"Aww, you're welcome. You know I've got your back, right?"

"Yes, I do. Thank you. I'll speak to you later." When I get off the phone with her, I put my hands together and whisper another prayer. How could I not be thankful? God didn't leave me hanging, and I can't take that for granted.

A soft knock on my door forces me to open my eyes as a nurse walks into my room with the same blue scrubs I saw earlier. "Good morning. You're awake." She sends the brightest smile my way before walking in.

"Good morning." I smile back at her.

"How are you feeling?" she asks as she pulls the blood pressure machine closer.

"I've never been better."

"Great." She checks my blood pressure, heart rate, temperature, and oxygen saturation. Then she takes off the stickers from my hands, feet, and chest before disconnecting me from the EKG machine and ending the beeping sound.

"I'm glad you're feeling great. The doctor will come in to see you later, but things are looking up and you might go home soon."

"Thank you so much... Mia," I say, reading her name badge.

"You're welcome. Oh, before I forget, there's someone here to see you. A woman."

I frown, wondering who it might be. "Oh... erm... is there any chance I could shower first before seeing anyone?"

"Do you mind if I help you with that?" A familiar voice comes from the doorway and I turn my head to find her standing there with her hair tied up in a messy bun.

"Mom?"

"Yes, honey." She walks into the room as Mia excuses herself and leaves us alone. "I knew you would be hungry, so I brought you your favorite." She places a plastic bag on the table and steps back.

The smell of the carrot chapati and lentil stew wafts into my nostrils, dialing up my hunger pangs and setting off rumbling noises in my stomach. I wrap my arms around my middle, pleading for it to be quiet as Mom stands awkwardly next to my bed with her head low and her hands fiddling with her bag.

"Thank you," I say under my breath, wondering if she heard me.

"You're welcome, honey."

The room returns to silence again as I turn my face away, choosing to look at everything else in the room but her. For someone who has spent almost all her life craving Mom's touch and presence, I thought I would know what to do and what to say in this situation, but my silence is surprising—even to me. *Lord, please help me.*

Let go, my beloved.

"I'm happy you're feeling better." Mom breaks through the silence and I turn to meet her green gaze. "If you ever need me, all you need to do is call me." She places a piece of paper on the table with numbers scribbled on it. "I'll always be praying for you, Heather." She sends me a small smile and then heads for the door.

My heart sinks as I watch her walk away. Her being here felt right, and it was the first time since she came back I didn't feel revolted by her presence.

Heather.

Yes, Lord. Please help me. I don't know what to say. What should I do?

Let go and rest in Me.

The still small voice speaks to me again, reminding me that this change is not by my own strength. I can't keep fighting anymore. Healing has to start from somewhere and today, I have to choose to make the first step—no matter how small it is.

"Wait," I say and she stops in her tracks, her hand on the doorknob. I fiddle with the sleeve of my hospital gown as she turns to look at me. "Please, I'd like you to stay."

39

EMMANUEL

I've always wondered how Esther felt before she went in to speak to the king. Yes, the Bible explains that she prayed and fasted for three days, but I'm sure she still had some hesitation, as her life depended on it. Or maybe she was truly confident that God would favor her (as He eventually did).

I'm having a similar moment right now as I prepare myself to speak to Dad again. Of course, this is nothing compared to what Esther went through, but it's important to me. Myself, Olanna, and Yin have been praying about it since yesterday.

I'm going back to the hospital to see Heather today, but I need to speak to Dad first. I messed up and I want to make things right. All I want is for God to make Dad reason with me, and then we can make some progress. But even if he doesn't reason with me, I'm still going to do what God wants because He is my audience of One.

I lock my car and walk up the stairs to the front door before pressing the doorbell. A minute passes and there's no response, so I press the doorbell again. If I didn't see Dad's car parked outside, I would have thought he wasn't home, but I'm sure he's ignoring me.

Slipping my hand into my pocket, I take out the spare key he gave Olanna and me in case of emergencies and in less than a minute, I unlock the door and enter the house. As I close the door behind me, a scripture flashes in my mind, also from Exodus.

"But the Lord hardened Pharaoh's heart, and just as the LORD had predicted to Moses, Pharaoh refused to listen."

The comfort I can take from that scripture is that God created man's heart. He has the power to soften and to harden and He can favor me today. "Dad?" I walk up his spiral stairs so I can check the bedroom first. "Dad?" I knock on the bedroom door, before opening it to meet his empty room, his king-sized bed neatly made up.

The house keepers do a good job during the week, but Dad always gives them the weekend off, so he must have made up the bed himself. I open all the rooms, including Olanna's room and my old room, but he's not in any of them.

When I run back down the stairs and into the living room, I find him sitting in a chair with his back to me and one leg crossed over the other. *Of course. I should have checked here first.*

I let out a sigh of relief as I walk over and lower myself on a chair next to him. For a minute, I say nothing as we both stare at the framed photo in his hand. It was the last photo we took as a family before Mom made her trip to Nigeria two years ago.

We were at the airport and none of us were in the mood to take a photo, but Dad has always been a firm believer in capturing memories with family. He asked a stranger at the airport to take a photo of us using his phone. We didn't know that would be our last photo with Mom.

Dad and I rocked up that morning wearing t-shirts and jeans, while Olanna outshone us looking all glam and pretty (like she always does) with her knee-length hoodie dress, hoop earrings, and starter-locs. Mom was wearing an ankara blouse and fish-tail matching skirt. She loved wearing skirts because—in her own words—"skirts make me feel free as a bird."

In the photo, Dad's hand is around Mom's shoulder, while Olanna is kissing Dad's cheek and I'm kissing Mom's cheek. I still remember how we all 'awwed' when the stranger handed the phone back to us. Those were the days when I thought I had the perfect family, the perfect future, and the perfect life. In my mind, nothing could go wrong—until it did.

"She always joked that I won't be able to handle raising both of you on my own if she wasn't around," Dad finally speaks, his voice croaky as tears slide down his cheeks and fall on the framed photo. "I agreed with her, but I always silently prayed that if one of us were to go first, that it would be me. I knew she was a better parent and I also never wanted to imagine living my life without her in it."

He wipes the tears away from the photo as tears blur my vision. "She was right," Dad continues. "I have failed in every way and the last two years have been a disaster. I promised her I would hold the fort until she got back. I just... I just never knew she wasn't coming back." He holds the photo close to his chest and sobs uncontrollably—a state I never thought I would ever see him in.

Pulling my chair close, I place my hand on his shoulder and squeeze. "Dad, you're doing a wonderful job," I sneak in between his sniffles. "Olanna and I love you. We admire you and we look up to you."

"Then why are you abandoning your family?" He looks at me for the first time since I walked into the room, his eyes begging me for answers. "What mistake did I make? What did I do wrong?"

"Nothing, Dad." I respond as tears fall down my face. "You did nothing wrong. You made your legacy and I respect you for that. I can never repay you for everything you've taught me. But sometimes... I feel like I only exist to fill your shoes and it shouldn't be that way.

"Mom poured out her heart for those women and children and she worked hard to create a better life for them. They need help, Dad. Someone needs to not only give them a better life, but to share the gospel with them. The harvest is plenty, but the laborers are few. God is calling me to do this work using the skills and talents he has given me."

"But how sure are you that this is what you're meant to do?" he asks and for the first time, I notice he has asked a question without raising his voice.

"Because God confirmed it. I prayed about it, talked through it with friends, meditated on His Word, did my research, and wrote out a business plan. When everything came together, I helped A Widow's Comfort with their last annual campaign event and the success from that gave me peace. That's how I know this is what God wants me to do."

Instead of a scoff or a frown or another retort, Dad wipes his tears, smiles, and then shakes his head. "I always knew you would be an ambitious leader. I just never allowed you to discover what you wanted to be a leader of." He leans back in his chair.

"Your mom and I always thought that you and Olanna wanted to take over the company. My dad wanted me to stay back in Bende and continue his agriculture business, but I had bigger goals for myself. My goals were much bigger than the borders of Nigeria, so I had to get out of there before they stifled my dream. I had to shoot my shot and trust God through the process."

He leans forward again. "I suppose what I'm learning from all this is that the apple never falls far from the tree. If I didn't let my father stifle my dream, why would I turn around and stifle yours?"

Relief washes over me as I choose my next words carefully. "So, are you giving me your blessing?"

He picks up his half empty glass of *SuperMalt* from the table and gulps it down in one go. "Let's hear your business plan," he says after finishing his drink.

I straighten my back, my breath catching in my throat. "What, now?"

"You said you wrote one out, right?"

"Yeah, I did, but I haven't finalized it yet."

He places his now empty glass on the table. "You said God gave you this dream, right?"

I swallow to wet my dry mouth. "Yes, He did." *Is he testing me?*

"So you don't need a fancy sheet of paper or document to tell me what your plan is. Relay it to me the same way He placed it in your heart."

Blowing out a breath, I spill out my plan to him as the information pops into my head. Doubts rise in my chest again as Dad gives me his full attention, direct eye contact, head resting on his cupped hand, and listening intently at my rambles.

"I want to form a partnership and open up a charity marketing agency, which will specialize in helping charities with branding, print design, digital marketing and event coordination. I also plan to provide coaching services to help these charities find the most cost-effective way to align their message with their audience.

"My client base will be Christian charities—both big and small whose work is to help advance the gospel. My long-term goal is to branch out internationally, specifically working with charities in Nigeria and Africa. I want to form connections with them and help extend God's kindness, grace, and love to vulnerable people."

Silence stretches between us as I wait for his response. "And what if I don't approve?"

I pause for a moment, considering my response. The old Emmanuel would have tried to negotiate, tried to bend my will to fit in with Dad's, but things have changed. I have an audience of One, so with my newfound confidence, I speak up. "If you don't approve, I'll do it anyway because I have a greater purpose and a higher calling.

"Spending my life trying to please you is not how God wants me to live. It's not about you, so from here on out, I'm only living to please God no matter who is offended. If you don't understand that, it's okay. But I know that someday, you'll see for yourself what God is doing."

"Akachukwu, wait." He stops me from standing up before rubbing his hands together. Minutes pass with us staring at each other and then he speaks again. "It's a promising idea and your goals sound achievable. If you put in the work, it could set off in the first few years. You mentioned it's going to be a partnership, which is a smart idea, but I have to ask, who is going to be your partner?"

My silence says it all and Dad continues. "Why her?"

"Because she has the drive and the determination. She has an entrepreneurial mindset, and she believes in working hard to succeed. We share the same core values. She's great to work with and I trust her. She helped me a lot when I was working on the project for AWC with Mr. Nwaeze. We would have never pulled it off without Heather's input."

Dad nods. "Well, I agree with all the qualities you have mentioned because Yin had nothing but good things to say about her, too." He rubs his mustache, another moment of silence passing before he speaks. "So, you like her that much?"

"I love her, Dad." The words escape my lips without me thinking about them. I can't take them back and I won't because it's the truth.

Dad lifts his head to meet my gaze. "Really?"

"Yes," I respond and Dad opens his mouth to speak, but I cut him short. "I know your last encounter with her wasn't the best. She was only trying to pass across a message I couldn't deliver myself." I pause, waiting for his response, but he just stares at me, so I continue.

"She's not insolent or rude, and she's not a home breaker. Please, Dad. I'd love for you to give her a second chance."

Dad places his hands on his lap and sighs. "Well... I have to say, it has been a while since someone challenged me like that. Her words have haunted me for the last twenty-four hours and they made me realize that I have to listen to you and Olanna more. I'm sorry that you didn't feel free enough to tell me how you felt about taking over Madu Health. I'm also sorry that you had to torture yourself by keeping it in for two years. Have you told Heather about the partnership yet?"

I shake my head. "She's actually in the hospital recovering from an accident."

Dad frowns. "In the hospital? What happened?"

"Yeah, it's a long story, but she's fine and I'm going to check on her when I leave you."

Dad nods and his demeanor falls again. "So who will take over the company now?"

I frown, baffled by his question. "What do you mean? You have another child. Her name is Olanna Gloria Madu, remember?"

Dad raises his brows. "Really? Olanna?" The shock in his voice is unbelievable.

"Yes, Dad. It has always been her dream to work for you and she's very keen."

"Yes, but being keen is different from taking over all these responsibilities. I just always see her as my baby girl who still has a lot to learn."

"She's still your baby girl, but she's also a very intelligent young woman. Train her and equip her with all the qualities she needs. Or are you hesitant because she's a woman?"

"*Mba,*" Dad shakes his head. "You know I have always treated both of you equally."

"Exactly, so work with her. She would make an amazing CEO. I have no doubt about that."

Dad smiles and pats my shoulder. "Thank you, my son. I'll take your advice and work with it."

Wow, this might be a once in a lifetime experience in the life of a Nigerian son. Not only has Dad apologized to me twice today, but he has also listened to my advice. Isn't God wonderful?

"I'm just going to miss having you around, you know?" He smiles.

It's my turn to pat his shoulder. "Dad, I'm not resigning as MD now. I'll let the business grow and I'll employ more people as it does while I'm supervising. When it's time for me to leave Madu Health, I have the perfect person to recommend to you," I say as Yin pops into my mind. He would make the perfect MD.

We both stand and hug each other. "I'm really glad we had this talk, son. I will invest in your business," Dad says when we break the hug.

"Really? Dad, I'll be fine taking any loans I need from the bank."

"*Bia nwoke m,* this is not a loan. This is a gift from a father to his son."

Tears blur my vision and I throw myself on him again, thanking him as he pats my back. *Thank You, Jesus.*

40

EMMANUEL

"**K**nock knock." I push open the door and step into the room, excitement building in my chest as I look forward to staring into her green eyes and taking in the brightness of her red hair again.

She lifts her head and locks eyes with me, and my anxious mind anticipates the moment she'll ask me to leave when she remembers how I messed up yesterday. But to my greatest relief, she sends me the biggest smile ever and stretches her arms out toward me.

Without hesitating, I place my bag on the floor and rush to her side, engulfing her in a hug and kissing her temple multiple times. She holds me tight and sobs quietly on my shoulder as I brush her hair gently, whispering comforting words in her ear. "I'm here," I say, over and over again.

I need her to believe those words. My actions might have hinted otherwise, but I made a mistake and now I know better. I need her to know that this time I'm serious about being with her. This time, I'm ready to fight for her.

After five minutes, she breaks the hug and stares into my

eyes. The anger I saw in them yesterday is gone and in its place is the sparkle I never thought I'd see again.

"My hero." She touches my beard, the warmth of her hands sending a comforting sensation through me.

I kiss her hand and wipe the tears running down her face. "My love."

"How did you know where to find me last night?"

I take both her hands in mine as I recall what happened. "God," I respond simply, trying to find the right words to describe the intensity of the experience.

"God told you I was at the bar and that I was in that room?"

I nod. "Yes. I called your phone and couldn't get through to you, so I went to your house and spoke to your mom and dad, who were worried about you. They told me about the argument and how angry you were when you left, so I offered to look for you. After searching around the block, I parked on the street opposite Ignacio's and developed the strong urge to go in. I asked... Roy, the bartender, if he'd seen you and he said no, but he was acting suspicious, so I stayed. When I saw your glasses on the floor, I knew you were there and I had to find you."

"Wow." More tears fall down her face. "Manny, I only went in there because I was angry. As soon as I walked in there, I realized it wasn't worth it and I wanted to leave, but Ignacio encouraged me to stay and he... he spiked my drink. The doctor told me there was ketamine in my blood and... and..."

"Shhh." I place a finger over her lips as she sobs. "Baby, it's okay. He has been arrested and you have nothing to worry about. He was involved in human trafficking and has been doing this to young women for years. He will go to court alongside all his accomplices. Justice will take its course. You're safe now, okay?"

She nods. "Thank you." She wipes her tears with the sleeve of her gray sweatshirt.

"I thought about what might make you feel better, so I

brought you this." I unzip my backpack and pull out a pink teddy bear holding a red heart.

Her eyes widen as she takes it from me. "Aww, it's so soft." She says before sniffing it. "And it smells so good. Is it scented?"

"Well, let's just say I got some help from Olanna, but I'm glad you like it." I zip up my backpack and place it on the floor again. "Do you know when they're going to let you go home?"

"Yeah, the doctor has already discharged me. My dad is on his way to pick me up."

"That's great. Have you eaten?"

"Yeah, my mom brought some food earlier, and she helped me get showered and dressed."

I raise my brows. "Your mom was here? Did you make up with her?"

"Well, I'm trying hard." She turns around and lets her legs dangle off the bed. "I've been fighting this for too long and I'm tired. If I had died yesterday, I would have never had the chance to forgive her. I want to stop letting offense control my life. I'm tired of being bitter and angry. I want to be happy and I want to make the effort no matter how hard it's going to be." She lifts her head and looks at me. "That's not impossible, is it?"

I shake my head vigorously. "Of course not. You've made the right decision and I'm happy God has brought you here. You'll get through this. I know you will."

She smiles and lowers her head again.

"What's wrong?" I ask, ready to dispel any doubts about herself or our relationship.

"Are you sure you still want to be with me?" Her words are soft, but the authenticity of the doubt in them is real. This is my chance. This is my time to let her know how serious I am. It all starts with what I tell her now.

Lifting her head and looking into her eyes, I take her hands in mine and let the words out of my mouth without holding back. "Heather, when my mom died, I lost a huge part of myself to grief. It sucked away my joy, my peace, and the hope that I could ever live a fulfilling life. I was heading down a destructive path, but God used you to change my life.

"You beat yourself up all the time for having struggles, but it was your struggles that inspired me to become more intentional about my relationship with God. Your struggles slapped some sense into me and gave me the courage to tell my dad what I've had no guts to tell him for years.

"So you see? You may only look at your life and see struggles, but I see testimonies of the wealth of God's kindness. You told me how hopeless your life was without Jesus, but here you are—saved, redeemed, and sanctified. God transformed your heart to love Him. How did you go from hating your mom to being willing to forgive her? Baby, that's a miracle." I cup her face and plant a kiss on her forehead as she smiles through her tears.

I turn her wrist over, so her tattoo is in full view, before regurgitating everything I learned from studying Ephesians chapter two last night. "Heather Mae Osborne, you are God's beloved. Your life has been masterfully crafted by Him and you are a work of art—a trophy of God's grace. You didn't get here on your own and you sure won't carry on by yourself. I've experienced the beginning of this glorious miracle and you want me to miss the full unveiling? Never. I'm not leaving you. I love you and I'm going to stay right here."

"Aww." She throws her arms around me and hugs me tight. "I love you too."

"Please be my partner," I blurt out as she breaks our hug.

"What?"

"My dad knows the whole truth, and he knows I love you."

"He does?"

"Yes, and I also told him I want to start up a charity marketing agency and I want you to be my partner."

She stares at me for a few seconds before drawing her eyebrows together. "You mean... like your business partner?"

"Yes. You have the social media marketing experience and I have the coaching and managerial experience. If we work together, we can reach more people with our expertise and impact more lives. I know your dream was to revive HO marketing again, but I wanted to ask whether you would consider working with me. You would still get to do everything you want to do and I have the connections to help bring in clients. What do you say?"

Again, she pauses, looks away and then clears her throat. "Wow, Manny, I'm so honored that you want me to be your partner but... I'd like to pray about it first. Is that okay?"

"Of course. Take as much time as you need. I'll be right here." I plant a kiss on her lips and hug her again, this time praying that nothing interrupts this special moment we have with each other.

41

HEATHER

The feeling you get when you're back in your own bed after spending two noisy nights tossing and turning in the hospital is indescribable. I never appreciated how peaceful it was to wake up to soothing morning bird sounds instead of the beeping of machines and the smell of medicine.

I also never appreciated how soft the carpet in my room is compared to the hard, cold hospital floors. Don't even get me started on how nice it is to take showers at home. Yes, I know hospitals have showers too, but something about using them made me believe I wasn't clean.

The most surprising thing about the last couple of days is that I left this house angry, broken, and ready to give up, but I returned even more empowered and hopeful about my life and my future. Not only did God reassure me about His love for me, but He was kind enough to turn things around between me and Emmanuel.

I've been thinking a lot about his offer to be his partner and I don't know if I want to accept it or not. I've dreamed about owning my own business for many years, but I never thought about the possibility of having a partner.

I've always wanted to be my own boss and run things my own way, but I enjoyed working with Emmanuel on the AWC project. He never treated me like an employee, but like an equal partner. He's not condescending, and he creates a safe space to share my ideas. Plus, I love him and it'll be a dream to own a business with the man I love. My only concern is if our relationship breaks down. What will happen then?

I let out a sigh and push myself up from the bed. Walking up to the window, I close my eyes and say a quick prayer. "Lord, You brought me this far. Please show me what to do. I don't want to ruin my relationship with Emmanuel."

"Meow!" Phoebe wiggles her way between my legs and I pick her up from the floor.

"You have something to say? Go on, then. Tell me what I should do." I place her on the table in front of me.

"Meow!" She stares at me, licking her lips and following my fingers as I snap them in front of her.

"I'm worried about things not working out. Do you think that's a valid concern, or do you think I'm crazy for talking to you and expecting you to respond?"

She leans forward and rubs her head against my cheek. "Yeah, I know, girl. I should shut up and pet you." I laugh before taking her in my arms and petting her.

My phone rings and I place Phoebe down before returning to my bed. Olanna is calling me and she'll be the best person to speak to, as she's always positive. "Hello?"

My smile fades when, instead of her usual cheerful greeting, sniffles come through from the other end of the line.

"Olanna, are you okay? What happened? Why are you crying?" I stand up as a million thoughts run through my head.

"Alex broke up with me," she sobs into the phone.

I gasp and bring my hand up to my chest. "What? Why? What happened?"

"I don't know." She continues sobbing as she struggles to catch her breath. "He was acting weird for a few weeks and every time I tried to hang out with him, he told me he was busy. Then he started ignoring my calls and canceling all our dates. After ignoring my text messages for a week, I went over to his house to see him and he broke up with me. He didn't even tell me what was wrong. He said it has nothing to do with me and everything to do with him, but it doesn't make sense. We've been dating for nine months and never had a huge argument that would cause us to break up. I love him, Heather. Why would he do this to me?"

For half an hour, I listen to Olanna pour her heart out to me and my own heart breaks for her. I would have never thought Alex would do this to her. They seemed perfect for each other.

After several attempts to comfort Olanna, she finally stops crying when I suggest a girl's night when she comes home to visit in two weeks.

"That will be great." She sniffles. "Please, don't tell Manny. I know he had his reservations about Alex, so I'll figure out a way to tell him myself."

"I promise I won't."

"Thanks, Heather. You're the best," she says and we end the call.

I sit in silence on my bed for a few minutes as shock takes over my body. Fear grips my insides and anxiety crawls all over my heart as the possibility of Emmanuel and I breaking up becomes more feasible. If Alex and Olanna could break up, what's the guarantee that Emmanuel and I will last? *Oh, Lord, please help me.*

"Heather, breakfast is ready." Dad 's voice pulls me out of my thoughts and I welcome the distraction by throwing on a t-shirt and sweatpants before rushing downstairs. A sweet savory smell hits my nostrils as I enter the kitchen and my mouth waters.

"Good morning, Dad." I meet him at the door and hug him from behind.

"Morning, honey. Did you sleep well?"

"Like a baby," I say, stretching as I enter the kitchen, and then I pause mid-stretch when I see Mom flipping the pancakes over the hob. "Hi... I didn't know you were going to be here today."

"Hi, honey." She transfers the pancakes onto a plate before taking off her apron and placing it on the countertop. "Sorry, I stopped by to check on you on my way to work. I still remember the way you liked your pancakes, so I wanted to make it for you. I hope you don't mind."

My gaze drops to the perfect golden-brown pancakes. "No, I don't mind at all."

"Okay, take a seat. I'll fix you a plate."

Dad settles in the chair at the top of the table as Mom gives him pancakes with strawberry toppings and chocolate sauce. "What topping would you like, honey?" She sweeps her hands over the selection of fruits and sauces on the table.

I glance over at the kiwis, strawberries, berries, grapes, and bananas. I've had a lot of chocolate over the last few days, so I'll skip the chocolate sauce. "Can I have a banana and caramel sauce, please?" I say, taking a seat on the right-hand side of Dad.

"Hmm, good choice." Dad nods and sips on his coffee.

Mom picks up a knife and slices the banana into round pieces before arranging them on the pancakes. She spreads some caramel sauce over it too and places it in front of me. My heart melts as I stare at the smiley face she has made with the bananas. That's exactly how I liked arranging the bananas when I was younger.

When I look at her, she sends me a soft smile before settling in the chair across the table from me. *She remembered.*

"Shall we pray?" Dad spreads his arms out, and we hold hands, close our eyes, and bow our heads. "Dear Lord, thank

You for the gift of today and for the food You have provided us. Thank You for bringing this family together again. Please bless our food today and let it nourish our bodies. Provide for those who don't have and through it all, may Your praises never cease from our lips. In Jesus' name. Amen."

"Amen," Mom and I say in unison. We dig into our food and Mom pours out a cup of coffee for me. For a few minutes, we say nothing, the only sounds being the clanging of our silverware against our plates.

"How is Emmanuel doing?" Dad breaks the silence before putting a piece of strawberry in his mouth.

"He's doing good." I smile, remembering all the hugs he gave me yesterday.

"I like him," Dad adds. "A man who went through all that trouble for you surely must care about you."

I smile. "Yeah, I know he does."

Dad pauses and looks at me. "So you two made up? You're no longer mad at him?"

I chuckle and shake my head. *I knew he was up to something.* "Yes, we made up and no, I'm no longer mad at him."

"That's great." Dad takes another bite of his pancake.

"I'm happy for you, honey," Mom's voice follows, low, but filled with sincerity. She smiles and her eyes crinkle as she picks up her fork.

"Thank you," I respond and the room goes back to silence before I speak. "He sorted out the issue with his dad and Emmanuel will finally start his own charity marketing agency."

"That's great," Dad says.

"Yeah, and he has asked me to be his partner." I place my fork down and search their faces for a reaction.

"How do you feel about that?" Mom is the one who asks.

I shrug. "I don't know. It's appealing because I love working with him. But I always wanted to have my own company and I'm worried about what will happen if we break up. His sister called me this morning to tell me her boyfriend broke up with her for no apparent reason, and that scared me."

"Hmm." Dad leans back in his chair. "Choosing to partner with someone is a big decision."

"Yeah, but please don't base your decision on what has happened to others." Mom adds. "Pray about it first and don't let anyone pressure you into making a decision. God will show you the right thing to do."

"Thanks…" The word *Mom* catches in my throat and refuses to let itself out, so instead of forcing myself to say it, I smile and focus on my food for the rest of the meal.

42

HEATHER

After breakfast, Mom and I clear the table and opt to wash the dishes while Dad flips through a newspaper. Without saying much to each other, Mom and I settle into the routine we had when I was younger—her washing up and me wiping.

She turns on the faucet and lets the water run into the sink while I grab a towel and stand next to her. The awkward silence is so thick, you could cut it with a knife. Every time she passes me a plate, she smiles at me, but says nothing. I want to start a conversation, but my brain refuses to form a sentence. *Lord, please, You have to help me with this one.*

When she passes me the last plate, I dry it and place it in the cupboard before forcing out the first thing that comes to my mind. "I didn't know you had a job."

She lifts her head to meet my gaze, her warm smile returning. "Yeah, at a bakery. Starting over is not as easy as I thought, so I have to work to stand on my feet again," she says as she turns off the faucet. "I just wish I could turn back the hands of time, you know?" Her voice breaks and she drops the sponge in the sink before covering her mouth with her hands and sobbing.

Her hands shake as the tears slide down her cheeks and for the first time in six months, my heart fills up with compassion for her. It's a strange feeling to have toward her because a few days ago, I was so convinced my heart was incapable of feeling anything toward her but hate.

Let go, my beloved.

As I close my eyes, God's warm presence washes over me and a lump builds in my throat. Instead of walking away like I've been doing for the last six months, I yield to what God is doing in my heart and let out all the emotions I've been suppressing for years. "It's okay." I open my eyes before wiping the tears streaming down my face.

"No, it's not." Mom leans against the sink and shakes her head. "I put myself in this mess and missed out on my daughter's life. I ruined everything for everyone because of my selfishness and I'm facing the consequences of my actions." She sniffles. "It's my fault and I deserve everything I'm getting—your anger and frustration toward me—everything. I'm paying for all the pain I caused you and your dad."

Her words cause realization to dawn on me. All this time I've been focusing on how I'm feeling without trying to look at the situation through her eyes. What would have happened if Dad refused to forgive me because of how disrespectful and horrible I was to him while growing up? Where would I be right now if he had refused to take me back? Probably broke, homeless, and living on the streets somewhere in New York.

"You didn't miss out, Mom." I surprise myself by saying the same word I struggled to say half an hour ago. When I take a step toward her, she turns to look at me.

"What?" Her green eyes are wet with tears and the hope stirring in them is clear.

"You didn't miss out on my life because I still want you in it." The words come out slowly, but God knows I have a million thoughts running through my head. The memories move from my life as a child, a teenager, a college student, and then they finally settle on the events of the night of my abduction. I would rather not think about it, but I know why God has reminded me today. Sometimes reminders like this are necessary, so I can take action.

"Really? You still want me here?" she asks and I nod.

"I thought I was going to die that night, you know?" The words spill out of my mouth as the details of the incident unfold. "I didn't know where I was or what he was doing to me, but I remember him tying my hands and feet and placing scotch tape over my mouth. He spoke in Spanish mostly, but the only time he spoke to me in English was when he warned me not to scream or he would kill me." My voice shakes as a cold shiver runs down my spine.

"Honey, you don't have to do this." Mom reaches out and holds my hands, but I shake my head.

"No, please, you don't understand," I respond as desperation laces my voice. "I *need* to do this."

"Okay." She nods and I lower my head before continuing.

"As I slipped in and out of consciousness, the only prayer I lifted to God was that He would rescue me, so I could get another chance to make amends with you." I lift my head to meet Mom's shocked expression.

"Yes, I was mad at you before and I didn't think you deserved my forgiveness. I wanted you to pay for leaving us the way you did. But laying helpless in that room reminded me about everything you went through in China and how harsh my words were before I left the house that night. I didn't want those words to be the last thing you remembered me saying to you because even though I was angry, I *never ever* wished you were dead.

"I only said those words because I was angry and I'm sorry. While I was in hospital, God reminded me about the gift of His grace, which is His unmerited favor. He also reminded me about His mercy, which means He has chosen not to give me the punishment I rightfully deserve because He loves me. How can I claim to believe in a merciful God when I don't even try to love like Him?

"I'm a sinner and I've made mistakes. But if God could forgive me for everything I did to Dad, then I'll be a hypocrite not to forgive you, too. For five years, I prayed for this moment. I begged God every night to bring you back to me and He did. I'll be a fool to turn a blind eye to this answered prayer.

"I'm sorry for all the hateful things I said to you, Mom." We close the gap between us and she squeezes my hand. "The truth is that I *want* to love you but... I don't know how to do that effortlessly anymore. So much has changed in the last sixteen years and I..."

"Wanting is the first step, honey." She cups my face in her hands as tears stream down her face. "Let's not put pressure on ourselves. We're just going to be intentional about making this work. Little steps is all it takes. Okay?"

"Okay." I nod before asking. "How do you feel about going to therapy? I'd really like us to unpack these emotions and deal with them the right way. I have a wonderful therapist called Meredith and she has helped me for almost five years."

"I'll do anything you want, honey. Anything to make this work," she says and we fall into each other's arms, sobbing and savoring our first mother-daughter hug in sixteen years. I hold her tight, crying on her shoulder as she pats my hair gently.

"I love you, Heather," she says. "I love you so much."

"And I love you both." Dad wraps his arms around both of us and we stay hugging each other with no intention to let go. Sixteen years of her absence is a long time. This is the closure Meredith was talking about. The healing starts now and I'm done wasting my time holding grudges.

43

EMMANUEL

Out of all the ways I could embarrass myself today, I let Heather bring me to a cooking class. Not only did she bring me to *any* cooking class, but she specifically chose a Spanish cooking class. Like, seriously? I haven't even finished perfecting my jollof rice recipe and here I am learning how to cook paella?

I don't know how or why I agreed to do this, but after everything I put Heather through in recent months, I would gladly embarrass myself a thousand times over for her. It's not out of guilt, of course (even though I'm guilty as charged), but out of the love and respect I have for her. So bring it on, girl. Boss me around all you want, I'm not budging. This man is here to stay.

"Manny, can you please pass me the onions?" Her voice drags me out of my thoughts as she stretches out her hand.

"Of course." I push myself away from the counter and walk up behind her before placing the bowl of chopped onions in front of her. Instead of returning to my spot next to her, I hover over her shoulder as she adds the onions into the hot olive oil in the skillet, followed by the chopped bell peppers and garlic.

I've always known she loves cooking, but watching her in

action and seeing the sparkle in her eyes, her determination to get this recipe right, and her boss-lady energy makes my heart so happy. I can't believe I almost let her go because of my—okay, we will not slip back into the past now. She has agreed to be my girlfriend again so this time I'm doing this the God-way. That's all that matters.

Giggles erupt from the couple on our right-hand side as chef Ricardo shows the man the easiest way to chop an onion. I smile and shake my head, almost giving myself a pat on the back because I may not be the best cook, but at least I know how to chop onions.

When the man showed up wearing a white shirt, trousers and a tie, I thought he had missed his way to a courtroom, but his partner complements him perfectly well in her pastel-colored clothes and sunshine energy. If I ever had the job of a matchmaker, I would never have thought to put those two together, but the tenderness in which they treat each other is undeniable. In the same way, I would have never thought Heather would become my biggest blessing when she first walked into my office seven months ago. But here we are.

"Okay, keep stirring your onions and let them soften for five minutes," Chef Ricardo says as he walks over to the next couple across the room from us. They don't look a day over twenty (perhaps college students) and they are the definition of "young love" and can't keep their hands away from each other. *Literally.*

"Wait for me to give you the go ahead before adding the chopped tomatoes and seasoning," Chef says before walking over to the older couple on our left-hand side. They seem to have a lot of experience with Spanish cuisine because they keep asking unending questions about specific ingredients I know nothing about.

After freeing himself from the older and wiser couple, Chef Ricardo walks over to our table and gives us a thumbs up. For whatever reason, Heather lets me add in the next set of ingredients, but she's watching me closely, so I have nothing to worry about.

"You're doing well, you know? You don't have to look so nervous." She squeezes my shoulders gently.

I straighten my back and scratch the back of my head. "Erm... I was hoping it wouldn't be that obvious."

She chuckles as we both chop the parsley. "You know you're very easy to read, right?"

I send her a sheepish smile. "Yeah, my mom used to tell me that a lot. I'm not sure if that's a good thing."

"It is for me. It's okay to be nervous, though." She stops chopping and her eyes flick up to look at me. "I just hope you're having fun."

I take her hand in mine and plant a kiss on her knuckles. "Baby, everything is fun as long as you're with me."

She scrunches her nose and groans. "Did anyone ever tell you that your lines are so cheesy?"

"Ouch." I feign a gasp and step back. "It's the same cheesy lines you fell for, though." We both laugh before she adds in the broth and brings the mixture to a boil.

Twenty minutes later, we add in the seafood mix and again, she lets me sprinkle in some peas on top. "I have to say this is looking better than I thought it would be."

"Of course. It will be perfect because I'm involved." She sticks out her tongue at me and I squint at her, trying to find a good comeback. But sometimes, it's okay to accept defeat. Especially when she's right.

"Yes, ma'am." It's my turn to chuckle as we get ready to serve.

"Here, baby, taste this, please." She turns to me with a spoon full of rice.

"Hmm. That is so good," I say before going in for a second taste, but I have to control myself before she asks me whether this tastes better than jollof rice. She should know by now that no matter how good other rice meals are, I will always stand with Nigerian jollof rice. It's a ride or die thing at this point.

"Thank you." The smile of satisfaction on her face is golden. How can I look at that smile and not want to keep making her happy?

Chef Ricardo once again walks to the center of the kitchen and claps. "Well done, everyone. You are practically professionals now. We have come to my favorite part of the cooking class. The part where we eat."

Everyone cheers as all four couples settle in the high chairs behind their workstation to dig into the colorful meal. In less than a minute, the sound of melodious Spanish music fills the room, followed by laughter and chatter.

"Hmm." Heather wafts the aroma into her nostrils. "This smells so good. The lemon slices and parsley garnish makes it so aesthetic." She takes out her phone and after ignoring my protests, she takes some photos and videos of us and our food. After what seems like forever, we finally start eating.

"I think I deserve a prize for not ruining the meal," I say, chewing the bits of food in my mouth.

"Really? You can have my love." She snickers and my mouth drops open.

"But...but I thought I already had your love?"

She tilts her head. "Okay, what about... a thousand kisses?" She wiggles her eyebrows, but I shake my head.

"I thought the kisses come as a package deal with your love?"

"*Ugh*, you're too picky." She picks up another forkful of rice.

"Okay, fine." I roll my eyes before lifting both hands in surrender. "I guess I'll take the thousand kisses."

"Good." She pauses and sends me a sly grin. "You can top that up with a new business partner, too." She says it so casually that I have to shake my head to convince myself I didn't have an auditory hallucination.

My fork falls out of my hand, sending a loud clanking noise across the room, but I don't even care. "Say what now?"

She snorts and covers her mouth to hide her giggle. "I said yes. I would love to be your business partner."

"Oh, that's amazing." The joy in my heart is so uncontrollable, I spring to my feet and pick her up in a hug before spinning her around. She giggles all the way through before planting a kiss on my cheeks.

"Sorry everyone, I just received the best news," I explain to the other couples and the chef before turning back to my girl. "What made you decide?" I take both her hands in mine, curiosity lacing my heart.

She only touches my face with her palm and says, "Let's just say, one thing God has taught me the last three weeks is that sometimes, He answers prayers in a different way to what I expect. Meeting you was no coincidence, Manny. God knew about you long before I did. For many years, I prayed for mud when He was preparing to give me pearls. I don't know about you, but I'll prefer pearls any day."

44

HEATHER

"You look happy." Meredith taps her pen on her notebook as her mouth curves into a broad smile. "Dare I ask about it?" Her eyes crinkle at the corners, the heat of her gaze so intense it feels as if she's sitting in front of me instead of being on my laptop screen.

Heat travels across my entire face as I cover my mouth to stop myself from smiling.

"Ooh, someone is in love." Meredith wiggles her eyebrows at me and I chuckle.

I nod, still covering my mouth, and when I compose myself enough to stop smiling, I put my hands down and exhale a long breath.

"If there was one word you could use to describe this current season in your life, what would that word be?"

I pause for a second. "Blessed."

"Interesting." Meredith adjusts in her seat. "In what way?"

"I'm blessed to be alive." I shrug as the events of that night whiz through my mind. "Blessed to be on the receiving end of God's mercy, even though I'm totally undeserving of it. Blessed that I now know what it truly means to be *alive*—not just existing, but living the life He has called me to live with confidence and without fear." A tear slides down my face–happy tears this time around and I smile through them, moving on to my next blessing.

"I'm blessed that God brought my mom back to me. Blessed that He gave me the ability to truly let go and forgive her. I'm blessed that He gave me back my family." My heart flutters as I think about the next blessing.

"I'm blessed that He brought me Emmanuel—my knight in shining armor. Setting up a partnership company with someone as experienced as him was the least of my expectations, and this particular blessing has shown me that God is the one in control. I believed that before, but I believe that even more now. God has blown my mind and I can't explain it."

When I finish, Meredith has a wide smile on her face and she's looking at me as if she's expecting me to say more.

"I'm done."

"I know," she says, still smiling. "I'm just amazed by how much growth you've achieved. You have no idea how much I've prayed for you, Heather."

"Really?"

"Of course." She says. "I pray for all my clients. Every single week. I prayed that God would open up your heart to let Him work in you, and He did. Your life is a testimony of God's love."

"It is, and I'm a trophy of God's grace."

"Indeed, you are and no one—living or dead—can rob you of that."

"What do you think about this?" Emmanuel hands me the piece of paper he has been using to scribble our company's name suggestions on. After three weeks of praying with Mom and Dad, my doubts slowly resolved and the more I thought about how this company would impact the lives of others, the more excited I wanted to be a part of it.

I still worry about whether things would work out long term between myself and Emmanuel. But if I let those worries consume me, I won't live out today to the fullest. I'm learning to put in my best effort and hand all my worries and cares to God. He will never fail me.

"Pistis Charity Marketing?" I frown, pushing the paper back to him.

"Yeah." He smiles as Olanna turns her head away from the TV to look at us. She has finally come home to cool off after her breakup with Alex, and it took a lot of convincing for us to stop Emmanuel from driving up to NYU and breaking Alex's bones.

"Why Pistis?" I ask.

"Yeah, why Pistis?" Olanna rests her head on her hand as Phoebe purrs in her lap. I fulfilled my promise and brought Phoebe over, but Emmanuel wants nothing to do with her, so I had to keep her with Olanna.

Emmanuel shrugs. "I like the idea of using a non-English word and 'Pistis' is the Greek term for faith. Some people translate the word to mean 'a firm conviction', which I thought was interesting."

"Okay?" I tilt my head, still trying to figure out where he's going with this.

He sighs and continues. "You remember that day when we found out we were both using the secret balcony at the office?"

"Yeah?"

"You told me that whenever I have a decision to make, I should ask myself whether I'm doing it because I feel guilty or obligated or because of my own values and convictions?" He pauses, shooting a glance at Olanna and then back at me. "Well... we can center this agency on our own values and convictions—our faith in Jesus, so Pistis."

"*Aaaaahhh*." Olanna and I drag out the word, and Emmanuel rolls his eyes.

"The least you girls can do is sound more enthusiastic."

I chuckle, and Olanna continues playing with Phoebe, which has been very therapeutic for her.

"Babe, I'm sorry. I love the idea and I think it's cute that you remember what I said all those months ago."

"But?" He raises his eyebrows at me.

I shrug before pressing my lips together to suppress a smile. "The word 'Pistis' reminds me of urine."

"Yeah, that's right," Olanna says with her back to us.

"See?" I hold back a chuckle. "Someone agrees with me."

"Oh, whatever." He folds his arms across his chest, and turns his head away. I love it when he pretends he's mad at me, because I know he's only looking for a kiss.

"I'm sorry." I stand up and plant a kiss on his lips before sitting down again.

"And just like that, you're forgiven."

"*Ugh*, get a room," Olanna says, and we both shush her.

"Remember this day when you fall in love again," Emmanuel retorts.

"Don't worry, I'm never falling in love again. Love is too complicated for me. I'm done," she responds without looking at us.

Olanna has had a rough few weeks and even though our girls night gave her a chance to talk through her frustrations as we did a movie marathon, karaoke, and a home-cooked dinner, the poor girl is still hurting, but we've made some progress.

Emmanuel opens his mouth to speak, but is interrupted by

his buzzing phone. "It's Mr. Nwaeze." He picks it up and places it on speakerphone. "Hello, sir. Good evening."

"Hello, my son. How are you?"

"I'm doing great, thank you."

"Sorry to call out of the blue. You asked me to remind you about our meeting with the team next week."

"Yes, I actually remembered, and it's on my calendar. It's the twenty-sixth at two pm, your time, right?"

"Yes, that's right. I'm so happy you finally decided to officially be a part of us. You have no idea how many lives are being changed. I wish you could take over and supervise everything like your mom did."

"You are doing a wonderful job supervising, Uncle Dennis. I trust you."

"Well, thank you and hope to see you and your madam next week."

Emmanuel looks at me and smiles. "I assure you she will be there and you can finally see why I can't stop talking about her." He winks at me and my cheeks warm up.

"What was that about?" I ask when he ends the call.

"Nothing."

I push his arm gently. "Come on, don't do that. What have you been telling him about me?"

"The truth." He shrugs. "That you're my *madam*." He uses the same accent Mr. Nwaeze used. "My *asempete*, *Omalicha*. Fine girl, with no pimples."

I chuckle even though I have no idea what he's saying. "Okay, I'll take all of those as compliments."

"Well, you should, because they are." He holds my hand, and an idea drops in my mind.

"Charis," I shout out and Emmanuel frowns at me, clearly confused. "Charis." I pull up my phone and type in the word. "What did you say your mom's name means in English?"

"Ooh, I know this." Olanna turns around. "Amarachi means God's grace."

"Well, look at you go. Spoken like the true daughter of Chijioke Madu." Emmanuel hails her.

"Did you know that the word grace in Hebrew is 'Charis'? Instead of using Pistis, what about Charis Charity Marketing in honor of your mom and to remind us and all the people we'll help that we are all trophies of God's grace?"

He grins. "Yes. We extend grace to others by showing kindness and love. Those are our core values. I love it."

"Yeah, me too," Olanna agrees.

"Okay, settled." I squeal and pick up the piece of paper we've been scribbling on. "So we've got a name. Now we need to hire a graphic designer who will work with clients on branding, logo designs, and printing."

"We also need to figure out which print-on-demand company we'll be using and the costs," Emmanuel chips in.

"Yes, you're right." I make a note at the top of the piece of paper. Then we pause as we both stare at the scribbles. I can't believe this is all coming together. We're going to be entrepreneurs.

"Manny, I just got a weird text from Dad," Olanna says and we both turn to look at her. "Why is he telling me we'll spend our daddy-daughter day at a leadership conference?"

Emmanuel and I send each other a knowing look before smiling. He shrugs. "I don't know. Maybe you can ask him." He chuckles just as Phoebe escapes Olanna's lap, running toward us and leaping on the table.

The unsuspecting Emmanuel pushes his chair backward as Phoebe struts in front of him. Olanna and I burst out laughing at his expense.

"Come on, babe. Just pet her."

"Errm... no, thank you. Did you see how she leaped onto the table? If she can jump that high, then she can jump on me."

"Oh, come on." I roll my eyes. "Just pet her. Here, like this." I show him how to stroke Phoebe's fur and beckon on him to move forward.

He closes his eyes and extends his finger, closing in on Phoebe until his finger grazes her fur coat. Then, just like she appeared, she jumps off the table and runs back to Olanna's lap. Emmanuel relaxes his shoulders and wipes the beads of sweat off his forehead as Olanna and I burst out laughing again.

I squeeze Emmanuel's hand tight and let out a sharp breath as we both walk up the stairs leading to his dad's house. My heart beat is pounding in my ears the same way you hear when there's a tense scene in a movie.

I tighten my grip around the non-alcoholic wine bottle Emmanuel bought. He says it's his dad's favorite flavor and he'll love me for it. I really hope he does, because this is the only peace offering I have. There's no backup.

Emmanuel has already assured me a thousand times while he was driving us here that Mr Madu was the one who suggested we have dinner today. But my anxious heart is too fragile right now. Everything has been going well the last few weeks and I don't want this to flop.

Olanna gifted me one of her African print tops, which she has never worn. I love the top because it's so colorful and it matches my hair. I had some reservations about how I would look with the African print, but all my doubts flew away when I saw the look of admiration on Emmanuel's face as I walked out the door.

I really need to build my collection of these outfits because the color looks good on me. I haven't worn makeup much since surrendering my life to God because I wanted to give my face a break from all those years of heavy makeup application.

But tonight I decided to go light and I'm glad I did. Emmanuel loves the red lipstick, so of course I have to give him that. I've put in all the effort on my part to appear peaceful, so I hope this goes well.

Lord, please, don't let this flop. I say a silent prayer as Emmanuel presses the doorbell. He turns to look at at me and his reassuring smile sends a calm through me. He looks so handsome in his blue shirt and white pants. I literally have to restrain myself from kissing him again.

Then, as if reading my thoughts, he bends over and plants a kiss on my forehead before whispering, "It's going to be okay."

The door opens to reveal a middle-aged woman dressed in a smart white shirt and black pants. "Emmanuel." A bright smile appears on her face as she hugs him.

"Aunty Martha. Good evening."

"Oh, you seem to grow taller every single time I see you." Her Nigerian accent is more evident this time.

"I'm pretty sure my height peaked when I was eighteen, but I'll accept anything to boost my ego." They both laugh and Emmanuel turns to me. "Aunty, this is Heather, my girlfriend." He pulls me close to him in that reassuring way he always does.

"Aww, you're welcome, my dear." She hugs me as well, her lavender scent going straight into my nostrils. "Please, come in. Your dad has been waiting for you." She walks into the house and then says something else to Emmanuel in a foreign language—which I'm guessing is Igbo.

"Yes, she is very beautiful," Emmanuel replies to her in English. "Inside and out." He looks down at me and my cheeks warm up.

The spiral staircase immediately catches my attention,

followed by the golden chandelier and the gray sofas. The warm, cozy atmosphere is to die for, and the interior design is so exquisite I should take out my phone and write some notes down for the future.

"You haven't been around on a weekday in a long time. You should come and say hi to us more often," the woman says as she pauses and turns to look at us.

"Yeah, I'm sorry about that." He rubs the back of his neck before sending her a sheepish smile. "Work has been crazy, but things are slowing down now, so I promise I'll swing by more often to see you and Uncle Matthew—that's the chef, by the way," he says to me.

"Remember, a promise is a debt, young man." The older woman sings-songs.

"And I won't stop until I have paid my debt in full."

She nods. "Your dad is on the phone with family in Nigeria. He says he will be with you shortly. Please make yourselves comfortable and I'll go check on Matthew to make sure everything is set for dinner." She smiles at both of us before heading out.

"She seems nice," I say as Emmanuel leads me to the sofas in the living room.

"Yeah, she's the housekeeper, and she supervises the rest of the staff. She's very friendly."

I open my mouth to respond when I'm interrupted by the sound of a closing door and footsteps coming down the stairs.

We both stand and I pull my blouse down before Mr. Madu comes into full view wearing his matching gray Kaftan and trousers.

"Hey, Dad." Manny walks up to him and hugs him.

I follow suit, not knowing whether that's too presumptuous of me, but to my surprise, instead of shaking my hand, Mr. Madu hugs me as well.

"Heather, good to see you," he says before stepping back to take in my full outfit. "I have to say that my son is already doing a good job of taking care of you." He turns to Emmanuel and pats his back.

"Thank you, sir. This is for you." I hand him the bottle of wine and he takes it from me with a grin on his face.

"Thank you so much. I'll get Martha to make sure this is served with our dinner." He places the bottle on the center table before gesturing for us to sit down. "It's been long since I had a home-cooked dinner with Emmanuel, so this is refreshing."

"Thank you for welcoming me here, Mr. Madu," I say. "You have a beautiful home."

"Ah well, to God be the glory."

I hesitate a little, but then force the words out before I can talk myself out of it. "I just want to take this opportunity to apologize for my behavior last time. I should never have spoken to you the way I did. I'm sorry and I hope you can forgive me because I love your son and I know how important his family is to him."

"I have already forgiven you, my daughter." He interlocks his fingers. "Everyone deserves a second chance, including myself, and the thing about God is that He gives us a million second chances every single day. So, in the spirit of following God's footsteps, we will start this relationship on a clean slate." He sweeps his hand across the room to make his point. "Because my children are important to me and they speak highly of you, so they must be right." He smiles and stands up. "Come on."

Emmanuel helps me stand up as I walk over to Mr. Madu and give him another hug. Just then, Martha walks in wearing a smile. "Dinner is ready, and the table is all set."

"Thank you, Martha." Mr. Madu says when we break the hug. "Heather, I hope you're hungry because my chef is the best and his food is a true palette explosion. We have okro soup, pounded yam, assorted meat, chicken, plantain, *ayamase* stew and, of course, jollof rice."

A surge of excitement rushes through me as we follow Mr. Madu toward the dining room. "I love food, so I'm looking forward to it." And I'm looking forward to the rest of my life.

EPILOGUE

Three Months Later

I can't stop myself from smiling as Mom walks down the white-carpeted aisle toward Dad, who is wearing a black tux. The train of her simple ivory lace dress flows behind her as she holds onto her white bouquet with the biggest smile on her face. The wind blows against her veil and it dances behind her as her little steps match the beat of the song playing from the speakers.

I've never been to an outdoor wedding before and it's amazing that the first one I'm attending is that of my parents. After completing their marriage counseling three months ago, it seemed appropriate for them to do this again and celebrate their new commitment to each other with close friends and family.

When we struggled to find an affordable venue, Emmanuel pulled a few strings, and we got approval to use the golf course for free. I didn't even know he played golf that much, but my heart loves him a thousand percent more for this.

The open field location is perfect, and we worked hard to set up the chairs on either side of the aisle, decorating them with white and green floral bands. There's a matching white taupe decorated with leaves from top to bottom, and we are using that as a backdrop. Trees sway from side to side all around the course, and not too far off in the distance are golfers playing.

I take Mom's hand when she arrives at the front, and then I hand her over to Dad as the music fades away. The officiant opens his Bible and starts reading from it, welcoming everyone to the ceremony and after a short message about the significance of marriage, he lets Mom and Dad share their vows.

Dad takes out a piece of paper from the pocket of his blazer and, after dabbing some tears on his cheeks, he speaks into the microphone. "Erica, you know I'm a man of few words, but I have to express how grateful I am to God that you're back in my life. I've always loved you, so I pray God will continue to help me love you the way He wants me to. Today, in front of our friends and family, I vow to stay faithful to this calling and to be the husband God has called me to be for the rest of our lives. So God help me." He laughs.

There are sniffles among the crowd and tears spill out of my eyes, but I catch them before they fall. I was there all those years ago when Dad suffered from the heartbreak of losing the only woman he has ever loved. I'm so happy for him and can't wait for them to start their journey again.

Mom takes the microphone and I hand her the piece of paper she wrote her vows on. "Jack, thank you for accepting me back into your life. There were many times along this journey where I made mistakes and paid dearly for them, but..." Her voice breaks as she continues.

"I thank God that out of everything I lost, I didn't lose your love. Your heart for God inspires me and I pray that this time, I can be the wife you need. You've been nothing but good to me and today, I vow that as long as God gives me strength, I'll be nothing but good to you. Today, I vow to love you the way God wants me to for the rest of my life. So help me God."

After her speech, there's no dry eye left in the audience. Teeyana, Amara, and Olanna are dabbing the corners of their eyes with tissue paper. Raymond, Jayden, and Emmanuel are doing a good job with holding the tears in, but even Teeyana's two-month-old baby Zion is whining on her lap. He must be sensing the whoosh of emotion sweeping through.

I hand over the ring box, and after exchanging rings, the minister prays for them. "... I now pronounce your union blessed in the name of the Father, the Son, and the Holy Spirit. Ladies and gentlemen, Mr. and Mrs. Osborne."

Everyone stands and claps as Mom and Dad walk back down the aisle while I follow them back to the cafe area. After Jayden, Raymond, and Emmanuel move the speakers into the building, the guests file in to get snacks and drinks.

"Congratulations." Emmanuel hugs me from behind and I look up at him.

"I'm not the one getting married, am I?" I chuckle.

"No, but it's the start of an exciting season for you and your family, so congratulations." He smiles and kisses my forehead before his phone rings. "Sorry babe, let me take this quickly. It's Martin from Chasing Hope."

"Okay, I'll wait for you here." As he walks off, I can't stop myself from admiring him in his striped gray suit. My man is fine and I'm not even ashamed to say it because it's true. We've been together six months now and every day I love him more.

"Hey, girl." Amara, Olanna, Teeyana, and the boys join me. After each of them gives me a congratulatory hug, I take the baby from Teeyana for my snuggles.

"Hello, Zion. Did you miss me?" I rub my nose against his as he reaches for my hair. "Wow, you're getting so big."

"You can say that again," Teeyana agrees, rubbing her shoulders. "I can't wait for him to start walking."

"And talking," Amara chimes in. "Then you'll want him to shut up." We all laugh and then we turn to look at Emmanuel who is still on the phone.

"We're so happy for you, Heather," Teeyana says. "It seemed like yesterday when I was encouraging you to believe what this tattoo says." She points at my wrist. "Now look at you, saved, redeemed, sanctified, and absolutely killing it for God's kingdom."

"Yeah, your story is so inspiring and you've been a huge blessing to us," Amara adds.

I shake my head. "No, you girls… and boys have been a blessing to me." The girls hug me again for a few moments before Emmanuel joins us.

"Hey, man. Was that Martin?" Jayden asks as I hand Zion over to him.

Emmanuel nods with a smile. "Yes, it was."

"How did it go?" I ask, excitement building in my chest.

"They've agreed. We're going to Madagascar." We let out loud cheers as the boys take turns shaking hands with and hugging Emmanuel. Teeyana and Jayden recommended our agency to the charity they volunteer for in Madagascar called The Chasing Hope Foundation and they just accepted to make us their official marketing agency. Another client in the bag.

"Congratulations, my brother," Raymond says. "Amara and I will be eagerly waiting for you in Naija after your Madagascar trip. Heather, you're going to come too, right?"

"Of course! I'm so excited." I lean into Emmanuel as he wraps his arm around me. "It'll be so fun to travel with you all."

AWC has been doing really well and lots of volunteers have joined the cause, so we've been reaching out to more women and children. We will visit our team and our clients in Nigeria when we get there.

Because of our increasing client base, we have hired a graphic designer and an events manager as well. We have a few long-term clients and we've also been getting referrals for the coaching services because of how amazing Emmanuel is.

"Olanna, will you come with us to Nigeria?" I ask and silence cuts through the air as we all turn to look at her. She has been quiet the whole time and I know she's still finding it hard to adjust to this celebration of love while dealing with her recent heartbreak. I told her she didn't have to come to the wedding, but she insisted, saying she would be a bad sister-in-law if she didn't share in my happiness.

"Nah, I'm good." She shakes her head. It's the response I expected, but I'm not ready to give up.

"Oh, come on. Getting out of New Jersey might do you some good, you know? It may give you time to reset?" I tilt my head and make my best pleading eyes gesture, but she only shrugs.

"I don't know. I'll... think about it."

"Yay, that's good enough for me." I hug her and everyone starts chatting again.

"Alright boys, this is my territory," Emmanuel speaks up. "If you ever want to engage in a competitive game of golf, hit me up."

Jayden opts in while Raymond steps back and scratches his bald head.

"I don't know. I was hoping to do something more active, like football." Raymond jogs on the spot and kicks the air.

Amara chuckles before leaning in and touching her husband's chest. "Honey, it's soccer, not football."

"Oh, please, Americans need to catch up with the rest of the world. You play with your feet, do you not? *Ehe*, so it's *football. Who soccer epp?*" Raymond says, followed by his kissing teeth gesture and we all laugh even though I have no idea what the last thing he said meant. The way he said it was funny, though.

"I'm with you, my brother." Emmanuel hugs Raymond. "I owe you a good game of football."

"Now you're talking," Raymond responds and after a few more minutes of chatting, everyone heads back to the reception area to greet my parents, leaving Emmanuel and me alone.

"So…" Emmanuel pulls me toward him until his mouth is only a few inches away from mine. "You want to have lunch with me on Saturday?" He plants a soft kiss on my lips and I pull him even closer.

"Babe, I would love to," I say when we break the kiss.

He props my chin up with his finger. "But?" he says, his brown gaze finding mine.

"But I have a date with my mom." I rub his arms, which are planted firmly around my waist. "She's moving in tomorrow, so we're planning to go to the hairdresser and then shopping for a few household items—just like old times. It was Meredith's idea."

"Really? That's awesome. Are you excited?"

I sigh. "Well, a little, but I'm also nervous about what will happen and if it'll actually be like old times or if—"

"Shhh!" Emmanuel places a finger softly against my lips and steals another kiss. "Don't worry about it, baby. You're doing the right thing. Healing is a journey and as long as you're intentional about every step you take toward the light, you'll be fine. God is with you and I'll be right here too, okay?"

A smile spreads across my face as my heart melts at his words. What did I do to deserve a man like this? Wait, that's right. Absolutely nothing. *Thank You, Jesus.*

THE END

A PLEA

Thank you so much for reading this book. I would be very grateful if you could please leave a review online. Reviews are very important because they help the book become more visible to others so they can be blessed by it too. Thank you again and God bless you.

GLOSSARY

Nwa Nwoke- my son

Chai, inu kwa m- Wow, can you imagine that?

Bia- Come

Abeg- Please

Joor- A slang adopted from the Yoruba language which means please.

Abacha- An eastern Nigerian dish also called the African salad. It is native to the Igbo people and it is made of dried shredded cassava, crayfish, palm oil and spices.

Nke a bu gi n'ezie?- Is this really you?

O bu m- It's me

Las las we go be alright– In the end, we will be fine.

Asoebi- a uniform dressing Nigerians typically wear to ceremonies as an indication of solidarity.

Isi Agu top- A vibrant and colourful traditional outfit worn by the Igbo people, so called because of the lion head pattern on the fabric. It is usually worn on special occasions like weddings.

Agbada- A four piece attire worn by the men of the Yoruba tribe which consists of a large free flowing outer robe, an undervest, a pair of long trousers, and a hat.

Ibu onye ala Igbo?- Are you from Igbo land?

I ghotara?- Do you understand?

N'aha Jisos.- In Jesus' name

Daalu- Thank you

Biko- Please

Chineke m- My God

Princessa- Princess

Rápidemante- Quickly

Nunca- Never

Soro Soke- Speak up

Mba- No

Asempete- The pretty one

Omalicha- Beauty

Okro soup- Okra vegetables mixed with oil, meat/fish and spices.

Pounded yam- Staple West African food made from pounding and kneading of boiled yams. Although the same texture can be gotten by mixing yam flour with boiled water.

Ayamase stew- A popular dish among the Yoruba tribe made with green bell peppers, palm oil, scotch bonnet, meat and spices.

Jollof rice- Spicy rice dish made with tomatoes, vegetables and meat in a single pot.

Naija- Short form for Nigeria

Who soccer epp?- How is soccer going to help me?

AUTHOR'S NOTE

The inspiration for this story came to me in November 2020 while I was on the tube travelling to work in London. I was drafting the second book in the series–*The One Who Loves Me* at the time and I was enjoying the drafting process for book 2 so much that I had the idea to write a third book in the series. When I thought about which character to follow, it made sense to choose Heather because I always felt there was so much more to her story.

I immediately knew I wanted to explore what it's like to follow Jesus after experiencing unresolved childhood trauma. Whilst it is a blessing and privilege to be part of God's family, I feel like the church rarely talks about the daily struggles new converts (and Christians in general) go through. It is easy to paint a picture of perfect obedience, where we always yield and we always do what is right, but we hardly talk about all those times we struggle, when we are faced with temptation and feel help-less. It is not by our own strength that we live a holy life. It is the spirit of God who helps us to intentionally choose God when we are faced with temptation. It is the spirit of God who helps us die to ourselves daily, so we can do what is right.

The central Bible verse for this book is taken from the book of **Ephesians 8:9** and it says *"For by grace you have been saved through faith. And this is not your own doing; it is the gift of God, not a result of works, so that no one may boast."* The one theme God kept encouraging me to write in this book was one that highlights not just the miracle of being saved, but also the miracle of staying saved. It's easy for us to think that it was because of our doing that we came to Christ or have stayed the righteous path, but the Bible preaches the opposite. We came to Christ because God brought us to Him and we stay in Him only because He keeps us. **Yes, we have a responsibility to respond to God's call, but ultimately, God does the calling, and He does the saving.**

This is something that Heather had to learn in her journey and I'm so honoured I got to write her story. I didn't realize how much I knew her until I started writing her point of view. We are all human and hurt people hurt others. Heather's childhood trauma and her experiences dealing with rejection from her own mother wasn't something I could relate to, but still, I felt I understood her as I have experienced my own fair share of disappointment and temptations. I know it's never easy to forgive especially if you've been hurt by someone you love, but I pray that if this is something you are struggling with, that God will heal your hurt, and give you the grace to forgive others as He has forgiven you.

Emmanuel's story was the hardest for me to write because he was a new character. It took me a while to get his voice and to understand what his motivations were. But with the help of my beta readers and my editor, I was able to nail down his character arc and that's when I realized how much I relate to his character.

Like Emmanuel, I, too, can be somewhat of a people pleaser and I can let others trample on my opinions because I'm too scared to offend them. I sometimes find it easier to let others have their way instead of speaking up for myself—especially if it is someone I respect. I never knew until I wrote this story that God was also speaking to me.

So to anyone who is also struggling to stand up for what God has called them to do, I pray that just as Emmanuel was able to find his voice and embrace his freedom in Christ, you too will be liberated from every obstacle trying to keep you away from the purpose God has called you to do.

Finally, if you're reading this and you're yet to surrender your life to Jesus Christ as your Lord and Saviour, here's an open invitation to do so today. It is not too late. The Lord's open arms are waiting, and He is calling you to come home. There's no pain He can't heal. Jesus has already paid the price for you. He wants you to abandon your pride today and run to Him. He has loved you from the beginning of time and He always will. If you want to take that bold step today, please say this prayer with me;

Dear Jesus, I come before you today with thanksgiving in my heart. I accept that you are God and I am not. I am a sinner, but You alone are the Forgiver of sins. Please come into my heart today. I surrender my all to you as my Lord and Saviour. Make me clean and teach me how to love and obey you. In Jesus' name I've prayed. Amen.

If you've prayed this prayer of faith and are willing to walk into your new life with Jesus, congratulations. Welcome to God's family. Please get plugged into a local church if you haven't already done so. Commit to studying the Bible with fellow believers and find a spiritual mentor you trust who will help you along the journey. If you would like to share a testimony with me, please reach out to me on social media or using the contact form found on my website: www.joanembola.co.uk.

Until the next book,

    Lots of love,

    Joan.

BOOK FOUR

IS GOD SOVEREIGN OVER UNCERTAINTIES?

While trying to overcome grief, Olanna Madu faces another blow when her college sweetheart abruptly ends their relationship. Now, two years later, Olanna is healing from the hurt as she navigates her new life as the CEO of her family's business. But when her ex shows up at her office as her new client, not only does the pain resurface, but also the feelings for him she once thought had died.

If Alex Obeng had a blank check to have any prayer answered, he would ask God to turn back the hands of time so he could explain to Olanna why he broke her heart. But his desperate attempts to reach out to her for the past two years have been futile. When Alex is sent to New Jersey to work with Olanna's company, it seems God has answered all his prayers until he stands face to face with her and can't bring himself to tell her the truth without opening his old wounds.

With their rekindled feelings growing stronger every day, Olanna has to decide whether to give Alex a second chance or protect her heart from getting burned...again. And as the pressure mounts on Alex to fight for the woman he loves, he has to choose between being vulnerable enough to tell her the truth and letting her go...again.

The One Who Holds Me, book four in the Sovereign Love series, is a dual timeline stand-alone novel about second chances and learning to trust in the sovereign goodness of a loving God who holds our future securely in His hands.

Coming September 24th 2024

Available For Preorder here

FREE SHORT STORY

Subscribe to my free monthly newsletter here to stay up to date with book news and to also get a free short story called *A Promise To Keep*, which follows a Nigerian couple—Dayo and Dara as they navigate the challenges of life while learning about endurance and what it means to experience the goodness of God.

ACKNOWLEDGMENTS

I experienced a lot of struggles writing this book but I would have never done it without my Heavenly Father. Thank You Lord for helping me finish this story. You put Heather and Emmanuel's story in my heart and now I'm giving it back to You. Please use it for Your glory.

To my parents and brothers, thank you for always believing in me, trusting the abilities God has given me and supporting me all the way. I have so much love for you all.

To my love and biggest supporter, Oladunni. You are my biggest blessing and God knew what He was doing when He chose you to be by my side. Thank you *ife mi* for never letting me doubt myself. You make this journey so easy. I love you so much.

To my beta readers, Tiffany, Iyanu, and Temitope. You have no idea how your useful feedback boosted my confidence in this story–especially yours Tiffany. I am so blessed to have people like you supporting me on this journey. May our good Lord reward you all abundantly.

To my editor, Michaela Bush, thank you so much for your patience and your incredibly good eyes for detail. This story wouldn't be where it is today without you.

To my cover designer, Elle Maxwell, you always blow my mind with your talent and creativity. Thank you so much for perfectly capturing Heather and Emmanuel the way I imagined them.

To you reading this book, thank you for giving it a chance. I hope it has brought you hope, and that it has reminded you of the Father's sovereign love for you.

Finally, I'll have to go back to my Heavenly Father—the One who sees me. My Lord, I started this journey with You and I'm finishing it with You. To You be all the glory, honour and praise forever and ever. Amen.

ABOUT THE AUTHOR

Joan Embola is a UK-based Cameroonian-Nigerian Christian author who aims to share God's love one word at a time. She writes books about diverse characters whose hope-filled stories point to the love and goodness of God in our broken world. She is a qualified Physician Associate and also the founder of Love Qualified, a ministry dedicated to encouraging others to experience the sovereign love of the one true God who has qualified us to be His beloved ones. She is a passionate lover and teacher of God's Word, as shared on her YouTube channel, blog, and podcast. When she's not writing or curled up with a book, you'll find her watching movies, YouTube videos, or making memories with her family and friends.

You can connect with her at www.joanembola.co.uk and on instagram, YouTube and her podcast. Subscribe to her newsletter to stay up to date with more book news, cover reveals, how to sign up for advanced reader copies, and fun giveaways.

DISCUSSION QUESTIONS

1. At the start of the book, we see Heather in a place where she is struggling to accept the new direction her life is taking and she sees herself as a failure. Have you ever gone through a season like this? How did you deal with it?

2. How would you describe the relationship between Heather and her dad? What did they go through and what did they need to overcome over the years to get them to this point?

3. At the start of the book, we see Emmanuel struggling to stand up for what God has called him to do because of fear of what he could lose. Have you ever been in this position? How did you deal with it?

4. How would you describe the relationship between Emmanuel and his dad?

5. The first time Heather and Emmanuel met, he wasn't very kind to her and he later attributed that to his frustrations. Have you ever been in a situation like this where other people around

you are affected by your own internal battles? How did you deal with it?

6. How would you describe the relationship between Heather and Emmanuel? Did they have a good foundation for their friendship and how did their bond grow stronger over time?

7. What roles did the side characters (Teeyana, Amara and Olanna) play in the lives of Heather and Emmanuel? How did these people influence them?

8. What lesson did Heather have to learn to get her to where God needed her to be?

9. What lesson did Emmanuel have to learn to get him to where God needed him to be?

10. Does the title of the book make sense to you? Do you get the overall theme that the author was trying to portray?

Made in United States
Troutdale, OR
11/03/2024

24405400R00206